I0596724

WHAT HAPPENS IN COLLEGE...

Vanessa M. Knight

What Happens in College...
Copyright © 2015 by Vanessa M Knight
Published by Inked Publishing

Cover Design by Okay Creations
Book Designed and Produced by Nancy Canu and Vanessa Knight

Edited by Nancy Canu

What Happens in College... is a work of fiction. All names, characters, places and events are the product of the author's imagination or are used fictitiously, and any resemblance to actual persons, living or dead, or to actual events or locales is entirely coincidental.

All rights reserved. No part of this work may be used or reproduced in any manner whatsoever without written permission from the author except in the case of brief quotations for use in critical articles or reviews.

ISBN: 978-0996217224

To my favorite and only son. I'm so proud of the man you've become.

Acknowledgements

There are so many people that made these books possible; it truly does take a village and a hunk (or two) of chocolate.

First and foremost, I'd like to thank my husband, Spyder, for supporting me and my dreams emotionally and financially. He's putting his money where my pen is... Does that sound kinky, or is it just me?

I also want to thank my darling son for giving me the teen point of view. He is my reality-check resource for the current college student. He always finds time to help and I appreciate that immensely.

I could never forget to thank my fabulous family and friends. You have seen me through the good, the bad, and the ugly (remember that little orphan Annie perm...ick). Thank you for your support and understanding through long hours and unwavering focus as I try to finish just one more book so I can relax. (Mom, I promise to relax after I write the next one.)

To my editor, Nancy Canu, for "getting" me and my writing style. You help make these books into something I can be proud of, and I thank you for that.

Thank you to the best critiquers in the world...J Leigh Bailey, Kelly Garcia, Nicole Leiren, and Stephanie Scott, and also to my wonderful friends, Sonali Dev, Cheryl Huth, and Cici Edwards. You all have talked me off ledge after ledge. You have given me strength and sometimes just a stiff drink, inspiring me to keep going when I wanted to quit and join the circus (thankfully, I was reminded I don't have circus-quality talents before I made that mistake). You make me laugh when I want to cry, and you make me write when I just want to watch TV. You are truly awesome.

And last but not least, I'd like to thank all of the readers. I can't wait to see where this series will go, and you allow me to continue writing so we can find out together.

$$\sim\!\gg\!\Psi\mathrm{P}\!\ll\!\sim$$

Chapter One

Karina

THE LIGHTS IN the house were dimmed, the music was too loud, and Karina Wolfe's roommate, Savannah Whitley, was wearing a dress short enough to read her lips.

"How are you dancing in that dress without giving everyone a peep show?" Karina raised her voice enough to be heard over the music and dropped onto the couch, balancing her plastic cup of water. First night at Ritter University, first party—even if it was off-campus at somebody's parents' house—first opportunity to embarrass herself. All good reasons why she had skipped the spiked punch and stuck with water.

"Well that's easy." Savannah fanned her blonde hair across her narrow back, the straight strands immediately slipping back in front of her shoulders. Everything about Savannah was narrow—and long—and tall. "I only slow dance, sway, and country line dance."

Gabriella Blanco pulled on the pink stretchy material that barely covered Savannah's lady bits, tugging it down about a half inch. "Sway?" She straightened up, the bling on her belt accenting the way her low-slung jeans clung to her hips.

"Sway. You know, back and forth. All that arm-throwing and butt-thumping is unnecessary. It's all just foreplay, anyway."

"If only her preacher father could hear her." Gabi gulped down half her glass of punch.

Karina laughed. "If only your boyfriend back home could hear you now."

Savannah gave Gabi a pathetic excuse for a glare. "Keep my daddy out of it, and Leland would be just fine. He knows how much I love him."

Karina sipped her water and wondered about the fake smile at the end—who was Savannah trying to convince?

Gabi dropped into the space next to her on the couch, her cut-off T-shirt with Latina Princess in pink glitter riding up over her flat stomach. "We're not sitting here long. We're going back out to dance." She pulled her long dark brown hair away from her sweat-soaked olive skin. All Karina needed was four hours in the sun, a boob-job, and butt injections, and she too, could look that good.

"You can go anytime," Savannah told Gabi. "Karina and I will go when we're good and ready, bossy-pants." Savannah had barely touched the drink in her hand. Her eyes were too busy bouncing from side to side. Maybe that's why the girl could dance for forty-five minutes and not break a sweat. There was no liquid in her system.

Karina didn't have that problem. She lifted her dark blonde hair off her neck, ignoring the sweat beading and dripping down her face. Her hair was barely past her shoulders and it was too hot—how did Savannah stand it? Her black jeans were stuck to the back of her thighs, and she tugged on the neck of her damp T-shirt to get some air on her skin. "How are you not sweating?"

"My momma, God rest her soul, always told me women don't sweat. We glisten." Savannah sipped her drink and Gabi rolled her eyes.

If it were only that simple. If only Karina would miraculously stop sweating because her mom said so. Her mom would love that, just pull some magic puppet strings and no more sweating… Check. Another pull of those strings and no more "slovenly" wardrobe, all jeans and T-shirts banished… Check. No more "horrible" attitude… Check.

A boy-band lookalike gazed in their direction across the dance floor. Karina smiled and nudged Savannah. "Speaking of fine. You have an admirer."

Boy-band swaggered up to the couch and leaned toward Savannah. "See my friend over there? He wants to know if you think I'm cute."

"Whatever for?" Savannah batted her eyelids and flipped her long blonde hair back over her shoulder.

"Because I'd like to ask you to dance, but couldn't handle it if someone as beautiful as you said no."

"Well, aren't you just adorable."

"Wanna dance?"

"Sure." Savannah leapt from the chair and followed the boy-band wannabe. Although the pickup line was bogus, it figured that the one girl with a frickin' boyfriend waiting at home was asked to dance by a gorgeous guy.

"I'm going back out there." Gabi downed the last of her punch as she jumped up from the couch. "Ready?"

"Give me a minute."

"One minute, and I'm dragging your butt out here." Gabi shuffled through the crowd to where their group of dorm mates was dancing in a large circle in the middle of the floor. Everyone was having a great time.

Their first party at their new college campus. Away from home. Away from parents. Their first chance to be on their own.

Bodies jumped and writhed on the makeshift dance floor when the bass thudded a new rhythm. The heat in the room rose, and even sitting off to the side, new sweat lined Karina's forehead. A guy bumped the back of the couch and landed on her lap. "Hey, sexy."

"Hey."

He lifted his longhaired head and blew on her with boozy breath. "Dude, did you go swimming? You're all wet."

"Yep." Karina sighed.

"Awesome." He leaned a hand on Karina's shoulder and stumbled to his feet. As he walked away, he tripped over a set of legs. "Cool. Hey, man, did you hear—there's a pool."

Drunk guys. Gotta love 'em. She puffed a burst of air at her bangs. Nope not working. Air. She needed real air.

Karina slid off the couch and angled through the gyrating bodies on the floor, heading for the sliding glass doors at the opposite end of the room. She squeezed and banged her way through the crowd, wrinkling her nose as cigarette and pot smoke mixed with the overwhelming scent of sweat. Num.

The sliding glass door was open when she reached the Promised Land. Air. Fresh air. Karina drank down the cool evening breeze, cold air sliding down her throat. Through the soft glow of outdoor lighting, she watched couples walking hand-in-hand down the sloping backyard to Ritter Lake on the other side of the trees.

So relaxing. She closed her eyes and sat back against the railing of the back deck. Shivers crawled up her arms as the breeze washed away the sweat—no—glisten from her skin.

Thump. Thump. Her body pulsed to the rhythm coming through the railing.

Thump. Thump.

Crunch.

Her arms flew out, looking for something to grab as she fell backward. Anything to stop her downward momentum. Nothing. There was not one thing to stop her. No way to stop the power of gravity. Wood jabbed into her side. Crap. Her eyes closed and her butt puckered as she braced for the cruel reality of hard ground and pointy wood.

Instead of an intimate introduction with the business end of an improvised spear, strong arms wrapped around her waist. Momentum stopped. Realization hit. She wasn't going to be making that last-minute ER trip this evening after all. She leaned into the large chest of her rescuer.

"Whoa," a seductive deep voice rumbled in her ear. He eased her forward until she was standing upright "Are you okay?"

"I think so." Karina tested her knees and figured she could manage not to fall in a heap. Damn deck. She lifted her head to thank her savior, and air wedged in her throat.

Wow. Her gaze locked on his hazel eyes and full lips. Both looked right at home next to chiseled cheekbones and a strong jaw. His brown hair was cut short on the sides, gradually getting longer near the top of his head. The only flaw she could see was a rounded nose—and even that gave him a unique attractiveness. A guy-next-door Adam Levine.

Did she mention she loved Adam Levine? Too bad she'd given up on dating and guys and anything associated with either, because this one would be just her type.

Danger. Warning.

Her type of guy tended to be hot. Stupid hot. The kind of hot that conned unsuspecting women into doing stupid things. Thank goodness she wasn't unsuspecting—anymore.

"Are you sure?" He ran a hand through his already disheveled hair.

What? She thought back—what was the last thing she said? No clue. "Am I sure about what?"

"That you're okay. You look a bit confused."

"Confused?" She might be a bit confused. On account of the hotness? No—because she almost got impaled. That was it.

"How many fingers?" He held three fingers up next to his head.

"Three."

"And now?" He lifted one finger.

"One."

"What's your name?"

"Karina." Yep. She was sure that was her name.

"Karina."

"Wait, how do you know if I'm right?"

"I don't. I just wanted to know your name." He slid a finger along her cheek, pushing a stray piece of hair behind her ear. "The confusion seems to be gone."

"Sorry. I'm fine now. What were you doing out here?" She turned away as heat crawled up her neck. Confused? Maybe a little. But her brain was not pinging from his touch along her face. Not even a little. She was confused after her brush with death. Yep, death by impaling. Yep, that was it.

"Um, I needed some air." He stuffed his hands into the front pockets of his blue jeans. He looked so good in those jeans. Narrow hips. Broad Shoulders. Did she mention the Adam Levine thing?

Okay, so she might have given up on men, but she wasn't blind.

"What were you doing out here?" He pointed through the door toward the throng of dancers. "The party's that way."

"Needed some air." She stole his answer. It was the truth, after all. She looked into his eyes. Kind eyes. Sweet eyes. Eyes that held her in place. Eyes that held... Red and blue lights flickered against the hazel. She turned around.

No way. It couldn't be happening. Not again. An all-night rave twerked through her stomach. This was supposed to be her chance to put the past behind her. Move on. A visit from Cedar Glen's Finest was not in her plans.

They'd find out. Everyone would find out. Everyone always seemed to find out what she'd done.

More lights swirled through the back yard as terror gripped her by the throat.

Karina sucked in a deep breath. "The cops." *Oh no, no, no—* "I need to find my friends." She flew through the open sliding door and searched the dance floor. The dancers kept moving, oblivious to the commotion outside.

Gabi spun and dipped in the center of the madness. Thank goodness. Karina pushed through the crowd and leaned into her. "We have to go. Now. Have you seen Savannah?"

"No." Gabi shook her head as she shouted over the music. "Why do we have to go?"

"Trust me." She pulled Gabi toward the stairs to the second floor and stopped. Around the corner, college students stared as the cops talked to the homeowner. When Karina originally thought about her first night away from home, she didn't think that night would be spent in the pokey.

"There is no underage drinking here, sir." The homeowner and the college student tried to reason with the cops. "Just having a small get-together."

"We'd like to check it out." The officer craned his neck, trying to see around the front door.

"Shit, cops." Gabi whispered behind Karina.

Karina's thought exactly.

"Don't you need a warrant or something?" The homeowner stepped into the doorway. Karina nearly cheered— *Keep it up, guy.* The warrant would keep the cops busy for a few minutes, anyway. Maybe they could get out of here before the cops started their walk-through.

"Let's split up," Karina told Gabi. "I'll head upstairs, you check this floor. Find Savannah and the rest of our floor and let's get the hell out of here."

Gabi slipped into the family room and Karina headed up another flight of stairs and down a darkened hallway. Family pictures lined the walls. Not that she could see any of the specifics in the dimness.

She opened the first door. "Savannah," she stage-whispered. No answer. No sound. She closed the door and turned around.

"Who are we looking for?"

A scream lodged in her throat as she jumped back against the door. Edible porch rescuer guy stood in front of her. His hands were up in a *don't shoot* gesture.

"You scared the crap out of me." Karina pulled away and walked to the next door. "What's your name?"

"Ryan."

"Savannah?" Karina opened the door and flipped on the switch. The girl stopped riding the guy on the bed long enough to shout some interestingly-worded instructions. Something about Karina getting her own room and things she could shove up her backside when she found that room.

Karina slammed the door. Well, Savannah wasn't in there, not unless cowgirl-chick lassoed and gagged her.

"Who's Savannah?"

"My roommate. She was dancing with some guy and then disappeared." Karina walked further down the hall and threw open the next door. Empty.

"Well, I'd be happy to help you find her, if you'd like."

"Sure." She closed the door.

"So, do you lose your roommate often?" He opened the nearest door and held it open while Karina snuck under his arm and flipped the light switch. Another empty room. She made the mistake of looking back at his gleaming hazel eyes. Eyes that stopped brain functions. Rendered her speechless. Dammit, she forgot he had those eyes.

"Karina?"

Shit. There was a question in there somewhere. She was sure of it. Oh yeah, lost roommate.

"I don't think so. Who knows?" She sighed. "I just met her this weekend."

"She might have headed back to this guy's room." Ryan opened the next door and turned on the light. Karina forced her eyes off him and peered around his gorgeous body to the empty room.

What if Savannah had gone off with this guy? She'd been dating the same guy since she could walk. And now she was off with some unknown guy. He could be a predator of sweet innocent girls.

Savannah was a sweet, innocent farm girl. A preacher's daughter, and one who had lost her mom at a young age, for goodness sake. What had Karina done, letting her go off on her own? What kind of crappy roommate was she? She let the innocent sheep wander off with the wolf. He could be a knife-wielding psycho— or a dick-wielding psycho— he was probably shaking his sword in her horrified face as she and Ryan strolled down the hall.

"She wouldn't go to this guy's room on her own. She's dating someone back home. She's in love with him." Karina flung open another door. "Savannah?"

Nothing.

"That doesn't mean anything. Maybe she's sowing her wild oats."

"Sowing her wild oats? What is she, ninety? I don't think oats have been sown since the Depression." She stopped in front of the next door. "Anyway, she's not like that. She's a southern pastor's daughter. Just because guys can't keep their thing in their pants, don't assume we can't."

Jerk. She opened the next door with a bit too much force. Bathroom. Empty.

"Men don't have a corner on the infidelity market. It's human nature. She might not have even told the unsuspecting fool that she has a boyfriend."

"Why are we still talking about this? She's not sowing her wild oats or anything else with anyone."

Disappointment slithered down her spine. He looked so pretty. It's a shame a jackass hid behind that beautiful smile. *Everyone cheats. It's human nature. Jerk.*

"We should separate." She pointed at a door to the left as she headed to the last one on the right. The further away the better. "You go that way."

He laughed and opened his door. Karina opened hers, the last door on this floor. The master bedroom. A head bobbed up from behind the floral couch along the side wall. Savannah. She was crouched behind the couch with a guy. *Crap.* Karina hadn't actually met Savannah's boyfriend— he went to another school— but Savannah had pictures of him in their room. And the guy standing next to her? Not her boyfriend Leland.

It was Boy-Band.

Savannah fidgeted with the straps of her baby-doll dress, and he was straightening his clothes.

Fire swelled in Karina's stomach, following the gasoline creeping up her spine. She couldn't decide what angered her more, that Savannah was cheating on her boyfriend or that Ryan was right. Although, she could admit, Savannah's infidelity didn't really bother her at all, but that crap-eating grin on Ryan's face when he walked into the room annoyed the hell out of her.

"Um…" Karina looked at Ryan. Yep. That darn grin was definitely boiling her blood. She turned back to Savannah. "We need to leave, now. Did you want to come back with me or will your new friend be walking you home?"

"No. I'm coming. Let me get myself together." Savannah straightened her dress. Not-Leland was pushing the tails of his shirt into his tan chinos. He ran a hand through his long blond hair, his bangs immediately falling back into his eyes. His only focus seemed to be Savannah.

Ryan nodded at Not-Leland. "Hey, I'm Ryan. You're Ski's cousin, aren't you?"

"Yeah, Joe," Not-Leland said before turning to Karina. "And you must be the roommate. I've heard a lot about you."

Really? How the heck could he have heard a lot about her, when he'd just dropped that cheesy pick-up line a couple of hours ago? From what she could see, most of that time was spent with Savannah's hands down his pants. She would be disturbed and surprised if her name was brought up during any of that mess.

"Well, we need to go." Karina ushered her roommate to the door.

"Okay." Savannah turned to Joe. He leaned in to kiss her on the lips, and she turned her head, his lips falling on her cheek instead.

"Call Me." Joe-Not-Leland turned and headed out the door into the hall.

"Do you have everything? We need to get out of here before the cops swarm." Karina pushed her into the hall and peered over the edge of the banister. She had no plans on getting thrown in dorm-jail or grounded or worse, real jail.

No cops.

"Yes," Savannah said, unable to meet Karina's eyes.

As they flew down the stairs, Savannah grabbed Karina's arm. "Don't be mad at me. There's something I didn't tell you." She looked at Karina, tears building in her eyes. "Leland and I, we have an arrangement. I didn't tell you because I didn't want you to think less of me."

"Arrangement? Can we talk about this later?" Karina pulled Savannah down the stairs, but Savannah just kept talking.

"The Vegas Arrangement. What happens at college stays at college. That way we can stay together, but still get the full college experience."

Karina stopped in the center of the stairs and gaped. Really? Of all the things she thought would fall out of Savannah's mouth, the "Vegas Arrangement" was not one of them.

"Don't be mad."

"I'm not mad. I'm just a little surprised." Karina stopped and waved to Gabi across the room. She pointed at Savannah and mouthed, *I have her.*

Meet you at the dorm, Gabi mouthed over the partyers, and headed out a side door with their rest of their group.

Karina grabbed Savannah's hand and bolted straight through the kitchen and out the back door. That familiar cool air hit her skin as they walked around the house, hugging the side and watching for cops.

"Are we in the clear yet?" Savannah and Karina moved to the sidewalk, blending into a group of spectators. Savannah turned to the man following behind.

Oh, crap. Karina forgot he was still there. "So, Ryan, right? You look a little old to be a freshman."

"I'm a junior."

"A junior," Savannah winked at Karina, "and you're with my roommate."

"Um...not so much. He's not with me," Karina snapped. "He's not my type."

She didn't go for jerks who thought everyone cheated... Wait, she did go for that type in the past. That's why she was avoiding them in the future. They led to nothing but heartache.

Ryan frowned. "Yeah. She's not my type." Why was he upset? She was the one who had to listen to his whacked-out theories for the past half-hour. And what did he mean she wasn't his type? Just because she didn't buy into his disgusting ramblings, she wasn't his type?

Not that it mattered.

He nodded to Karina. "I should get back to my friends. It was nice to meet you both. And...um, Karina...I'd be happy to explain my assumptions on wild oats, anytime."

"Funny." She rolled her eyes, wanting to be pissed. She wanted to hate him, but he was so darn adorable. "Thanks for your help."

Really, he wasn't so bad—he did help her find Savannah. It wasn't his fault her roommate was in flagrante.

Whoa. That was the type of thinking that got her in trouble in the past. A jerk was a jerk. The way they found Savannah might not have been his fault, but his crappy attitude was. Back home had been overrun with crappy attitudes, so she had no plan to surround herself with more of them.

"My pleasure." He disappeared into the backyard.

"What did that mean?" Savannah whispered.

"Nothing. We need to get hell out of here." Karina turned and headed down the sidewalk, back to campus. She missed her car. The college didn't allow freshman to have cars. Hell, they weren't even allowed to have keys to the outside of their building for two months. It was like being back in grade school. One of the downfalls of going to a private Christian college. "So do you want to talk about this 'Vegas Arrangement'?"

"There's nothing to talk about. Leland and I have an agreement. We're exclusive during breaks and summers. However, while we're at school, we can date whomever we like. We just, A, can't get serious about anyone and, B, can't talk about it."

"I don't mean to pry, but are you sure that's going to work? Doesn't it bother you to think about him with someone else?"

"I don't think about it. This gives us a chance to get all the others out of our system. When we're done we'll be together, so it will all work out."

Karina knew her mouth was open. Speechless. She was speechless.

"Don't look at me like that." Savannah rolled her eyes.

"Like what?"

"Like I told you there was no Easter Bunny." Savannah pulled on her dress one more time, and straightened the hem.

"I'm just surprised."

"I know. It's just...you don't understand. I spent the past eighteen years in a glass prison, watching others living their lives without restraint. Enjoying all the things I was denied. I was representing my daddy in everything I did. No parties. No secular music. No movies above a—" She gasped. "—PG rating.

"My only glimpse at a real life came from cartoons and Leland. I've never been with anyone but him. I've never lived." She sat down hard on one of the benches lining the campus sidewalk. "I'm finally away from my daddy's eyes. I'm finally on my own to live my life the way I want. I'm taking this chance. And when school's over, I'll probably marry Leland."

"Probably? You don't sound so thrilled."

"I don't know. It thrilled me when I was younger, now I'm not so sure."

"Have you thought about breaking up with him?"

"Yeah. A lot. I don't know. I do love him. I figure taking this chance to experience it all will make me love him even more."

Karina nodded her head. She didn't have the heart to tell her that the idea sounded about as good as two Germans playing with big cats on stage. Both incidents would lead to injury. Of course, maybe it could work for her—stranger things had happened.

~»ΨΡ«~

Chapter Two

Ryan

RYAN WALKED BACK down the stairs. The police were still at the front door, so he had a few minutes to grab Brent and get out. News of the visitors in blue must have gotten around, because the room was practically empty.

Most of them were freshman, anyway. Too young to drink. He never should have come—he knew this was a bad idea when Brent suggested it. Sometimes Ryan didn't know why he hung out with the guy. Oh yeah... He was the president of their fraternity, and he played a mean game of golf. True, he was an acquired taste—a complete jackass around women, but a helluva lot of fun when there was no estrogen present.

Tonight, though, they were surrounded by women, and the six-pack Brent downed before the party had him in rare form. That was the real reason Ryan needed to be there tonight—he was playing babysitter and designated driver.

Not that the evening hadn't been fun. So far, Ryan had seen a few nice-looking women in the freshman class, including the redhead Brent had sitting on his lap in the corner. But none compared to Karina. He liked that she fought with him. Hell, he hadn't believed half the crap coming out of his mouth, but he loved pissing her off.

Most women were too busy ogling his father's money to fight with him. They had no idea he would walk away from his father and his money in a minute, if he could.

"Well, well, well, if it isn't Ryan Kent. Aren't you a bit old to be crashing a freshman party?"

Speaking of gold-digging... "If it isn't Parker Breckenridge. I'm a junior. It's not that big of a deal."

"I suppose." She ran her nails down the length of his arm, and he nearly jerked it out of reach.

He resisted the urge to rub away her touch. "I was surprised when I heard you chose to attend humble Ritter University. I figured you'd go to some Ivy League school. I'm sure the pick of rich husbands dwindles here. You know, small Christian college..."

"Oh, but there's you, darling."

"I hardly doubt you came here for me, Park."

"Why not? Our parents have been trying to set us up for years."

"You know why that will never work."

"I know no such thing. Anyway, your mom said you'd watch over me. My big, strong protector..." She moved her claws to his chest. There had been a time when he found Parker hot, and then she'd opened her mouth to speak. Killed all attraction. Now, they were quasi-friends. He put up with her overt passes and materialism—after all, her parents and his were best friends—and they tolerated each other since they both spent many hours together at the country club and other parental functions.

"Of course, I'll watch out for you Parker. You're like a sister to me."

"Ouch." She placed her hand on his cheek, her full lips drawing into an over-pronounced pout. "That hurt."

He removed her hand and she rolled her eyes. "I bet you'll get over it."

"Your loss, darling." She stood next to him as they perused the disbanding party. "See anything interesting?"

"Interesting?"

"See anyone worth removing that ginormous chip from your shoulder and sharing a movie or a meal. You know, the generally accepted first date choices." Parker sighed.

"I'm not talking about my love-life with you, Parker. I seem to remember we tried that before, too. That ended badly."

"Whatever. It wasn't my fault she couldn't take a joke."

"You called her tramp-clamp, affixing herself to me for my money." Never mind that she really had been. But he'd never tell Parker that.

"She wasn't good enough for you, anyway. How could you waste six months on her? I don't know why you insist on attracting the poorest, most pathetic girls in the room."

"Park." Tension crept up his neck and wrapped around his head.

"Fine." She tossed her hair. "Your father didn't like her much either."

"You know I don't give a fuck what my father likes."

"Don't shoot the messenger. I apologized and I swore I'd stay out of your love life. What more can I do? Anyway, it was different then, your mom didn't like her either, and watching you and your father argue wasn't good for her."

"I know." He rubbed a hand down the back of his neck. Watching his mother wither away had nearly killed him. But somehow, she'd found the strength to keep going. Somehow, she was cancer-free for over a year now.

"How is she doing? I just hear snippets from my mom."

"With her last check-up she's still clean."

"Good." Her eyes roamed the room. "Well, I'll see you around, darling."

She sashayed toward the sliding doors just before Brent walked up with the redheaded freshman on his arm. He leaned into her and kissed her lips before saying. "Honey, can you go get me some more punch?"

"Sure." She turned, and Brent tapped her on the ass. She giggled as she bounced toward the table covered in plastic cups.

"Looks like you found someone. Who was the smoking blond?" Brent asked as he eyed Parker's ass up and down as she walked out the door.

"Parker. And I didn't find someone. She's an old friend." Ryan didn't care who Parker dated, but she was off limits to Brent. Brent might have money, but he had no class, and while Parker might be a pain in the ass, she was like a sister to him. He promised his mother he'd watch out for her, and he planned on keeping that promise.

"Hmmm. I wish I had old friends that looked like that. You do her?"

Ryan rolled his eyes. Is that really all Brent thought about? Oh, yeah—it was.

"I'm joking, dude. Get the pole out of your ass and take a joke."

"I'm heading out. Are we bringing the newbie with us?"

"Hell yeah. She's all primed and ready to go. Didn't you find one for yourself?" Brent scanned the remaining undergrads.

"No."

"I could see if she has any friends she can bring with her?"

"Not interested, Sinclaire." Ryan headed toward the sliding glass doors.

"Fine, but a little froshy ass might get that snarl off your face." Brent yelled as his minion brought him a beverage. Ryan flipped up his middle finger as he continued to walk out the door into the cool August air. He popped the door locks on his Mercedes just as two adults—probably the parents—ran up to the cops. The real homeowners. Brent stumbled out to the back yard with two co-eds carrying him. Lucky shit. Got out in the nick of time.

Ryan pressed a button and the window rolled down.

"Matthew, who the hell are all these people?" the parents yelled as they rushed in the front door.

Ryan gunned the engine to drown out the yelling, and to remind Brent to hurry the fuck up. He was tempted to hit the gas and get the hell out before things went bad. And given the number of cop cars pulling down the block, things were going to get bad real quick.

Brent crawled in the back seat, his followers squishing in beside him. "Let's hit it."

Ryan shook his head as he pulled away from the curb. He couldn't help but wonder what Karina was doing now. Had she taken Savannah home? Or had they gone to Joe's room for a party?

Not that it mattered. She wasn't his business. So why the hell couldn't he stop thinking about her?

~»ΨP«~

Chapter Three

Karina

SUN SLID THROUGH the wall of windows in the cafeteria as Karina picked up a sandwich for lunch the next day. Last night had been great, hanging out with the rest of the women on her floor. They seemed nice. So far, everyone had been nice. But wasn't everyone nice until the shit hit the fan? Then you really saw their true colors. It was never good.

After the party last night, Savannah, Gabi, Megan and a few others sat up most of the night talking. Karina managed to keep the focus away from herself with well-timed redirects and the mention of snacking. Anything to keep the conversation off of her. No one needed to know about her life before Ritter. In fact, the whole point of coming here was to forget about it. Forget it ever happened.

Life before Ritter… What's that?

She made her way up the back stairs and into the open door of her room. The sound of Savannah cooing into the phone wafted to her ears. Darn, she thought her little lunch-run would have given Savannah time to get all that kissy-face out of her system. Karina tried to block out the sound.

"…of course I miss you so much. I don't know how I'll survive until Thanksgiving. Maybe we can get together for Labor Day? Oh yeah, I definitely miss that thing you do with your tongue…"

Karina stopped in the doorway. *Please make it stop. Turn around. Run. Run far.* Savannah waved to Karina in between gag-inducing display of affection.

She wanted to shout, "Get a room." But technically Savannah was in her own room. Karina dropped her sandwich onto her desk and crinkled the wrapping. Anything to block the sound. Anything to keep her hands and eyes busy.

She couldn't bring herself to look at Savannah without thinking about the things Leland would do with that tongue. Crap. Maybe she was a prude or something, but it wasn't just that she was embarrassed by the thought of his KISS tongue-imitation. She was jealous.

No guy had ever cared enough to make sure she enjoyed herself. Granted, she hadn't technically slept with anyone, yet. But she'd experimented with her boyfriends. They just never experimented back. Maybe that's why she never went any further. Why give up the milk, when they wouldn't even pet the cow for free?

She shook her head. Maybe she needed a new idiom. She was sadly aware she was the cow in that scenario. But that's what she'd felt like. The guys she dated were never into her. They were into her reputation, the reputation given to her by Craig.

Craig.

Her one true boyfriend. Her first love, or so she thought. She honestly believed they had something special. She thought they'd go to college together and eventually build a life together. White picket fence and all.

Well, that had blown up in her face. Spectacularly. And if that meant she avoided good-looking men like the plague, well then she'd keep her distance.

Of course, she would love to coo into the phone with someone special. Have inside jokes and shared secrets. She'd love to have someone to talk to about her family, about the bullshit of the past…

Stop. Been there. Messed up that. She'd tried the whole damn thing and it always ended. Ended with another shred of her dignity ripped away. She didn't have much left.

She focused on the turkey on rye. *Num.* Turkey. *Num.* Rye. She was so busy blocking out the call, she didn't notice Savannah was no longer talking on the phone.

Karina turned around to a small snuffle coming from the scrunched-up human ball on her roommate's bed. Another gasp escaped from the shaking body.

"Are you all right? What happened?" She abandoned her meal and ran over to Savannah's bed.

"I'm fine. I just miss him." Savannah sat up and ran her tissue over her red-stained cheeks.

"You'll see him soon. I heard you mention Labor Day. That's only a few weeks away." Karina placed an arm around her shoulders, leaning her head on Savannah's cotton T-shirt.

"Yeah, I guess. We won't be able to see each other though. My brothers are busy and won't be able to pick me up."

"What is all of this? Did you miss church or something?" Gabi glided through the open door and sat on Savannah's bed.

"Of course not," Savannah snipped. "I just got off the phone with Leland."

"Ooh," Gabi snarled and swiveled her hips. "Told him about Joe the sex machine, huh? He didn't take it well, did he? Guys don't like to share."

Karina attempted to give Gabi the evil eye. The one that said, *shut the hell up*. Gabi turned to her with a shrug that said *what?*

"That's not it at all. I just wish we were together. I never should have told you about Joe. You make it sound so vile."

"Hey. I think it's great. You are way too young to be committed to one man. I just figured with your open relationship, you'd share each other's conquests. Hell, it could make for great phone sex. Oh baby, he rode me like a stallion." Gabi pranced around the room, twirling her invisible lasso. "Do you wanna spank me for bein' bad?"

"Ew, you are vulgar." Savannah laughed and spanked Gabi's ass. "We decided not to share our stories. I don't want to hear about any other women and I don't think he does, either."

"I bet if you were with another woman, he'd love to hear about it." Gabi ducked as Savannah's pillow flew at her head. "What? Guys are into that."

Savannah dropped her head to her knees and sighed. At least the tears had stopped.

"Anyway, I have a great idea on how you can forget all about your man troubles. My brother's friend Keith invited us to play games at the Mehnk Student Union. They have pool tables, video games, bowling, and bunch of other shit. Keith's a sophomore, frat boy, adorable. The best part is he has some really hot friends."

"So we're solving my man trouble with more men." Savannah shook her head. "No thank you."

"Absolutely. What's the saying? The best way to get over an old horse is to get under a new horse...or something." Gabi dropped to Savannah's bed, stuffing her feet under her.

Savannah huffed and pushed Gabi's feet off the bed. "Don't put those stinky things on my bed. Now I have to wash the blankets again."

"They don't smell. For goodness sake." Gabi lifted her bare foot to Savannah's face.

"For the love of God." Savannah pushed her leg away. "If I wanted to smell something nasty, I'd take a whiff of the garbage chute."

Gabi rolled her eyes and jumped over to Karina's bed. "Are you happy now?"

"I'll be happy once my bedding's in the washer." Savannah pulled a pillow out of the case and started stripping the bed.

Karina jumped up as bedding was pulled from under her ass.

"So, anyway, tonight—guys—Mehnk."

"Hot guys?" *Danger! Danger!* Karina cringed. She couldn't exactly explain her hot-guy ban to her friends. "I don't know about that."

"What else you got to do? Read?"

"I'm reading a great story. The guy..." Karina went to grab her e-reader, but stopped as Gabi shoved her fingers in her ears. Seriously, in her ears.

"La. La. La," Gabi sang. Apparently, she had learned everything she needed to know in kindergarten... And behaved like she was still there.

"You're going. Maybe you'll see your boy-toy, Ryan." Gabi crossed her arms. "I didn't get a look at him. I want to see what the dreamy rescuer looks like."

"He was adorable," Savannah added. "I wasn't too busy to notice that, but I should stay in tonight."

"Did I hear hot guys?" Megan Stewart asked as she sat down on the floor by Karina's bed. Her cutoff Indiana Colts shorts were hidden by an oversized Pacers T-shirt, and her fire-red hair was tied in a knot on the top of her head.

"Hot guys. Six PM. You in?" Gabi asked.

"Heck yeah," Megan said.

"No thanks." Savannah turned to her phone.

Karina grabbed her tablet and dropped onto her bed. "I'll stay with Savannah." Thank you, Savannah, for a good excuse to stay home.

"Why aren't you going out tonight? Is everything okay?" Megan must have noticed Savannah's tear-stained cheeks because her tone went all maternal and smooth.

"She's fine. The phone won't ring while we're gone. You have to go. We're all going. You don't want to be left out. Only the cool people are going. Aren't you cool?" Gabi pulled out the sing-song tones.

"Peer pressure. Really?" Savannah rolled her eyes as she shook her blond hair.

"Come on, Savannah. It won't be any fun without you," Megan whined.

"I'm sure you'll have plenty of fun." Savannah leaned back against the headboard.

"Please. You have to go."

"Pretty please with sugar on top. We'll even wait till your blankets are out of the dryer." Gabi shook her head at that last part.

They all whined and pestered her relentlessly until Savannah heaved a theatrical sigh. "Okay. I'll go if y'all leave me alone."

Darn it. And with just a dash of peer pressure, Karina's reason for staying home was gone.

~§~

The Mehnk was packed. The four women walked into the shiny atrium and there were students everywhere, spread out around the tables and chairs scattered around the glass-ceilinged reception area. The layout focused on the large white-brick fireplace that led up, at least fifty feet, to the atrium ceiling.

Hallways broke off from the main area to the different parts of the building. A large archway led to the Meeting rooms and Grand Hall, another passageway led to the school's main cafeteria, and another hall led to a set of stairs with a sign that said, "Scoreboard".

The girls headed toward the sign, walking down the dark set of stairs and descending into the popcorn-infused air.

Ding-ding-ding.

Beep. Beep.

"Round one, fight"

Pop. Pop.

Multiple foosball, air hockey, and pool tables lined the left-hand walls of the dusky room. To the right were three lanes of bowling, with at least twenty-five video games—everything from *Ms. Pacman* and *Street Fighter* to *Dance, Dance Revolution*—separating the two areas.

Neon signs and televisions lining the walls cast an eerie glow over the patrons shouting to be heard over the rock music blasting from the jukebox. College students sat on bar stools next to bar-height tables, drinking non-alcoholic beverages—the only drinks available from the café at the far end of the space.

The women looked around the crowded room, hoping to find Keith and his friends. Even though only one of them knew what he looked like, that didn't stop every woman from craning her neck. Heck, maybe the guy wore a T-shirt with his name on it or something. Who knew? And it didn't hurt to look. To be prepared.

"Hey girl," a wanna-be surfer dude with brown hair and a rounded face shouted. He wrapped his wiry, sun-tanned arms around Gabi. "How's my little sis?"

"Is he your brother?" Karina asked. If they were related, those were some good family genes. He might be skinny, but his lips were full and his eyes were deep set. The smile he threw their way probably had girls lining up out the door.

"No, but I've known her since she wore diapers." Surfer dude rubbed his knuckles on the top of Gabi's head, noogie-style.

Karina's brother hadn't given her a noogie in years—well, maybe months. Not that she missed it. Her brother's knuckles were famously hard—just ask the eighth grader he punched when he found Karina and said eighth grader exchanging their first kiss. Her first kiss ever.

"Wow, you did not disappoint, Gabs. Way to supply hot friends. I'm Keith." He grabbed Karina's hand and planted a kiss on the back. If the attempted smoldering look he gave as he slid his wet lips over her hand wasn't so smarmy, she might have ended up standing in the line out the door.

He slobbered on each girls hand, and then pulled Gabi toward the pool tables and began the introductions. "Gabi, this is my friend Ski, and this is Danny. Their other roommate is roaming around here somewhere."

"These are my friends Karina, Megan, and Savannah." Gabi pointed to them as they each gave a little wave, and the Gabi Show unfolded. Hair was tossed. Eyelashes were batted. The men hung on every move. Karina was in awe.

"What are we playing?" Gabi asked as she grabbed the white ball and spun it in her hand, massaging the orb. The hormone-ridden male eyes ate it up. Except for Ski, who was completely oblivious as he racked up the balls before he pulled out his phone and started texting. Either he was gay or he had a girlfriend. Of course, with Karina's track record, she'd probably never know.

"A little eight-ball, who wants to play?" Danny asked.

"I'm in." Gabi smiled as she dropped the ball to the table. Her flirting skills were exquisite. Did she go to class for that, or did it just come natural?

Karina would love to sign up for Flirting 101, she'd even take the advanced Learning to Talk to Guys 102. Maybe then she wouldn't be such a train-wreck. Not that she planned on talking to a whole bunch of guys given the whole man-hiatus, but it could happen someday, and wouldn't it be nice to be prepared?

"All right, Gabi and I against Keith and Ski. We will annihilate you," Danny the roommate boomed, pointing a finger at the end of a tattooed arm at Keith's chest. He leaned down and whispered to Gabi. "Are you any good, sweetheart?"

"Watch and learn." She smirked and flipped her dark brown hair.

"We'll let you go first, since you have a handicap," Keith mocked.

"Am I to be the handicap?" Gabi joked as she ran the chalk slowly over the tip of her cue. Danny practically drooled. "Being that I'm a girl and all."

"No," Keith said, "I was actually referring to Danny over there."

"Yeah, sweetheart, you look like the type of girl who knows how to handle a big stick." Danny leaned against his own cue.

"It is my specialty." Gabi purred and batted her pretty little eyelashes.

"Oh, good grief." Savannah rolled her eyes.

"Hey. That's my boy's sister. Keep your mind out of the gutter." Keith punched Danny in the arm.

"I'm going to head over to the video games. Anyone in?" Savannah rolled her eyes again.

"I'll go." Megan and Karina said together.

"You can't all leave me." Gabi whined. "Karina, please stay."

Karina knew somewhere there was a girl code that said you didn't abandon a fellow lady with a group of guys. Especially unknown strange guys with drool hanging down their chin. Although she had a feeling Keith would beat the crap out of anyone that got too close to his "little sister".

Gabi's eyes pleaded. Darn girl code. Karina shrugged. "Sure. No problem."

Karina leaned against the wall and watched Savannah and Megan walk away. She wasn't a huge video game player but sending Ms. Pacman aimlessly around a fluorescent board was a helluva lot more fun than holding up the wall.

Gabi leaned in to align her shot, swinging her hips from side to side. Her neckline lowered just enough to give a glimpse of her cleavage. Karina was tempted to grab napkins for the men huddled around the table, drool pouring down their chins. She could charge a fee for this good of a show. It just kept getting better and better.

Gabi sank the three-ball into the corner pocket on the break. "Well, it looks like we're solids."

She proceeded to sink every single solid ball, one after another, and finished by sending the eight-ball into the center pocket on the other side of the table.

"I think we win," she crooned with a mock-innocent grin. The guys just stared, mouths hanging open. As the realization hit that she had cleared the table, their expression changed from fascination to humility and finally worship.

Wow. What doesn't that girl do well? Karina thought. If she didn't like her so much, she was certain she would hate her.

It was funny how men became mush when certain women were around. Karina had, never managed to pull off that effect, no matter how hard she'd tried. She was sure it was because she hadn't perfected the eyelash-bat. She always looked like she had something in her eye. She'd even tried the seductive look once, but upon investigation, she found it made her look like she was constipated. Not exactly the look you're going for when trying to woo a guy.

"That's my girl," Danny announced as he wrapped an arm around her shoulder.

"I'm going to run and grab some drinks. Do you want anything, Gabi?" Karina couldn't sit still any longer. It was time to make herself useful. Or scarce.

"I'll come with you." Gabi set the cue on the end of the table.

"I'll take a Monster." Danny racked the balls and turned to Gabi. "Be quick. It's best two out of three."

"We'll just be a minute. Can I get you anything?" she asked Keith and Ski.

After a couple of head shakes, Karina and Gabi headed toward the drink bar. Danny must have seen his friend, because his booming voice yelled, "Hey, dude. Get the hell over here so I can kick your ass. You still owe me a game."

All Karina could see were broad shoulders as the new guy lifted his arm and gave Danny the one finger salute. He didn't turn around but continued talking to the gaggle of women who were hanging on every word and gesture he made. A male Gabi. Awesome.

"My, my, he looks nummy," Gabi whispered as they approached him. "I wonder if his front is as tasty as his back."

"Come on, man, bring your new friends with you." Keith bellowed.

"Hold on…"The friend turned around and Karina's heart stopped. "Hi, Karina."

"Hi, Ryan." Karina sighed. Of course jerk-extraordinaire was not only here, but also friends with their new pool buddies. Perfect.

"Ryan Kent? Long time, no see," Gabi said. A knowing smile crossed her lips. "I heard you have a knack for finding lost friends."

"Gabi, hey, my reputation has preceded me then." He smiled. An annoying, arrogant smile. Maybe his smile wasn't arrogant. Maybe that was just Karina, but everything about this man screamed pompous jerk. From his lean muscular body to his dreamy, smiling eyes. Shit, none of those traits screamed arrogance. But they were there—somewhere.

"How have you been?" Gabi asked the pompous jerk.

"Good. I haven't seen you in months."

"You know each other?" Karina asked.

"From the Oak Brook Country Club."

"Ah." Karina nudged Gabi. "We should go."

"Are you coming back?" Ryan asked, while the gaggle he abandoned shot razor blades through Karina and Gabi with their psycho, possessive eyes.

"We're just grabbing a drink. Can we get you anything?"

"No. I'm fine." He sauntered toward the pool table. "But thanks."

Gabi fanned herself with her hand once he was out of hearing distance. "Wow. Had I known you were hot for Ryan Kent, I'd have told you to go for it. He is fine."

"I'm not his type. Anyway, he seemed to be more into you than me." She nearly winced at the disappointment in her voice. This was not a disappointment. He was a jerk—a jerk with bad hair. She sighed. She really needed to work on finding better hideous faults.

"He was looking at you, not me. I just did most of the talking." They stopped walking and Gabi turned to look back at the table. A smile spread across her face. "And anyway, he's still looking at you."

Karina didn't want to do it, but her head wouldn't listen. She touched her chin to her chest. Then to her shoulder. Then around to look at Ryan. To find him talking to his friends. She was right, he had no interest in her. And that was for the best, because she had absolutely no interest in him. None.

His ears were too small for his big head. She sighed. Faults, she needed to find better faults.

She grabbed Gabi's arm and dragged her toward the bar counter. "Would you just order? I'm sure he has a girlfriend or a harem."

"Jealous?"

"No." Absolutely not. Jerk. Bad hair. Small ears. Who needed that combination in their life?

As they walked back to the table, drinks in hand, Karina asked, "What about you and Danny, anything there?"

"What? No. I just met him."

"I think he's got a thing for you."

"Nah, he's just a flirt. Some of these frat guys are just a bunch of womanizers. I have no interest in that."

They made it back to the table and found Ski and Keith arguing about who would shoot first. Gabi gave the energy drink to Danny. The look he gave her was hot and dark. Oh, yeah, he was the womanizing type— Karina knew that look.

"Hey, Ryan." Gabi called over to womanizer number one after she and Gabi sat at the nearest table. "Where are your groupies?"

"On to their next fascination, I'm sure."

Karina watched Ryan lean over the pool table. The jeans he wore fit him nice, showing off his assets. His corded arms bulged as he drew the big stick back and forth. *Crash.* Balls flew around the table.

Danny leaned over the table in front of Gabi, his eyes roaming up and down her body. "Ryan's going to play this round before he has to go, but we got next."

"Sure." Gabi smiled as Danny walked away.

"Now, what would your girlfriend think of your popularity, Ryan?" Gabi asked.

"I wouldn't know. I don't have a girlfriend," Ryan shot back.

"See. No girlfriend." Gabi whispered. That girl sure had a gift for bluntness.

Karina shook her head, ignoring the pleasant way her stomach fizzed at the idea of an unattached Ryan.

Just then, a girl from her dorm—Parker—slid behind Ryan. "Hi, honey." She purred and tossed her curly blonde hair. "How have you been?"

"Hi, Park," Ryan said as she threw her arm around his neck.

"Darling, I didn't know you knew my dorm mates. Aren't they fabulous?"

"Parker, I didn't know you thought I was fabulous." Gabi angled toward Parker and crossed her legs.

"I was trying to be nice. I didn't think calling you a home-wrecking whore would go over well."

"Hey." Keith got in between Gabi and Parker. Brave man.

"It's okay." Gabi laughed. "I can't help it if this snapback snatch can't hold onto her boyfriend."

Parker stepped back, eyes slicing daggers into Gabi. "I can't help it you like my castoffs."

"Oh for goodness sake, blondie, it was in eighth grade. Get over it." Gabi sighed and took a drink of her soda.

"What was in eighth grade?" Ryan looked back and forth between the two women.

"Nothing," the two girls said in unison.

Well, at least they agreed on that.

Parker turned her eyes to Karina. "Karen, right? It's so good to see you."

"It's Karina," Ryan said as he leaned down to take another shot.

"Of course it is." She cooed and skimmed her nails up and down Ryan's arm. "You be nice to my man. We mean a lot to each other."

"Ry, where you been hiding this one? I don't believe we've met. I'm Keith."

"I'm Parker." She hummed and turned to Danny. "And you must be Ryan's roommate, Danny. I have heard so much about you."

As Parker flitted about, ogling Ryan and his friends, Karina's blood boiled. *Not dating, my ass.*

Thankfully, Megan and Savannah returned from their escape to the video games. "Are you ready to go?" Megan asked.

"I am." Karina jumped from her seat. Thank God.

"Don't leave. I want a rematch," Danny pleaded with Gabi, who was right behind Karina.

"Raincheck."

"Okay. See you around."

Karina didn't hear anything else as she spun and headed for the door, too angry to listen to anything more that was said. Why did she care if he was with Parker? It's not like he was hers. Heck, she couldn't even stand the guy. In fact, he and Parker were perfect for each other.

~»ΨP«~

Chapter Four

Ryan

RYAN WATCHED KARINA leave. He tried to concentrate on the game of pool he was supposed to be playing—but the way she moved, the way she talked, the way she laughed—he couldn't get his eyes to cooperate.

Although she hadn't laughed for him. Not once. That needed to change. He was making that his personal goal—make Karina laugh. He probably had some work to do before that would happen. Maybe a little groveling.

She hadn't seemed all that happy to see him. He might have laid on the attitude a bit thick when they met. But he'd been having so much fun with her. And she didn't put up with his shit, which was unusual. And so damned entertaining.

"Grab your stick, Kent." Danny threw the cue at Ryan.

He caught it before it beaned him in the head. "Nice throw, asshole." Ryan walked to the table, leaned over, and lined up his shot. A solid color ball dropped into the pocket. Nice.

"So, what are we playing for, anyway?" Ryan walked the table and centered for another shot.

"The usual." Ski ran the square of blue chalk along the tip of his cue. "Dinner."

"Damn straight. You'll be buying me and Ryan dinner tonight, my man." Danny watched from the sidelines, rubbing up against Parker.

Damn Parker. Why couldn't the frat brothers just stay away from her? He was serious when he said he was going to protect her. His brothers were not good enough for her. Well, not all of them, but Danny the Psi Rho man-whore wasn't good enough for her.

Ryan missed his shot. Damn Parker. "Park, don't you have friends that are missing you, or something?"

"I'd rather be here with you and your friends." She flipped her blonde hair over her shoulder. "Anyway, I'm waiting for a friend. I'm meeting her here."

"Yeah, Dad, let her stay here awhile and play with us." Keith leaned in for his shot, hitting a stripe but spinning it along the edge of the pocket.

"So, Keith. How do you know them?" Ryan asked. Not that he cared. Mild curiosity at best.

"Them?" Keith snagged Danny's energy drink and took a sip.

"Karina and her friends."

Danny bent down and lined up the shot. There were two pool sharks in the house—Danny and Ski. Those two could clear a table in one turn. That's why Keith and Ryan always went first, otherwise they'd never get a chance to play.

"I went to school with Gabi's brother," Keith said.

"That's right, the brother went to public school or something." Ryan sat on a bench as Danny sank ball after ball. This was going to be another fast game. Which was probably good. Ryan had fraternity bills to be paid, a checkbook that needed to be balanced and a bunch of shit he'd never get to once school started.

"Yeah, he went to public and the rest went to private. I guess he didn't like all the bullshit. He didn't talk about it much."

"At least he had a choice." Not like Ryan. He'd tried to get his parents to let him go to public school a few times over the years. No luck.

"Oh darling, your life wasn't all that bad." Parker leaned up against the table. She had no idea the life he'd led. She was too busy dealing with her own parental issues to see what he'd lived with. Or maybe she just didn't mind being told what to do and when.

He minded. He'd always minded.

"I'll see you boys later. My friend's here." She swayed her hips back and forth as she walked out of the room. Thank God.

"So are we going to hang out with them again?" Danny finished off the last ball and stood up from the table. By "them" he meant Gabi. Danny seemed to have a semi-one track mind with her.

Not that Ryan could say anything—stones and glass houses and all. He was having a hard time getting his mind off Karina. And no matter how hard he tried, he couldn't help but hang on the answer to Danny's question as well. He'd love to see Karina again.

"Time for dinner." Keith tossed the cue on the table. "I'll set something up for next week."

Ryan wouldn't miss that for the world.

~»ΨP«~

Chapter Five

Karina

THE NEXT DAY, Karina, Megan, and Gabi stepped out into a dazzling August day. The sun beat down, warming Karina's bare arms, and she inhaled the sweet scent of the summer salvia scattered along the edge of the sidewalk.

She pulled the sliding strap of her ice blue tank top back onto her shoulders. "I told you—he's a jerk, end of story." Not even the delicious summer weather could get her mind off of Ryan and his hellion succubus.

"I don't think he's into her. He seemed like he wanted Parker to go away just as much as we did," Gabi shot back.

"I guess." She didn't want to talk about Ryan. Well, she did. But talking about him was not helping her forget him. And she had to forget him. She was on a man-fast. No more of their bullshit clogging her arteries. It didn't matter what he felt or didn't feel. He was a minor inconvenience in an otherwise happy existence. So what if he was smoking hot?

Smoking hot? Crap. She needed an attitude adjustment when it came to that guy.

"I can't believe Savannah didn't want to come. When is she planning on getting her books?" Megan bent down and broke off a stem of salvia.

"She stayed back because Joe was stopping by for a nooner. I'm sure my room will be inaccessible and tainted." Karina couldn't believe that her roommate was seeing Joe again. Or the way she blew off his kiss the other night, and the kissy-kissy slobber-face she'd had with Leland the next day. Karina thought for sure they'd be over. But no. Joe was becoming a permanent fixture.

"How can the room be tainted? She changes her sheets if she sneezes on them. She scrubs the floor once a week." Megan scuffed her feet along the sidewalk.

"Who said she was going to use her own bed? Karina's bed tainted by dick-snot and maybe a side trip to Karina's desk. Gross." Gabi laughed as Megan gagged.

"You're disgusting." Megan threw the salvia at Gabi and shook her head.

Karina stopped short, glaring at Gabi. "Nice." Her poor virginal bed. Her sweet innocent desk defiled by a nympho roommate. "I have to sleep in that room, you know."

"Just don't lay on any wet spots. You'll be fine." Gabi turned toward the bookstore and tugged Karina's arm. "You can always hang out in my room for a while. I have nothing going on."

"Fine, but that doesn't help with the dick-snot problem."

"Could you please stop calling it that?" Megan sped up. "I'm going to gag."

"Which part offends you...? The dick or the snot?"

"I'm done with you." Megan laughed and ran along the path toward Holmes Hall, the building that housed the bookstore. The other two watched Megan sprint ahead and then turned to each other. A grin spread on their faces as they shook their heads in unison.

"Oh, no. You're not running away," they yelled and ran after her. Once they caught her, both of them grabbed Megan's shirt.

"We love you. *Mwah. Mwah. Mwah.*" Gabi and Karina made a show out of kissing Megan as she covered her head with her arms.

"Go away, you freaks." Megan giggled as she pushed the other two away.

"Nope. You're stuck with us." Karina wrapped her arm around Megan as they started walking again. "Anyway, I may need another place to stay to avoid my room. When we agreed that a scrunchie on the doorknob would indicate a man was in the room, I didn't think the elastic band would become a permanent door hanger. After all, she has a sorta-boyfriend."

"True. I thought Joe was a one-time deal. You know, the whole no-getting-attached since Leland is waiting." Megan commented.

"Apparently he's a three time deal, thus far anyway," Karina said.

Megan blinked. "Haven't they only known each other four days?"

"Exactly. We've only been here for four days, and already my room has been fraught with sexcapades."

"I'd like to be fraught with sexcapades." Gabi sighed, as Karina nodded. She too would like to be fraught with sexcapades, but that brought her full-circle to the man-fast. Damn.

A long line of students waited along the side of the Holmes Hall, their heads bowed as they played with their smart phones.

"You have gotta be kidding," Karina huffed as they walked to the end of the line. The back of the line. More like a mile-long wait.

"Are they giving crap away? That is the only reason I can see why this line would be this long." Gabi craned her neck over the mob of bookstore patrons.

"Might as well get comfortable." Megan sighed and sat on the grass. Gabi and Karina followed suit. Not like they had a choice.

When they ran out of conversation, all three got out their cell phones. *Candy Crush. Words with Friends. Temple Run.* Karina's mind went numb waiting for the line to move. Waiting to reach the Promised Land...a store that would take hundreds of dollars of their parents' money in exchange for the books that would be anchored to their hip over the next four months, and then sold back to the bookstore for fifty bucks.

An hour and a half of loitering and senseless handheld entertainment later, and the women entered the bookstore with their class schedule in hand. Signs identifying the departments, courses, and instructors hung on the nondescript white walls above the respective stacks of books.

This should have been easy. Karina twisted the piece of paper as she walked the aisles of books for the English department. English 101. Didn't everyone have to take English 101? She wound her way up and down the aisles again, this time spreading out toward the foreign language section. She came up to the book she needed for her German class. The small stack stuffed between the heap of Spanish and French books should have been hard to find. However, the damn thing practically jumped off the shelf into her hand. Yet, the English book...the language of the country where she stood...was impossible to find.

Shouldn't there be a mountain of books for that class? She peered at the paperwork in her hand. The crinkled list of classes wouldn't direct her to where to go, no matter how hard she stared at the piece of paper. She shook her head and read her schedule again. Maybe she'd misread something. She checked the English department bookshelves again, hoping her eyes would latch onto the elusive tome.

Tome. She laughed. Maybe she knew enough English to skip the class. Wishful thinking. The proper use of the English language had never been her strong suit, something she would have to address if she wanted to be a lawyer.

"Are you lost? Can I help you find something?" She jumped at the deep voice behind her. She looked around and found an adorable guy with reddish-blond hair. His green eyes sparkled when he flashed a beautiful, pearly-white smile.

"I am lost, please save me," hung on her tongue, but she pulled it back. She already felt brainless since she couldn't find a simple book in a bookstore, no need to advertise her stupidity. Although she really needed this book and he *was* adorable, with sweet eyes and cute dimples. "I guess so."

She debated batting her eyelashes. He might think she was having a spasm or something. She knew her limitations. "I'm looking for English 101. I can't seem to find the book." She held her class schedule out toward him.

"I can help, English is my major." He resituated his own set of books and grabbed the piece of paper. His hand glided along hers and tiny sparks pinged along her skin. "One PM on Tuesday and Thursday? Doctor Morefield. I have her for English. She's an avid linguist, and she wrote a captivating book on the subject. Have you read it?"

"No." Karina smiled at his excitement. He seemed to love words. Hopefully Karina would love her major just as much. "Are you new here?"

"Yes, I'm a freshman."

"So, you're taking English 101?" she asked as he handed her schedule back to her.

His fingers caressed soft and slow along her skin before he pulled back. "No, I placed out of it. But I noticed the book when I was grabbing my own." He walked to the end of the aisle, and then around the corner into a small nook at the back of the store. "The class has so many students that they put the books back here, out of the way. It's hard to find."

"Thank you. I don't know what I would have done without your help."

Why would anybody look in the large cubbies at the back of the store for a darn book when all the others were stacked in the front?

"Well, I hope to see you around campus. I'm Kyle."

"Karina—and thanks again." She watched him walk away. Not bad looking and sweet. Kyle, hmm…. Nice guy. Helpful. Not the usual jerk she seemed to fall for. Maybe her luck was changing.

College might not be so bad after all.

~»ΨP«~

Chapter Six

Ryan

AN ANTI-CLIMACTIC MIXTURE of English and business classes filled Ryan's Monday morning. Tuesday wasn't looking that much better—in other words, a morning mandating severe caffeine intake. Unless he wanted to fall asleep in class.

So far Ryan had been unimpressed with his courses. Today, though, he'd be going to his architecture course. The bonus for putting up with the rest of the crap classes. He was also hoping to get a glimpse of Karina, but so far that hadn't happened. He hadn't gone out of his way to find her. He wasn't that far gone. Yet.

He shook his head as he opened the glass doors to the Languages building, heading for his German class. Despite the fact that he should have spent the past few days on fraternity business, he couldn't seem to get her off his mind. Granted, he was trying to replace a hot blonde with frat finances and planning. There was no contest. But now he needed to get his head back in the game and concentrate on his classes. Of course, he had a feeling German Composition wasn't going to hold his interest enough to remove her body from his thoughts.

And it was one hell of a body. Medium-length dark blond hair fell over a nicely sized chest and cute waist. Her legs were long and face was gorgeous. At least he thought so. The unattached guys from their night of pool only had eyes for Gabi.

Ryan got it. She was Latin heat. Slim waist, big chest, gorgeous and seductive. Gabi was hot. He could admit that, but she wasn't what he looked for. Hell, he was starting to think he'd just been looking for Karina all this time. Too bad she hated his guts.

Ryan walked into the jam-packed German Composition classroom. German phrases spewed from his classmates mouths even as they stumbled on the words. Professor Vierow wouldn't allow anyone to speak any other language in her classroom. Only Deutsch. Not that the students didn't talk in English most of the time anyway, since the woman couldn't hear out of her left ear—the result a tragic firework accident that seemed to bode well for her English-dependent students.

"*Guten Tag,*" Professor Vierow said, and then launched into a rant—in German, of course—of classroom rules and regulations, her bun jostling as she bounced from desk to chalkboard. The sad thing was that this was her in a calm state. In a few weeks she'd get so excited about the information she was teaching, she'd somehow get her four-foot five-inch frame on top of her desk and pontificate on the virtues of the German language.

Ryan just wanted to learn the language so he could work internationally for his father's company. Or better yet, put an ocean between him and his father's influence. Maybe spend the summer in

Constructing Berlin, a huge summer program of exploring local architecture, and building everything from temporary pavilions to gazebos. He wanted to go, but he had to be realistic. His father would never let him follow frivolous dreams of drawing pictures of buildings. He had family responsibilities.

That didn't stop Ryan from working toward a proficiency in the language or continuing to learn all about drawing those pictures. It was the one thing he loved to do.

"*Hier.*" Ryan raised his hand when Professor Vierow called his name. One word that sounded the same in German or English. He listened to the familiar names of his classmates. Since the university only required two years of a foreign language, most of the students generally stopped once they had enough credits for graduation. He wasn't majoring in German, but he was one of the few who went on to junior level, so he knew all the students in his class.

"Karina Wolfe."

"*Hier.*"

How had Ryan missed her? He never thought she would be in third-year German, that's how. Mistake number one. He turned around and watched her push her dark blonde behind her ear, face buried in her textbook. When she lifted her gaze, he saw recognition wash across her face, her smile turning to a scowl.

Yeah, she really was not happy to see him. He needed to work on that. She went back to her book and whipped to the next page. Okay. He might have said a few things that were outrageous—wild oats, human nature. He could understand why she might have taken it the wrong way. After all, she didn't know him at all, and he was rambling incoherently about her roommate's relationship. Well, it wasn't incoherent. She seemed to understand what he'd said just fine. That was probably the issue. If it had been incoherent, she'd be giving him a fake smile not an indignant glare.

He half-listened to the professor outlining the requirements for the term—a weekly four-page paper, two ten-page papers, and a daily journal. Well, the good news was he'd learn quite a bit while he tried to keep his entries and papers fresh. He loved throwing obscure words into his homework to keep Vierow on her toes. She seemed to like it, too.

The hour dragged. It had to be longest German class he'd ever sat through. The professor moved on from class demands to random class participation. She walked around asking everyone about their weekend, and reprimanded them when they didn't have the words to give a thought-provoking answer.

When he heard Karina's name, he lifted his head. Her face reddened as she attempted to answer *auf Deutsch, bitte*, and not in English. She seemed to hold her own, but that was never enough in this class. She'd learn. They all learned.

"Frau Wolfe. Auf Deutsch, bitte...nur in Deutscher sprache." Professor Vierow shook her head as she explained again that they could only speak German.

"Ich kaufte Bücher... at..." Karina stopped. Terror, frustration and panic oozed form her widened eyes and fidgeting hands. It broke his heart as she stumbled over words and dodged the professor's demands.

"Ich kaufte auch Bücher in der Buchhandlung," Ryan said.

Dammit. He'd said that out loud. He couldn't stand watching her suffer, and she was only talking about buying a book at the bookstore. Of course, he hadn't expected to Bogart her conversation, but she'd probably be thankful to be out of the spotlight.

"Sehr gut, Herr Kent. Welche Bücher hast du gekauft?"

Ryan rambled about the books he'd bought until the professor moved on to her next victim. He didn't see anyone else new to Vierow's class, so he had a feeling the rest would be ready for whatever onslaught came their way.

He turned to Karina. Well, crap. Indignant glare had morphed into slicing daggers. He could practically see smoke curling from her cute ears. Why was she mad? He helped her.

Unless she was secretly a masochist and enjoyed being skewered by faculty members? That must be it. He couldn't think of any other reason to still be mad at him.

As the class ended and the students filed from the room, Ryan fought his way through the throng of bodies to Karina. Speaking of masochist…

She glared and tried to escape through the side door as he approached. He was faster. "Hey, Karina. Did you enjoy your first German class with Professor Vierow?"

"I've had better." She kept her back to him as they followed the other students out the door. When they left the room, she turned to him, her arms wrapped around her books. "Which way are you going?"

"Planning on following me?"

"No. I'll go the opposite way."

"The anger… The least you can do is say thank you." He threw his best smile at her.

"Thank you for embarrassing me? I could handle myself."

"I didn't mean to embarrass you…"

"You know what? Don't worry about it." She spun and started down the busy hallway. She wore indignation well. In fact, she looked downright edible. Her hip-hugging jeans and T-shirt—there was something about the way her hips swayed. He really needed to see someone about the masochism.

He ran after her again. "Hey, Karina. Hold up."

"What?" She stopped and sighed.

"I'm sorry."

"For what?"

"For embarrassing you—for embarrassing myself the other night. I was an ass."

"Which night?" She sighed again

"Wow, I didn't realize there was more than one night to apologize for. The night of the party. I was just, you know, joking around."

"Oh, so a person's inability to be faithful is funny?"

"No, just a bad joke."

"Well, at least you can admit it." A small hint of a smile crossed her face.

He ripped a piece of lined paper from his spiral notebook and waved the impromptu white flag next to his head. "Truce?"

"Truce." She smiled as she walked away. Well, he finally got a smile out of her. Things might not be as bad as he thought.

~»ΨP«~

Chapter Seven

Karina

THE FIRST FEW weeks of school, Karina threw herself into homework
and studying. When she wasn't having fun with her friends, she was
trying to keep up with her classes. She had hoped the school would ease
the freshman into the curriculum. Yeah, right. That was a pipedream.
They'd hit the ground with a thud.

Of all her classes, German was giving her the hardest time. Although
an advanced German course seemed like a good idea back when she
picked her classes, it was a crusher. When they told her she had to take a
test to determine her placement, she never thought she'd place in a
third-year nightmare. It seemed like a great idea at the time—only one

foreign language course instead of three. Hindsight and all…

She sat in German as the teacher handed back her second paper. It looked like a damn crime scene with all the red marks splashed across the page.

"Son of a bitch," she muttered to herself. At least she thought it was to herself. A few of her classmates turned their heads, eyes wide with disgust. She wanted to ask if they were disgusted because she swore or if it was because it wasn't *auf Deutsch*. If she knew the words for son of a bitch in German, she would have said them.

"Everything okay?" Ryan asked. Over the past few weeks, the two of them had become quasi-friends. Gabi dragged her to social event after social event with Keith's friends, which naturally included Ryan. Between playing pool at Scoreboard and volleyball at the gym, and of course German, they'd seen each other every day.

But who *hadn't* she seen every day—not even once, actually? Kyle. It wasn't a big school. Four thousand students. Not huge compared to other colleges, and he was a freshman, same as her. So you'd think they'd bump into each other once. One chance meeting. But no.

"No, things are not okay." She definitely said that out loud, darn it.

"What's wrong?"

So many things, but first things first. "How did you do on the last assignment?"

"I did fine." His latest masterpiece had a bright and shiny ass-kissing A sticking out from his textbook. "I take it you didn't do as well."

"No," she said as she stared at the latest D+ at the top of her assignment.

"May I?" he asked and gestured at the pages.

"Sure, why not."

He skimmed the document. "It just looks like you need to go over conjugating verbs. No big deal. I can help you, if you'd like."

She hated looking desperate…hell, being desperate, especially in front of him. He'd already made it clear that he thought she was an idiot.

He'd proven that over and over again with his smart-ass BS.

Although he had apologized, with a white flag and everything. Their truce.

That was the bigger problem. She didn't want to ruin the truce they had going. It was nice to be able hang out with him and not want to hit him. The thought of listening to his condescending tone while he told her all the things she did wrong…? Ugh, seventh circle of hell. However, she looked at the bulging letter on her paper and sucked down her pride. "That would be great. Thank you. When would you like to start?"

"How about during lunch today? We can head to the Mehnk and grab something to eat."

Friends. They were friends now. And she needed help from her friend right now. Lunch and a little tutoring was no big deal. Right?

Sometimes she missed being a no worries, trusting sort of person. Craig had made sure of that. Not that he meant to, but sometimes she wished she'd never met him. Never asked him out. Never…

"Okay, the Mehnk sounds great," she said, looking at all the red marks clouding the paper. No wonder he wanted to start right away; she needed all the help she could get, as soon as possible.

~§~

"This happens in the future, so you want to use future tense." Ryan changed the verb with blue pen. He'd gone through the whole paper and reworked and fixed the problems. Not that Karina would be able to turn in the changes and get credit, but it might help with future papers.

Might was being optimistic. Everything he said and showed her seemed so logical, so obvious right now, but when it was time to write the next one she had no idea if she'd be able to put all that knowledge to good use.

He dropped the red-and-blue-spattered mess on the table. "So, you think you can handle this next time?"

"Maybe." She stared at the changes.

"Well, I can help you with the next assignment if you want."

"That's okay." Bile rose in her throat. Maybe she should just bail on the class. Have an extra few hours a week to do something else, anything else. If the damn thing wasn't a requirement, she would. But she needed the class to graduate. So this term, next term—she'd have to take it sometime. Might as well be now.

"Oh." His face dropped as he closed his book. Not the best way to keep the truce going. Insult the guy's ability to help.

"I just don't want to bother you." She shoved her own books into her bag. "I'm sure you have better things to do then help me get my homework done."

"Not really, and I want to help. We're friends, right?" He played with his book, opening the cover and then slapping it down. *Tug, thwap. Tug, thwap.*

"Yep." She smiled. It wasn't a bad idea. She could stay with the class, get it over with and spend time with Ryan. Not that she *wanted* to spend time with him, but they were friends now. Spending time with friends was natural. Even if the friend was ridiculously hot.

Dammit. Not hot. He had flaws. What were they again? Something about ears or hair?

"That would be great, if you don't mind helping." She stood up, slinging the strap of her bag onto her shoulder.

"My pleasure." He led her up the stairs to the atrium of Mehnk Hall, and they walked over to the darkened windows. Rain beat against the glass lining the hall. When did it start raining? Her umbrella was back in her dorm. Of course. She really needed to check the weather app before she left her room in the morning.

"Would you like a ride home?" Ryan held open the door to the entryway.

"I'm heading to class." She moved the bag from her right shoulder to her left. Tuesday and Thursdays were hard. She didn't have time to go back to her room, so she carried all twenty pounds of books around all day.

"I'll drive you to class." He wrapped his fingers around the strap on her shoulder and lifted. The weight vanished as he transferred the bag to his own shoulder. His muscular shoulder. No—her friend's shoulder. No muscles.

"Are you sure you don't mind?"

"Wait here. I'll be right back." He ran out the door into the downpour with her bag, and a few minutes later he pulled up in front of the building.

She ran out to the car and slid onto the soft leather seat. "Thanks."

He grabbed her bag from the backseat and handed it to her. "Anytime. Where to?"

"English, please." She inhaled as he shifted the car into drive. It smelled like him. Musk and sandalwood. No food wrappers or garbage on the floor. Not one thing was out of place. He turned down the street to the Liberal Arts building, the windshield wipers swishing back and forth in rhythm.

"Your car is pretty clean."

"It's not my car." He pulled into the lot and drove to the back, right by the side entrance to the building.

"Steal it?"

Ryan laughed, a deep rumble that that curled Karina's toes. "No, my parents gave it to me."

Parent issues. She could relate. She pulled her bag close as she opened the door. "Thanks for the ride."

"No problem."

She jumped out and splashed across the parking lot. Once she made it inside and stomped into the building, she turned around to watch Ryan pull away from the curb.

"So, did you get a ride?" An umbrella-holding Savannah walked over to her roommate.

"Yep." Karina walked toward their shared English class.

"Wasn't that Ryan?"

"Yep." Ryan was not a conversation she wanted to have with Savannah or anyone else.

"Isn't that sweet."

"Yep."

"Almost like you two were meant to be." Savannah left her umbrella at the back of the room and followed Karina to their seats.

Sliding into the stadium seating, Karina shook her head. "Because he gave me a ride to class?"

"He likes you."

"As a friend."

Savannah rolled her eyes.

"He's good at tolerating me. Remember, I'm not his type." Karina sighed. Those words would haunt her.

Dr. Morefield started the class and the Ryan discussion was over. Thank goodness. She didn't want to talk about him anymore. Chasing boys that didn't want her wasn't fun and only ended in heartache. Her heartache.

She needed to focus on something else. Anything else but Ryan Kent.

~§~

The weekdays fell into a familiar routine. Classes and tutoring sessions kept her occupied during the day. Nights were filled with studying, friends, and the occasional party. Since she started working with Ryan, her last paper fetched a C and her studying time had been cut in half.

Although she didn't really mind the studying. Ryan actually made it fun. There was no condescending tone, no arrogance, and—who'd have thought?—she was actually learning something during their sessions.

"Usual teams?" Ryan spun a volleyball on his finger as the group hit the volleyball court. Karina, Gabi, Savannah, Megan, Ryan, Danny and Keith were dressed in their sportswear finest and ready to destroy each other. Karina smiled as she counted the odd number of players.

Someone would need to refrain from the evening of bumping and spiking. Oh, darn. "We're missing a player. I can sit this one out."

She grabbed her tablet from her backpack, sitting down on the hard metal bleacher. It had been weeks since she was able to sit and play with an app or read something that wasn't a textbook. She turned the electronic page as they argued over the flight of a ball that landed out of bounds. It was nice to be on the sidelines, completely oblivious to the turmoil below her.

"Hi, you're Karina, correct?"

She looked up. Kyle. Damn, he was cuter then she remembered. Her mind hadn't done him justice. Sweet. Dreamy. Adorable. Her body sighed as her arms went slack—and her tablet tumbled from her limp hand.

Before she could grab it, Kyle caught the wayward item midair. "Whoa. You don't want to break this." His smile intensified as he passed it back to her.

"No. I don't. Thanks." She tried to control her breathing, her cheeks warming at her clumsiness. Way to make a good first impression. Okay, second impression.

"You're very welcome."

He was such a nice guy. She'd looked for him every time she left her room over the past few weeks. The quad, every hallway, every building, but like an A in German, she just couldn't seem to find the prize. Now, faced with his side-swept terra cotta hair and bright green eyes, she couldn't imagine why she hadn't gone door-to-door to find him.

"I'm Kyle McDougal. We met at the bookstore."

That he thought she wouldn't remember him was so sweet. It wasn't like she thought about him constantly for the past two weeks. Oh wait, she had. "I remember. Would you like to sit down?"

"No, thank you. I have to get back to the track upstairs. My friends and I are training for the Ritter Run for the Cure next month." He pointed to the running track on the second level of the recreation center. "But I wanted to take a break and see if you'd be interested in going out to dinner with me sometime."

"Sure." Her heart raced as he stuttered through his proposition. She couldn't decide which she liked better, that he was running to collect money for cancer or the fact that he was stuttering as he asked her out.

"Does Friday around six fit into your schedule?"

"Tomorrow night. Sure. I'm living in Dickinson. I'll be in the foyer at six." She tried to hide the huge smile that wanted to break free. She had to play it cool...

"I will see you then." He waved as he ran down the bleachers and up the back stairs to the track. She watched until he disappeared up the stairs.

She found Kyle, and he asked her out. Oh my. If she wasn't afraid of scaring people away, she might break out into a happy dance. She couldn't wait to tell Savannah, Gabi, and Megan.

She knew she should be afraid, but there was something so pure about him. So perfect. So kind. She could see herself with this guy, and for the first time in a very long time, she wasn't scared.

~»ΨP«~

Chapter Eight

Ryan

RYAN WAS DISTRACTED from the moment he saw McDougal walk toward Karina. He knew Kyle McDougal from his English class, but never gave him much thought. However, he hadn't known the twerp had an interest in Karina. If he had, he sure as hell would've paid closer attention.

He tried to watch the ball and them at the same time. What could she possibly want with him? His sisters always told him that men were only good for two things—killing bugs and opening jars. McDougal's skinny body and gangly arms didn't look tough enough to handle either one of those tasks.

Karina lowered her head as her cheeks flushed. What was McDougal saying to her? What did he say to make her smile, laugh and blush so easily? What did he have in that scrawny little body that could compete with Ryan? Dammit.

Ryan shook his head. He was being such a dick. It wasn't McDougal's fault that he fucked everything up with Karina. Managed to find himself dangerously close to the friend zone.

As he watched Kyle walk away, his stomach knotted. Kyle looked happy—so did Karina, for that matter. He wanted to ask her what happened, but he wasn't sure if their relationship had entered into the zone where personal questions like that were acceptable.

Vaguely, Ryan saw Danny jump into the air to meet the ball, and the slap as his hand made contact vibrated in the air. *WHAM!* Like the old cheesy *Batman* TV show, the volleyball connected right with Ryan's nose.

"Shit," Ryan yelled and reached for his gushing nose. Well, he might have said a few other choice words, but he was just hit by a damn ball. He'd earned the right.

Room spinning. Nose throbbing. Time was lost. He looked up and found himself sitting on a bench, a towel pressed to his face. The towel dropped to the floor.

Damn, I was holding it. He had never lost focus like that before. The soft feel of terrycloth returned and he pressed it to his aching nose. *Ouch.*

Karina pushed his bangs away from the carnage. His face was leaking, his nose was all jacked out of joint, yet his skin tingled where her fingers had just trailed so softly.

"Thanks." He wiped the towel along his nose, trying to clean the area. *Ow. Ow, ow, ow.*

"Are you okay?" she asked, and he nearly winced. He couldn't stand pity, especially from her. He wanted to be the hero with her, not the pathetic loser she had to coddle. "Let me help you."

"I'm fine," he snapped, and she pulled her hand away like he'd singed her fingers. He wanted to take the words back, but his sisters' voices echoed in his head. *No take-backs*. It was out there. Now—damage control.

Shit. It took weeks to get her to show him that sparkle in her eyes and he went ahead and fucked it up. He hadn't meant to be rude. He just... He just had to know.

Ryan met her gaze. "I'm sorry. I shouldn't take my facial pain out on you."

He saw her hesitate, but a small smile emerged. "It's okay. It looks like it hurts." She cringed and moved the towel to his cheek, but her smile didn't falter.

It hurt, but not that bad, so he'd take it. He hated to admit it, but a small smile and pity was better than the look of disgust from a few weeks ago. She moved in closer, wedging herself between his knees as she continued to clean his face. The situation was innocent, the gesture, sweet and considerate. His face ached as blood continued to trickle. Yet he was having a helluva time controlling his groin as she moved side to side with each stroke of the towel.

Focus.

Focus.

"So, what was with that guy?" He tried to keep his tone nonchalant. After all, it wasn't a big deal. It's not like he cared all that much... Yeah, if he said that enough, he might actually start to believe it.

"Kyle?" She flicked a glance up toward the running track. Thankfully, douchebag was gone, but somehow Ryan still wanted to gag at look on her face. "We met at the bookstore. He's nice."

"Oh, so you're friends." Relief flooded his lungs. The way she said *nice* seemed friendly enough. Friends he could work with. If she was dating that douchebag, that might be... annoying. Of course, McDougal would be an idiot not to go after Karina. She was smart, gorgeous and... shit, Ryan needed to step up his game before douchebag made his move.

"Well, he actually asked me out." Her eyes landed back on Ryan. "I can't wait."

"Great." He hoped he said that with conviction. Douchebag had made his move. Dammit.

"Rub some dirt on it and get your butt back here." Danny dribbled the volleyball and tossed it into the basketball net hanging next to the court. Megan laughed and hung on his every move. That was new. The poor girl was heading for heartbreak. Danny wasn't nice-girl material and Megan was a nice girl. Too nice for his frat brother.

"I'm really sorry about earlier." He looked into Karina's hazel eyes, where bursts of blue and green played around the pupil.

"It's fine," she said as she folded the bloody towel and laid it next to his bag on the bleacher. "You can keep that." She smiled at him as she stepped backward. A real smile... ugh. He was such a sap.

She raised her head to look at the running track as she walked to her place on the bleachers. Happiness transformed her face as she waved. Obviously, the douchebag was back.

Ryan's jaw clenched as he walked back onto the court. Distraction. He needed to find something to get his mind off of Karina. It was going to be tough. Volleyball would have to do the trick because beating the crap out of douchebag would probably piss Karina off.

~»ΨP«~

Chapter Nine

Karina

"IT'S FINE," KARINA protested. Savannah's phone was ringing—again—and Karina turned her head to look at it. Tried to, anyway, but Savannah put both her hands on Karina's cheeks and twisted her face back in place.

"Your hair is not fine," Savannah snarled as she reached over and hit ignore on her cell phone—again—before going back to torturing her innocent roommate with the curling iron. "You are so ungrateful. This is your first date with Kyle. You want to look good, don't you?"

"Ouch." Good, yes. Bald, no.

"Beauty is pain." Savannah fluffed the ends of the latest curl.

"She looks fine." Gabi peered over her tablet and shook her head.

"Kar, you are brave to let the Southern Belle get you ready for the big date. I wouldn't let that Confederate Cosmetician near my face or hair. I think she's added a full foot to your height."

"I'd never touch your face or hair 'cause there ain't no hope for you and Lord knows what diseases you've acquired from them frat boys you hang out with."

"Hey. You hang out with those frat boys, too. I seem to recall you were playing volleyball and pool and bowling with those very frat boys." Gabi shook her head.

"I just hang out with them. I ain't trying to get with them."

"I'm not trying to get with any of them."

"Really?" Savannah spritzed some hairspray on the curl she was cooking. "You looked mighty cozy with Danny the other day."

"We're friends." Gabi poked at her tablet.

"What kind of friends?"

"What kind of friends are you and Joe?" Gabi stopped typing and squared her shoulders.

Savannah finger-brushed a curl along Karina's face. "Don't you have your own room?"

"Yeah, but I don't have a roommate, so it gets boring. I'd much rather stay here with you."

Karina loved these two women, but sometimes they were like Mentos and diet soda—all explosion and relatively harmless, but who wanted to deal with the mess or clean-up? "Are you done yet? I'm going to be late." She squirmed as she sat cross-legged on her bed. When she originally asked Savannah to help her get ready, it seemed like such a good idea. Now, as her legs tingled with lack of blood flow, she was wondering if she'd made a mistake.

The peanut gallery casting doubts from behind her electronics at the end of the bed didn't help any.

Savannah sighed sharply. "You have a half hour. And you're meeting him downstairs. What is that—a sixty-second commute time?" Savannah fluffed the soft curls and spritzed the waves into place with more hairspray.

"What if I hit traffic? I don't want to be late," Karina mumbled.

"Traffic." A loud cackle came from Gabi. "You can't wait downstairs. You'll look desperate."

"It must be a bad idea to head down too early if Gabi and I agree on it. We don't agree on anything." Savannah pulled Karina's bangs apart and sprayed one final burst of hair product. "You're all set."

Karina stood, terror haunting her eyes. She could see curls from the corner of her eyes. Nightmares of Little Orphan Annie slid through her mind. That was not a good look for her. Crap. What if Gabi wasn't just being whiny? What if Karina's hair was frizzy stripper hair, and she would have to bend down to get through doors?

This was her first date with Kyle. What had she been thinking, trusting Savannah?

She walked up to the mirror and smiled in abject relief. Soft waves framed her face, making it appear longer, making her appear older. She never realized how young her face looked. But... damn. "It looks good. It's not that high, Gabi. The way you were talking I thought I'd have to crawl to fit under doors."

"I know." Gabi smirked. "I just wanted you to think about how you put your hair's life in her hands." She walked up behind Karina. "You look amazing."

"Kyle will be putty in your hands," Savannah said.

"Well, if you do it right he won't be putty. He'll be harder." Gabi wagged her eyebrows up and down.

"Honey, you have a sailor-worthy libido and a shipyard-worthy mouth." Savannah's phone rang again, and she grabbed the screeching nuisance and hit the ignore button. She was gonna wear that thing out.

"Trouble with the husband?" Gabi sat on the edge of Savannah's bed and returned to the magazine on her tablet.

"Joe's not my husband. And get off my bed. I'm gonna have to clean the sheets again."

"Wait, I thought you only washed the sheets when I defiled them with my stank feet. Now I can't even sit on them? You're insane. And by the way, I was talking about Leland since Joe is merely a boy-toy. But it sounds like there may be a story here."

"Gabi, be nice." Karina met Savannah's eyes. "What's wrong?"

"I'd like to talk, but…" Tears welled in Savannah's eyes. Actual tears. Savannah wasn't much for emotions. She kept most of her emotions close to her name-brand vest. "I am in no mood for teasing."

"We're not going to tease you. We're friends. We don't make fun of the serious stuff." Karina glared at Gabi.

"Well, um… So, Joe wants to take me out to dinner."

"So, go eat dinner," Karina said. Was dinner a bad thing?

"Yeah, it is customary to make a man pay for spaghetti before you eat the salami," Gabi added.

"That's just it. I don't want dinner. This isn't a relationship. I've told him over and over again. We're just having fun, but he wants to complicate things with dinner and movies."

"That bastard." Gabi threw down her tablet.

"I knew you wouldn't understand." Savannah unplugged the curling iron with a yank. She whipped the cord around the wand and threw the styling tool into her cosmetic bag on the floor. Karina had no idea how it didn't melt all Savannah's makeup and hair care products.

"I'm sorry, Sav." Gabi inched to the edge of the bed. "I'm just playing."

"What are you going to do?" Karina asked.

"I don't know. That's what I need you to tell me." She sat on the bed next to Karina. "What do I do?"

"Hey, if you're not comfortable going to dinner… don't go to dinner. Don't do anything you're not comfortable with." Gabi crossed the room and placed her hand on Savannah's. Karina heart tugged as her two best friends played nicely.

"But what if he doesn't want to see me anymore?" Savannah asked.

"Then he doesn't want to see you anymore. It's a chance you'll have to take, but I'm with Gabi. Don't do anything that makes you uncomfortable." Karina wrapped an arm around her shoulder. "With that bit-o-wisdom, I'm heading downstairs. Wish me luck."

"You don't need luck. You're as cute as a boxful a puppies. He'd be an idiot not to worship at your gorgeous feet." Savannah got up and went to the counter, wiping it down.

"Really? Have you not met many men? Most are idiots." Gabi picked her tablet up off the bed.

What if he was an idiot? What if Karina misread the signals? She wasn't good at all this... this... dating stuff. She had a history of missing things. Big things.

"But I have a good feeling about this guy," Gabi said, almost babbling. "He doesn't strike me as an idiot."

"He doesn't, right?" Karina smiled as she checked her reflection. "I got this. Are you okay, Savannah?"

"I'm fine. I'll figure it out."

Gabi headed out the door but turned around. "Do you want to go to dinner?" she asked Savannah.

"With you?"

"There's a bunch of us going. Megan isn't. She's got another volunteer gig. She's stuffing envelopes or some crap. I'd rather stuff pizza in my mouth. We could drop you back here when we're done, or you could come with to one of the gag-inducing frat houses."

"Tempting. But I think I'll stick around here." Savannah didn't even twitch when her phone rang.

"Well." Gabi scowled at the phone as she walked out of the room. "Good luck."

"Thanks." Savannah stared at the screen.

"Joe again?" Karina reached for her roommate, whose shoulders were hunched.

"Why can't he take the hint?" The phone beeped with a new

voicemail. Savannah hit speaker on the receiver.

"Hey, Sav. It's Joe. Are you avoiding me? I was hoping we could go out tonight. You know, do that movie or dinner... You know. Whatever. I'm heading to the Mehnk with my roommate, if you want to stop by. If not... How about I stop by after dinner and we can go to a movie? I think they're showing a movie at the science center. Well... I'll see you later. Bye."

Karina sighed. The guy was persistent, she'd give him that. "What are you going to do?"

"Not be here." Savannah slid on a pair of sandals, this time hitting ignore almost at the same time the phone rang.

"Well, I'm heading down," Karina told her. "Are you sure you'll be alright alone?"

"I'll be fine. You go and have fun."

Karina left while Savannah glared daggers through her phone. She hated leaving her alone. Hated walking away. But it was her first date with Kyle. The first time they'd be alone together. Her roommate had to understand. Right?

That Girl Code ran through her head—what was it?—*Sisters before misters*? Dammit.

She stuck her head back in the room. "Savannah, I'm going to go down and tell Kyle we can reschedule."

"Oh, no you don't. I'm fine. If you don't get your cute butt down those stairs and have a great time, I'll be so mad at you." Savannah armed herself with the hairspray and headed for Karina. "You're not wasting my hair masterpiece on me." Savannah moved a piece of hair behind Karina's ear and sprayed her one more time. "Anyway, I'm going to head out and find me a new man."

"A new one? Don't you have enough trouble with the ones you already have?" Karina licked the sour hairspray residue from her lips. Gross.

"True." Savannah tossed the bottle under the sink. "I keep hoping the next guy won't have so much drama."

"Good luck with that."

"Go." Savannah pushed on Karina's shoulders until she was in the hallway. "I have things to do."

Karina ambled down the stairs and stood in the foyer of Dickinson Hall. Her nerves sparked and popped. She slid restless hands down her peach silk shirt and acid wash jeans. The shirt was a small concession to her helicopter roommate who was appalled at her blatant disregard for first-date etiquette. As usual, Karina wanted to be comfortable, casual—so she wore jeans. As usual, Savannah wanted to be in charge.

She looked around the ever-changing lobby. Signs touting everything from Women's Basketball to chess club to Pep Band, the campus radio station, lined the wall beside the dark blue mailboxes. She checked the clock on the wall above the TV in the common room— 7:05.

One minute and he'd be late. Well, that's how it worked in the Wolfe household. Anything over five minutes was late. Even with the five-minute leeway, she was always late. It drove her father crazy. Yelling would ensue. Of course, these days he couldn't even look at her, so she didn't have to worry about those arguments anymore. It was tragically hilarious what she'd give to hear her father yell about those mundane disappointments. Back before she became a monumental disappointment.

Kyle walked in, green eyes gleaming. His dress slacks and blue polo shirt looked dressier than her jeans. Thank God she wore the silk shirt. Savannah was right. Not that she'd ever tell her that. His eyes found hers and a smile lit his face. He walked over to her and wrapped her in a quick hug. "Hi, Karina. You look amazing."

"Thank you. So do you. Were you able to find the dorm okay?" Dumb question. This was a small campus, with about twenty-five buildings. It was impossible to get lost. Kyle nodded at her, his eyebrow arched. Apparently, it was too much to ask for him not to notice a dumb question.

She made a quick change of subject. "So where are we going for dinner?"

"Dickinson? We are right here."

Disappointment over another campus meal sat like a stone in her gut until he placed a hand on her back, guiding her toward the cafeteria. Karina allowed herself to be guided, happiness fluttering in her stomach and displacing the stone. His gentle hand. His kind heart. She loved being with Kyle. She didn't care where they were.

They stood in line discussing campus food and the high cost of an education. Karina's parents and government loans were footing her bill. Kyle was relying on loans and scholarships, since his parents couldn't afford to help pay for school.

Speaking of money. Crap. What was college dating etiquette? Did she pay for her own food? Did he pay? They both selected the lasagna dinner, and then she stood behind Kyle in the cashier line. He paid for his meal and walked toward the tables. There was her answer. After she paid for her dinner, she followed Kyle to a table on the other side of the room.

"So, Karina, who are you?" Kyle scooped a forkful of lasagna into his mouth.

"Huh?"

"You know, where are you from? What's your major? What makes you tick?"

"Well, I'm from a suburb of Chicago," Karina said, unwrapping her flatware. Was this what first dates were like? "My major is pre-law and I have no idea what makes me tick. How about you?"

"Pre-law, impressive. I'm from Eau Claire, Wisconsin. My major is English and writing makes me tick." Kyle smiled at her.

"What have you written? Are you any good?" Karina took a bite of the lasagna, and the spongey noodles immediately lodged in a tooth.

"Did you know that good and well are both adjectives and adverbs, and that the only reason to use one over the other is connotation?"

"I'm sorry?" She tried to suck the noodle from her molar without contorting her face.

Kyle gave her a sharp look, like she was being slow. "You can ask if someone is any good at something, but never whether a person writes good... proper English dictates a person writes well. Anyway, it's actually bad form to ask. Every writer thinks they write well. Some just have no concept of what makes a great writer. I haven't been published, yet, but I would like to think that I write well. I have an interest in the classics. Most poser-writers have delusions of writing grandeur because they've read grammatical drivel. You know, romance or other mindless fiction." His top lip curled in a snarl for a moment before he shook it off. "Which literary style do you prefer?"

Karina thought about that for a moment. She didn't know what literary style she preferred, but she loved romance and other mindless fiction. But before she could speak, Kyle continued.

"I love Realism. It was a fresh perspective from a time literature was overrun with overly emotional romanticism. Writers like George Elliot were all about realism. Did you know that George Elliot is actually a woman?"

"No, I didn't," Karina managed to say before Kyle continued.

"It's not a big deal. I just find it interesting. Tolstoy is another one of my favorites. I like them all, but I'm not a big fan of Stephen Crane. Maybe if *The Red Badge of Courage* wasn't so grammatically lacking, I might find it enjoyable."

Karina nodded instead of trying to interrupt. Probably for the best—she liked *The Red Badge of Courage*. The imagery was vivid. Their taste in books seemed to be way off base.

But that was okay, right? A couple didn't have to share *every* interest, that way they both added something to the relationship. Right?

"Sorry, I've been monopolizing the conversation." He smiled, and her doubts of a second ago melted. "What do you do when not studying pre-law?"

"I read," Karina said slowly, "spend time with friends. We listen to music. Play video games or head over to the rec center. I love playing racquetball and volleyball—my friend Gabi and I play a lot."

"I'm not a big fan of video games. I think they're ruining our society." He shook his head, a frown clouding his face. "I mean, I suppose it's okay when you're young, but once a person is out of junior high, there's no time for that type of nonsense."

"I guess." She wasn't a gamer, not like some people she knew, but she loved playing a game every once in a while. Sometimes she just needed some nonsense in her life. "I like to play when I take a break from studying."

"I see. I think some people just rely too heavily on that mindless entertainment. They have replaced actively participating in life with a life within the confines of a digital world," he said, crumpling his napkin and dropping it on his empty plate. How did he finish his burger and fries so fast? "I'm a proponent of fully engaging in life. I like games of strategy, games that provide a challenge. What type of music do you like?"

Karina shrugged. "I love all types of music. Heavy metal... rap... classical. How about you?"

"We have something else in common." A bright smile lit up his face. His eyes sparkled. He was so darn adorable. And it was all because they had so much in common. "I love classical."

"My tablet upstairs has all my music. I'll have to show you my collection sometime." She dumped her empty plate onto the kitchen conveyor belt as they walked out of the café and headed toward the front entrance of the dorm. "Thanks for dinner. I had a great time."

"Me too. Would you like to do it again on Wednesday?"

"Sure. Meet me in the lobby at six." Her mouth twitched as she tried to keep up the blasé facade. This was no big deal. At least that was what she wanted him to think. Outside, calm and cool. Inside, emotions danced Gangnam-style.

We're going on a second date.

We're going on a second date.

"I'll see you there." He slid his fingers along her arm and lowered his lips to hers. Soft. Pliant. Gentle. His lips brushed hers. When he drew away he said, "*He stepped down, trying not to look long at her, as if she were the sun, yet he saw her, like the sun, even without looking.*"

"That's beautiful."

"That's Tolstoy. You're beautiful. I'll see you Wednesday. Sleep well."

"Good night." She watched him walk out the door. Beautiful. He called her beautiful.

A smile was plastered to her lips as she headed up the stairs to her room, pretty sure there were actual stars swimming in her eyes. Like one of them old-timey cartoons she watched when she was a kid.

She walked into an empty room. No Savannah. Hopefully her roommate was having luck finding a new guy to take her mind off the old guys. Not that Karina understood how that would help, but Savannah seemed to believe it, so who was she to judge.

She stared at her empty room. She would have loved to go over every single detail of her date. Dissect every moment—especially Tolstoy, especially that kiss.

But maybe this was sign she should go to bed. Yeah, right. Sleep was never going to happen tonight.

Chapter Ten

Ryan

RYAN SAT AT a back table in the quiet room for studying at the library. No bookshelves lined the white walls, but there were tables and chairs scattered between the potted plants in the small space. This was where people came to study with a group—or to make out or hide. Since he wasn't with a group and he had no one to make out with, he must be hiding. Maybe he was. But homework kept his mind off other things.

The red oak table was covered with pencils, rulers, and crumpled paper. This damn paraline drawing assignment was killing him. He loved his architecture class, he had to beg the administration to let him take the course, but this assignment was a pain in the ass.

Maybe that's why he loved architecture so much; it was a challenge. A challenge that forced him to devote all his free time to working on drawing after drawing. Hell, he was studying on a Friday night—what did that tell him?

His stress wasn't all about the assignment, to be honest. It was the thought of Karina having dinner and doing who-knew-what with that douchebag. And Kyle McDougal was a douchebag. Ryan had managed to validate that with the girl who sat behind McDougal in their shared English class.

According to her, Kyle had hit on most of the females in the class. None of them had taken him up on it. Yet. But given enough time and enough Casanova bullshit, he'd be scoring with some unsuspecting junior soon. Where did that leave Karina?

It didn't matter. She had to make her own choices. She was smart. She'd figure out McDougal was a dick. He just hoped it would be sooner rather than later.

"Hey, Ryan. What are you doing here on a Friday night?" Bianca Summerset from the Zeta sorority stopped at his table. She picked up a crumpled paper and started to unfold it.

"Studying." He grabbed the paper away from her and moved it back to the pile. His failed attempts were his. No one else needed to see them. "I have a full load this term."

"You have a full load every term. You need to lighten up."

"Maybe next year."

"I don't know how you do it. I'm swamped with a standard load." She fumbled with the books in her hands. "So, are you taking time off to go to dinner? I was just heading out to get something to eat, if you're hungry."

Although the offer was tempting—he was hungry, she was hot—she wasn't the one he wanted. "Not tonight."

"Oh, okay. Will you be at the Psi Rho party tonight?"

"Yeah, we've got a great party planned." Tonight was an ode to all things gelatin. Gelatin wrestling and gelatin shots. The true kickoff to college partying. Every fridge in the frat was stuffed with trays of green, red, and blue wiggly stuff.

"Well, great, I'll see you there."

"Great." He turned back to his dimensionally-challenged drawing as Bianca swung her hips in retreat. Why couldn't he be into someone like Bianca? She was nice, simple, hot. She wouldn't challenge him, wouldn't argue. Shit, he was getting bored just thinking about that nightmare of a relationship. Where was the fun in that?

As he erased yet another set of lines, somebody said, "Hi. Mind if I sit?"

It was Friday night. Didn't anyone slack off at this school? This time it was Savannah, dressed in black from head to toe Ryan waved at an empty chair. "Sure. Going to a funeral?"

"No, I'm blending."

"Blending?"

"Yep." Savannah put her bag on the table and walked back toward the front of the room. She picked up a garbage can and set it down next to Ryan. "For your practice sheets. May I?"

"Go ahead." He expected her to open them—well, maybe just one—but she didn't. She tossed all his practice sheets into the garbage and then sat down across from him.

He motioned at her all-black outfit. "So, are you holding up the bookstore later?" He couldn't remember her ever wearing that much black. Ever. She was bright colors, verging on cheery, all the time.

"I'm hiding from Joe."

"Did he do something? I could kick his ass," Ryan offered.

"No. Nothing like that. We just want different things."

"Not good. Want to talk about it?"

"Nope." She pulled out her English book and a binder, setting them on the table with a thump and a sigh. She yanked a pen from her bag and stared at it, eyes narrowed. This was a woman who needed to talk. There was no way he'd start, though. One of the many lessons he'd learned living with a house full of women was don't push a conversation. If a woman wanted to talk, they'd engage.

"I hate to bore you. It's stupid."

And there was engagement. "Try me."

"My boyfriend from back home, Leland, and I have an arrangement..." Redness crept up her neck as she undoubtedly remembered he was there for the unveiling of said arrangement. "Well, you know about our arrangement."

"Well aware."

"Then I met Joe. He's nice and fun and sexy." She raised a hand to her mouth. "Don't tell anyone I said that."

"Our secret." His lips curled. He couldn't help but like Savannah. She was Southern charm embodied.

"Anyway, the whole point was to have meaningless flings until we find our way back to each other, but..."

"Joe is more than a meaningless fling."

"He wants to be more. He wants to take me out to dinner and a movie. But I can't let him be more."

"Why?"

"It's stupid." She played with the pages in her binder. "But I don't want to be unfaithful to Leland."

"No, it's not stupid. But you should think about this before you dump Joe, no matter what put you in this situation. Here you are—you're on a great college campus with a bunch of new people. You aren't married and you have an opportunity to sample what's out there."

"But what if I change my mind about Leland? That would break my heart."

"Yeah, it probably would. But isn't it better to find out now instead of ten years from now, when you're married with two kids?"

She slumped in her chair. "That is annoyingly logical."

"I'm like that."

"Annoying or logical?"

"Both. Ask Karina." He ran a pencil over his drawing.

"She left for her date tonight."

"I figured." His lines darkened as he pressed the pencil deeper into the page. This was not a conversation he wanted to have with Karina's roommate. Hell, he didn't want to have it at all. He didn't need a reminder where Karina was tonight.

"So, when are you going to ask her out?"

Ryan's hand jerked, but he was able to rein it in before it became noticeable. He hoped, anyway. "Ask her out. Why would I ask her out?"

"Because I've seen the way you look at her. You look at her like she's a milker and you're a cow that ain't been milked in weeks."

"Interesting metaphor aside, she's out with douche…" He had to stop calling him that. "…with another guy. I don't share."

"I didn't think I did, either." A sad smile crossed her face and disappeared. "But hang in there. She'll come to her senses about you."

He wasn't so sure about that. They say you never got another chance at a first impression, and he'd made one helluva first impression. He picked up a ruler and redrew one of the lines he'd erased earlier. If he couldn't enjoy his social life, he'd enjoy the part of school he could control.

"What are you working on?"

"A drawing for my architecture course."

Savannah stared at the lines crossing the page in front of him. "I thought you were a business major."

"I am. I asked to be in this class as an elective." More like begged, but no one needed to know that. In the end, the thousands of dollars his father donated over the years gave him the ammunition to gain department permission to attend the architecture classes. Now he just had to make sure dear old Dad didn't find out.

"If you want to be an architect, just change your major."

"It's not that easy when your father already has your office set up at the company he founded."

"That sucks."

"Tell me about it."

"You know, Ryan. You're really a nice guy. You should show it more often. You know, get rid of that asshole reputation."

"I'll take that under consideration." He smiled as she bent her head to her book. Only his sisters ever told him he was nice. And they usually had him in a headlock when they said it. It wasn't a word associated with the Kent family. Well, except for his mom.

Warmth travelled down his spine as he thought, maybe, just maybe he took after her instead of the cold-hearted bastard he called a father.

~»ΨΡ«~

Chapter Eleven

Karina

LATER THAT NIGHT, Karina sat on her bed streaming a movie on her computer. She glanced at the clock. Ten o'clock. Where was Savannah? She'd tried Savannah's cell phone a couple of hours ago, but it was difficult for her roommate to answer when the phone sat on her bed. Turned off.

Who went anywhere without their phone? Even the elderly carried a phone. If infants could talk they'd carry one around too, for emergencies. She knew Savannah was avoiding Joe's calls, but leaving her phone here was dangerous. And really annoying for the roommate looking to talk to her.

She leaned back to watch as Channing Tatum sprawled on the stage, dry-humping the enviable air. Was it normal to envy air? He spun and ripped his shirt off his bulging muscles. Even though he tore the fabric off his chest, she couldn't help but envy the shirt, too. She had issues.

She brought a handful of popcorn to her mouth. It was probably a good thing Gabi was out at the frat and Savannah was doing who-knew-what with God-only-knew who. The thoughts running through Karina's mind weren't appropriate for polite company.

Especially since she was still humming from her night with Kyle. He was so sweet. Maybe a bit of a snob when it came to books, but that was his major, his passion. Everyone got a little crazy when it came to their passion. It was adorable. She loved a man with a dedication and excitement for something.

He said she was beautiful. She'd never been called beautiful before. Well, except by her father and stepfather, but they didn't count. Parents had to say sappy stuff like that to their kids. It was in their handbook or something.

Craig never said she was beautiful, but given his leanings that didn't mean anything. And then there was her second boyfriend, Robby. He'd always told her she was hot, but hot was not beautiful. Looking back, the way he'd said "hot" sounded tawdry, skanky—his abracadabra to get her clothes to magically disappear. Though his illusions were good, the one positive that came from the whole situation was that she never slept with that Slytherin sorcerer.

As Channing talked to his movie love interest, a key jiggled in the door lock and Savannah walked in, backpack slung over her shoulder.

"Where were you? Did you find your next love..." Karina's words trailed off as Ryan walked in behind Savannah. Crap. She threw a blanket over her Betty Boop pajamas and red fuzzy booties. Not a good look.

Matthew McConaughey screamed about fucking as he gyrated into a mirror. Karina flew across the bed and slammed the laptop shut. "Hi," she squeaked as heat travelled up her neck and took residence in her face.

"You're home already." Savannah threw her bag on her bed. "Come on in, Ry. Apparently it's movie night."

"I was just watching *Magic Mike*." Karina face pulsed and she tried not to think about how red she must be.

"Apparently. Any naked women in that one?"

"No." Typical Ryan. She threw a pillow at his head as he dropped his backpack and sat on the floor next to her bed.

"How was dinner?" Savannah asked.

"It was fun. He asked me out again."

Savannah leaned her book bag against her desk. "That's good, honey."

That's good, honey? That's it? Karina thought her friend would be a little more excited for her than that. Disappointment skittered down her spine.

Savannah grabbed a bottle of water from the mini-fridge and handed it to Ryan, who opened the bottle and guzzled down almost the whole thing. When had they become so in tune to each other?

"Where were you guys?" Karina asked. Not that she really cared where they were together. Maybe Ryan was the new boy-toy. He probably didn't require dinner beforehand. He just needed a drink of water after. Like a dog. A great replacement for Joe. Jerk.

"We had a wild and crazy Friday night." He pulled another drink of water and smiled at Savannah.

Damn boy-toy. Karina's blood boiled. She didn't want to hear about their wild night. How could Savannah have gotten with Ryan? *Her* Ryan. Well, not her Ryan but their Ryan. Their buddy.

And Ryan. How could he get with Savannah? Dammit. Why did she even care? It definitely wasn't jealousy. She had no right to be jealous. If Savannah wanted to have an affair with a jackass player, it wasn't Karina's problem if he wanted to be another scrunchie on her bedpost. Fine.

"Yeah, crazy." Savannah grinned. "We closed down the library."

Not that Savannah needed another scrunchie on her bedpost. Wait. In the library? "You did it in the library?" Karina couldn't believe it. She couldn't believe they had sex in the library. She read books there. How could she ever face the building again without wondering where they'd been naked.

"Did what in the library?" Ryan's eyes widened with what looked like real confusion, but only for a second. Now he was looking at her like she'd accused him of something horrible.

"We worked on homework in the library," Savannah said.

Ryan finished his water, and his laugh made Karina wince. "You must think I'm an absolute asshole." He tossed the bottle in the trash as he jumped to his feet.

"I'm sure she didn't mean…" Savannah said.

"Forget it, Sav. I have a frat party to get to. Maybe I can con more women into having meaningless sex with me. Especially if I know they have a boyfriend back home. Those are my favorite." Ryan grabbed his bag and threw open the door. "See you in class," he said over his shoulder.

Crap. The door slammed shut as silence strangled the room.

"What was that?" Savannah's hands flew to her hips.

"You were complaining about Joe when I left and then you showed up with Ryan…"

"So, I must have slept with him? Wow. Now I feel like I'm the town slut."

"Why? You're not a slut. I'm not mad at you."

"Why are you mad at all? You're the one treating us like trash. You practically called us both sluts. And why do you care? You're not dating him." Savannah got her shower gear and stomped out of the room.

Karina's throat closed as the tears fell down her cheeks. "I'm sorry," she whispered to the air as she flopped back on her bed, exhausted. She'd messed up another relationship. She'd hurt Savannah and Ryan.

She was a walking disaster.

Rolling onto her side, she stared at her tear-squiggled room. She liked her room. She was going to miss it. But she should have known she would fuck it all up. It's what she always did. She envied people who talked about lifelong friends. *Ha.* In her world, there was no such thing. People always abandoned her at the first sign of trouble.

Maybe this was for the best. She rolled off the bed and found a crate, started shoving her clothes into the cube. Tears burned hot down her cheek, but she didn't care. Maybe it was best they went their separate ways before Karina got too comfortable. After all, she was starting to rely on her quirky roommate. In her experience that was never good. Karina would rely on her and then she'd blab all her secrets, ultimately chasing Savannah away. Just like everyone else in her life.

Savannah walked in the room, one towel wrapped around her dripping body and another around her hair. She stood there and watched Karina drop another armload of clothes into the crate. "What are you doing?"

"I'll be out of your way in a few minutes. I'll stay with Gabi until I can find a new room."

"Why?" Savannah threw her shower stuff on the floor and unwrapped the towel from her head.

"I have to move out."

"Why?" Savannah actually looked confused.

"Stop asking that."

"Stop doing things that don't make sense."

"We had a fight." Tears streamed down Karina's face. "I can't live with someone who hates me."

"I don't hate you. I'm angry, but I'll get over it. You'll apologize for being an ass and we'll move on. Right?"

Karina stared at the shirt in her hand. Was that how it worked? She'd never had it work that way before. Once she let down her friends—and she always did—they stopped being her friend. They talked behind her back and called her names to her face. They threw eggs at her car and TPed her house. "I guess so."

Savannah plopped onto her bed and sighed. She picked up her phone and turned it on. "Bless your heart."

"I'm sorry. I didn't mean to hurt you. I didn't mean to call you a slut. Or him."

Savannah stared at the mini-screen as the phone powered up. "I went to the library to get away from Joe, and the phone wouldn't stop ringing so I left it here. Ryan went to the library to study. We saw each other there and started talking. The most tantalizing thing that happened is we studied our homework. Then we came back here. Nothing happened. Ryan's like a brother to me. Not that you deserve an explanation, byotch."

Karina smiled. *Byotch.* She knew she wasn't that angry when Savannah started to swear colloquially. Well, colloquially Northern. "I really don't think you're a slut at all. Forgiven?"

"Hand over the popcorn and start up that movie and we'll call it even."

"Deal." Karina handed her the bowl and walked over to her laptop.

"You really should apologize to Ryan."

"I know. I will." Karina woke her computer. She never wanted to hurt him. She had to apologize. She had no idea what to say, but she had better figure it out. She needed a plan when she made the grovel-call, if he'd even take her calls.

"So, how was the date, really?" Savannah pulled Karina out of her dreams of pleading. Maybe it was more of a nightmare. She hated to beg, but she hated Ryan being mad at her even more.

"What?"

"The date? Kyle?"

"Fantastic. He called me beautiful."

"Well, at least we know the man has good taste." Savannah scooped a handful of popcorn into her mouth. "Good popcorn. What's in here?"

"Reese's Pieces."

"You got good taste, too."

Karina smiled as she started the movie. Yeah. She was feeling pretty good about her taste, too. Kyle was amazing and everything was just going to get better. Despite the little hiccup tonight, she was feeling good. Good about school, her friends and her life.

For the first time in a long time she felt things were going her way.

~§~

A week later, Karina was still happy, optimistic, just loving life. Her last date with Kyle had been wonderful. Although he was taking things a bit slow; they were still in goodnight-kiss phase. Last night, though… Last night the kissing had gone further. Deliciously further, but it was still in that innocent phase. It was nice to not be just another pair of tits.

Her classes were going well too, even German. She made it through her morning classes and headed to the Mehnk with Ryan to begin their tutoring session.

"A B-minus. I can't believe it. I don't know how to thank you, Ryan." She'd pulled the assignment out of her bag four times to make sure she hadn't dreamed it.

White and brown squares lined the floors of the main cafeteria. Small black and red tiles were dispersed through the white wall tiles. Shiny red cabinetry and counters with a variety of food stations lined the front of the café, everything from pizza to burgers to a pasta bar and salad bar. There wasn't much missing from the collegiate buffet.

No wonder students gained the dreaded "freshman fifteen" that first semester away from home. Cupcakes, cookies and various foods were all readily available with the simple slide of a student ID.

Ryan shrugged. "It's no biggie. It helps me write my papers, as well."

"Can I at least buy you lunch?" Karina surveyed her lunch choices. The greasy stench of French fries and nuked frozen pizza permeated the stifling air. They might have everything available, but that didn't mean everything was good. She grabbed a pre-made sandwich, a soda and a bag of chips. It was pretty hard to screw up a turkey sandwich. "It's the least I can do after Friday night."

"I told you, it's no big deal."

"You say that now, but Friday you were pretty pissed."

"Yeah, I'm not fond of being treated like a man-whore by my friends." He dropped a plate of pizza on the counter. Grease was pooled on the top of the cheese substitute. How could he eat that?

"I'm so sorry." Guilt snaked around her temples.

"I mean, I get tired of being treated like a piece of meat. There's more to me than a gorgeous body for women to drool over. I get it. Look at the guns." He smirked as he raised his right arm, flexing his muscles. He did everything but kiss said guns.

"Whatever." She laughed as she set her food on the counter for the cashier, sliding his lunch until it was next to hers.

"You know this isn't necessary."

"It would make me feel better. Anyway, it's just lunch. I seem to remember you bought me lunch a couple times over the past few weeks, so I owe you a few, anyway."

"I'm not keeping track. I don't mind."

It bothered her that Ryan had bought her lunch, when her boyfriend hadn't bought her a meal. Not even once. Every dinner had been romantic and wonderful and the romantic quotes were swoon-worthy, but she still was buying her own meals. Frustrating. However, she was trying not to think about it. Not everyone had the money Ryan had, but still, it would've been nice for Kyle to offer to pay for her five-dollar sandwich. Just once.

"Did you hear from your sister?" Karina settled across the table from Ryan.

"No baby yet. Rachel says any day now."

"So you'll be Uncle Ryan. Do your other sisters have kids?"

"No." A smile lit up his face. "I'm pretty excited. Kristen is the oldest, but she's working on her PhD and she's just too busy to start a family. And Kacey— Kacey is Kacey. She's in grad school at NYU, partying. But Rachel is the good one. She graduated from Ritter, married the guy she dated all four years and is giving my parents their first grandchild."

"Are you going to go back home when she delivers?"

"I'm planning on it." He folded the piece of pizza and took a bite. "How was your parent's trip? Didn't they go to Mexico or something?"

"Yep, Mom and Stan just got back. They loved it. "

"Nice. What about your real dad? You don't mention him much."

"There's not much to mention." Karina picked up her drink. She didn't want to talk about her relationship with her dad. It always led to questions about how things had gotten so bad. She didn't want anyone at Ritter to know the whole story. Eventually someone would probably figure it out, but for now, she loved her life of anonymity.

Anonymity kept the glares away, kept the disgust away. No one would ever understand. Hell, her own father didn't understand. Her old friends didn't understand. They blamed her for Craig's expulsion. They didn't even care that she was expelled, as well. Her life had been a minefield of exploding relationships, where the only ones left on her side were her mom, Stan, and her brother Mike. Even her sister Kathy treated her differently after the shrapnel settled.

"My father and I don't get along. We had a falling out last year and things never went back to the way they were. How about you? You mention your mom and sisters, but you rarely mention your father."

"Yeah." He twirled his can of soda, a frown settling on his silent lips. Apparently she wasn't they only one hesitant to share daddy-issues. "It's a long story."

"I've got time." She laid her hand on his. The heat and strength of his fingers conflicted with the vulnerability in his eyes. He looked up at her. The intensity of his stare. The raw pain. She wanted to reach out and wrap her arms around him. She wanted to ease some of the pain, the slumping shoulders, the empty stare. Unfortunately, her boyfriend probably wouldn't appreciate her comforting another man. Especially one that looked as good as Ryan.

Really? Looked as good as Ryan?—*Ugh*. Sometimes she was shocked at the stuff that flew through her head. Thank God mind-reading vampires weren't real. Yes, because the mind reading was the scary part of the bloodsucking vampire story…

She pulled her hand from his and grabbed her drink. Another gift from God, vessels of caffeine gave naughty hands something to do beside hold a strong, capable hand. She'd watch those hands play, work and comfort. She could just imagine what other things those hands could do. Too bad her soda didn't keep her mind busy, because she couldn't stop the pictures of Ryan and those naughty hands.

What was wrong with her? When did Ryan become fodder for her imagination? Channing Tatum. Now there was a man for the imagination. After all, he hadn't announced that she was *not his type*.

"When I was a senior in high school, my mom was diagnosed with cancer." Ryan grabbed a napkin and wiped his hands. Karina's mind focused as her heart wrenched. "It was so hard… the doctor's appointments, the fear, watching her get weaker and weaker and not being able to do anything. I didn't want to go to school so far away, but she insisted. She wanted me to attend school where she went. So, I came here." He took a deep breath.

"That's one of the reasons Parker and I became friends. She was still in high school, and lived a few miles away. She kept me in the loop with the appointments and how well my mother was doing. She took care of my mom when my sisters and I couldn't be there. They got really close. Anyway, the goal in my house was to maintain peace. My father used that to his advantage."

His fingers wrapped around the paper napkin, knuckles white. Tension built in the lines forming at his eyes. "We were so busy making sure we kept the peace for Mom, we let my father dictate everything. When she got better, he just kept dictating from his throne. He has no clue what any of his children want or need. He's more concerned with his plans, his future, his reputation." He tossed the napkin onto the table and threw back a swig of soda.

"Is that why you won't change your major?"

"Savannah told you about that, huh?" Ryan traced the condensation on the can.

"You might have come up once or twice in our conversations."

"Really? What else has she said about me?" His eyes found hers. A playful grin lingered on his lips.

"Just that you're like a brother to her and you're secretly a nice guy."

"Hmmm." He took a bite of his sandwich. "And what did you say to that?"

"I told her that I already knew your secret. You try to hide behind that façade, but you're a closet softie."

"Honey, I guarantee if you got me in a closet, I would not be soft."

She laughed and shook her head. "I'll take your word on that."

She loved these lunches. It was the most uncomplicated part of her day. Bringing up the subject of tutoring occurred to her—but why talk German when she was enjoying the conversation so much?

"So, you had another date with Kyle. How did that go?"

"How did you know about that?" Karina asked.

"I went to the Rec Center yesterday night and ran into Gabi."

"It was fun. He's so old-fashioned, taking everything so slow. We're going out again tomorrow. It's weird to be around such a nice guy."

"Great. He sounds wonderful." Ryan finished his piece of pizza, leaving the crispy crust on the plate.

"Yeah, I think so too."

"What are you doing Friday? I mean… you, Megan, Sav and Gabi. What are you guys doing Friday?"

"I'm not sure." Karina grabbed the crust. The pizza might be a puddle of grease, but the crust was crunchy heaven.

"Then we're going out. You need to come by the frat."

"We've been by Psi Rho." Karina finished her sandwich as Ryan grabbed her bag of chips and started eating what was left in the bag. She never ate the whole bag, so Ryan started asking if she minded if he finish them. He stopped asking last week. The answer never changed.

"Yeah, but not when I'm there. I'll introduce you to the finer points of frat life."

"Let me guess... Drinking, burping and farting."

"We don't fart in front of guests, most of the time." His hazel eyes sparkled as he laughed.

"Charming. I can't wait." The funny thing was that she was looking forward to it all. Well, maybe not the possibility of farting. But she couldn't wait to see into the world of Ryan Kent.

~§~

Time seemed to move in slow motion, especially when Kyle called to postpone their date until next Wednesday. He had a huge English paper and couldn't get away. They'd been dating for three weeks, and yet she'd be spending another weekend dateless. He liked to study on the weekend—the libraries were quieter. At least that's what he said. He apparently liked the quiet of alone time. She would have still liked an invite. Studying together was better than partying alone.

"Who cares if he didn't ask you out for the weekend? We have things to do, anyway." Gabi stuck her arms through her Ritter sweatshirt, pulling it down and covering her red sports bra. "We're going to see a movie at the science center and then off to the frat. It will be fabulous."

"The science center..." Karina nearly groaned. "I don't feel like watching *The Universe and Me*, or any other lame sciencey movie. Why can't we go see a real movie? I hear they're playing the first *Pirates of the Caribbean* somewhere for Classic Movie Friday. Let's go there. It's got Johnny Depp. You can never go wrong with Johnny Depp." Karina dropped her brush on the counter and walked away from the mirror.

Why bother? She wasn't going to see Kyle or anything.

"They're playing *Pirates* on the giant screen in the science center." Gabi rolled her eyes as she ran a hand over her bare stomach and down her low-waist skinny jeans. She posed in front of the mirror. "Do you seriously think I'd drag you to some sciencey crap? Next time read the posters. I mean, how could you miss the information under Orlando Bloom's adorable face?"

"Because I was too busy looking at Johnny's adorable face."

"You need to learn to focus on the important things." Gabi fluffed her hair, not that she needed it.

"Like where *Pirates* is playing this weekend?"

"Yes, now you get it." Gabi twisted her neck toward Karina and smiled.

"I'm going to sit this one out," Savannah said as she leaned into the mirror over the sink. She poked and prodded her blond hair. "I have a date."

"Why are we just hearing about this now?" Karina watched Savannah pull at the long-sleeve floral dress covering her body. A little long for her normal Friday night date, but her clothes had slowly become less revealing lately, probably due to the cool Midwestern air swirling each night.

"I didn't want you two making a big deal out of this. It's a date. Nothing more."

"With Joe? Like a dinner and movie date?" Karina knew her mouth was hanging open. Finally— dining with Joe. About damn time. Not that she'd tell Savannah that.

"Not Joe." Savannah dug through the bag on the floor and took out a round brush. She ran the bristles through her shiny golden hair.

"Not Joe? Do tell." Gabi stopped and dropped onto the chair next to Savannah's desk.

"It's no biggie. He's a sophomore and he's adorable. I met him outside my Math class. His name is Peter and he has the cutest little cheeks."

"Which ones?" Gabi honked her hands, waist-high, in the air.

"You're vile." Savannah smiled. "But both."

"So does this mean Joe is over?" Karina braced herself—poor Joe. The boy had it bad. He asked about Savannah all the time and Karina blew him off again and again.

"I aim to break up with him. I just haven't done it yet." Savannah grabbed her wristlet and gave one last look in the mirror.

"I thought things with Joe were going well. He hasn't asked you out on a real date in over a week," Gabi said.

"Things are fine, but I don't want to get serious with anyone. So it's time to move on. You two have fun at your movie."

Savannah ran out the door with a wave. Karina stared after her, mesmerized. She couldn't decide if her roommate was handling the situation well or digging herself into a deeper hole. Not that it mattered what she thought, she barely had her own life together.

Megan banged on the doorframe of Karina's room. "Ready, girls?"

Gabi and Karina followed their dorm mate out into the golden evening, the setting sun hanging low in the sky. Crisp September air tickled Karina's nose, and the musty scent of falling leaves surrounded them as they took the five-minute walk to the science center. The summer flowers had been cut back, anticipating the long cold winter ahead.

Karina pulled the sleeves of her track jacket down to her wrists as they crossed the soft grass of the quad, detouring around the trees and benches. On any given day, students flocked to the area to play simple ball games or discuss important relevant topics with friends. Important relevant topics? Yeah. It was more like gossip, but whatever.

"So, is anyone meeting us there?" Megan asked.

"Like who?" Karina knew the answer. Megan tried to hide it, but she absolutely lit up when she was around Danny.

"I don't know. Ryan, Keith—or maybe Danny." Yep. There it was.

"I don't know who all is coming, but I talked to Danny and he said a few of the guys might meet us up there. I'm surprised you came out with us, Megan, since you've been ditching us lately." Gabi pouted and completely missed the smile that passed across Megan's face when she said Danny's name.

"I'm not ditching you. I've been volunteering with Adopt-a-Pet Charities and the Student Volunteers. You could always come with me and help."

"That sounds like work." Gabi huffed.

"Sometimes, but some of the things we do are fun, and think of all the good you'd be doing for the poor abandoned and hungry animals."

"I'll think about it," Gabi said.

"Translation—no." Karina laughed.

"That's so nice that you're volunteering, Karina." Gabi pushed on Karina's shoulder.

"I'll go if you go."

"You're both going. Tuesday night." The fall wind howled and Megan wrapped her sweatshirt tighter around her shoulders as Karina and Gabi rolled their eyes. "You two are like children."

"We're not." Gabi stuck her tongue out. Proving how little she resembled a child. Not.

Part dome for astrological observation, part classrooms, the gray-brick science center building was one of Ritter's newer acquisitions, thanks to a grant given by a former student and nuclear physicist. Karina couldn't believe she remembered that—she must have been paying better attention during that campus tour than she thought.

The door north of the dome-covered astronomical silo led to the foyer, with its six-foot-long double helix DNA strand, and they followed the stream of students into the front lecture hall. A thirty-foot screen had been dropped from the ceiling at the front of the room.

The girls walked down the pitched stairs toward the screen, waving at a few girls from the dorm. What were their names again? Oh yeah—Denise and Aimee. Danny and his crew were nowhere to be found.

Karina followed Gabi and Megan into one of the front rows. "Are you sure the guys are meeting us here?"

"Of course. Danny has a thing for me. He'll be here. Hey, ladies." Gabi sank into the empty seat next to Megan and Aimee. She was so matter-of-fact. A guy liked her and it was nothing. Just another day. How could Gabi miss the scowl that slid across Megan's face, though?

"Hey. What are you up to tonight?" Aimee ran a hand through her cropped black hair. Her light brown eyes and deep reddish-brown skin glistened as she grabbed a handful of popcorn.

"Not sure, probably Psi Rho. Wanna come?"

"Sure." The overhead lights dimmed as the projector flickered, and a second later Ryan, Danny and Keith dropped into the green stadium chairs next to Karina. Danny bumped Ryan's shoulder forcing Ryan's arm to knock into hers on the shared arm rest. This should be interesting.

"Nothing like getting here at the last minute..." Gabi whispered, leaning around Karina.

"Don't blame me." Danny punched Keith in the shoulder. "Romeo over here had to pretty-up his hair. He's worse than a woman."

"You're just jealous that I got style and you look like shit. Any way, you never know when you'll bump into a hottie." Keith elbowed Danny.

Danny elbowed him back. "Any hottie we may bump into will run from your girl-hair."

Keith's long hair wasn't Karina's style, although she knew quite a few girls drooled over him. But then again, Danny and Ryan had quite a few groupies too.

"And you think you could get a woman when you look like He-Man and Freddy Kruger's love child?"

"He-Man was rocking. I could live with that." Keith squared his shoulders and grinned.

"Whatever." Danny rolled his eyes.

"I smell a wager. Twenty bucks says I will pick up a smoking chick before you." Keith pulled out his wallet, yanking open the Velcro and pulling out a twenty.

Karina blinked. Velcro. Really? Didn't guys retire Velcro wallets in grade school? Around the time they were able to tie their own shoes.

"Are you two barbarians kidding? This sounds like a bad romantic comedy," Gabi whispered over the pre-movie intro.

They both ignored her. Keith asked, "Who judges whether they're smoking? I've seen the barkers you bring home. Hot mess doesn't equal hot."

"Fuck you. Ryan decides." They both looked at Ryan.

"Hell no, keep me out of this." Ryan shook his head as Karina stared at them. Was this really how guys talked? She couldn't picture Kyle behaving so childishly. Maybe that was why she liked him so much.

A girl behind them hissed. "Shhh… we're trying to watch the movie."

Karina shook her head and fixed her eyes on the screen. She didn't know Denise and Aimee well enough to know if they were offended by the nature of the talk-smack-betting. Who needed horses when there were so many jackasses?

"Switch with me," Danny begged Karina, leaning around Ryan to get her attention. She turned to Gabi, who nodded yes.

"Maybe the children will behave if we separate them."

Karina slid past Ryan and sat down between him and Keith. Danny punched Keith as he moved to the seat next to Gabi and settled in. With the toddlers separated, Karina could finally concentrate on the pirate shenanigans up on the big screen.

Even while Captain Jack Sparrow convincingly wreaked havoc on Port Royal, Karina couldn't help but wonder what Kyle was doing. Was he studying? Hanging with his friends? Would he have come to the movie if he wasn't busy?

She twisted in her seat, checking the rows behind her. The darkness of the theatre made deciphering features impossible. She turned back around and found Ryan glancing her way. He smiled and then faced the screen again, his arm dangerously close to her arm on the armrest separating them.

Warmth tingled along her spine as she realized how close she was to Ryan. Arm to arm. Shoulder to shoulder. Her heart thudded in her chest. Darn it. She whipped her arm onto her lap.

Popcorn. I need popcorn. She leaned over Ryan and Danny, tapping Gabi's knee. Of course, now she was getting closer and closer to Ryan. That was bad. Just bad.

She wasn't his type. She needed to remember that.

"Anyone up for popcorn? My treat," she whispered down the row. A mixture of yesses and hell yeahs floated down the aisle.

"I'll be right back."

Karina left the darkness of the lecture hall and headed past the DNA strand to the brilliant lights of the popcorn stand. She stood in line staring at the list of snacks available for purchase.

Nothing registered. Ryan. All she kept think about was Ryan. Why? He'd made it clear she wasn't his type. Heck, she had a good guy waiting for her. A guy who thought she was beautiful. A guy she'd just kissed a few days before and was taking her out next week. She needed to focus on him and the healthy relationship she was building.

Once she reached the front of the line, she ordered two extra-large popcorns and a few sodas to pass around.

"Hungry?"

She knew that voice. She dreamed of that voice and the guy attached to it. She spun around. Kyle. "Hi. You're here. I didn't see you in the theatre." It was bad enough she'd looked for him. Now, he knew she'd been looking for him. Pathetic.

"Yeah. There's not much else to do around here when you have no car. I came with a few friends." He flashed the beautiful smile that set his green eyes ablaze. "Who are you here with? Who are the guys?"

She couldn't help but smile. Apparently she wasn't the only one looking around the theatre. "Just a bunch of friends. Did you want to join us?"

"No, thanks, I don't want to ditch my friends in the middle of a movie."

"How about after the movie? We're heading over to Psi Rho." Karina shifted from one foot to the other, not sure how to juggle the popcorn and sodas. Screw it. She put everything on the counter.

"No thanks. I need to finish that English paper for Monday, but I'm so glad I ran into you." He looked her up and down. "I do have a question."

He grabbed her hand. So soft and warm compared to how cold her hands were from the jumbo sodas she just set down. "Did you want to go out on Sunday? I don't want to wait until Wednesday to see you."

A shiver flew down her spine, starting from the hand he touched and pooling between her thighs. He was so amazing. And he couldn't wait to see her. Her.

"I would like that." Her eyes fixed on his.

"Great. I'll pick you up at six."

"See you then." She watched him stride away, shaking her head to clear the hot-fuzz clouding her brain.

He was kind, intelligent, considerate… and he was her type, everything she was looking for in a man. And she found it in him, no one else. She smiled as she gathered napkins and straws. She needed to get these drinks back to the group before they sent out a search party.

~»ΨP«~

Chapter Twelve

Ryan

RYAN WATCHED AS Kyle followed Karina out the door. Great—the douchebag was going to find a way to latch onto their evening. The thought of watching the two of them make out all night pissed him off. He stared at the screen. Foot bouncing. Waiting. Watching for Karina.

Bounce.

Bounce.

Bounce.

Dammit. Maybe Karina needed help. Maybe she couldn't carry all the food. She was probably standing at the concession stand waiting for someone to help. After all, douchebag couldn't possibly have enough power in his teeny tiny muscles to carry a balloon, let alone a few sodas and a giant size popcorn.

He reached the main foyer in time to see Karina's hand sliding between Kyle's nasty hands. Her dreamy, starry-eyed look spoke volumes. Then Kyle walked away, a smirk stuck on his pretty, douchebag face. After a couple yards, he turned back and looked Karina up and down. *Ugh.* Not that Ryan blamed the asshole. Karina looked amazing. Jeans that hugged her curves in all the right places. A jacket covering a skin-tight tank top. Just enough was showing to get his mind racing. How soft her skin must be. How warm.

Crap. Not helping. He needed to refocus.

Douchebag. Ryan would like to place a fist in that face. He blew out a long breath. No matter how good that might feel, it wouldn't accomplish anything but piss Karina off.

"Do you need a hand?" Ryan asked as Karina stuffed two large popcorn tubs between her chest and arm, popcorn pieces tumbling down her chest and falling to the floor.

She jumped, more kernels falling, sliding along her cleavage. "Yeah. Thanks."

How he'd love to be that one piece of popcorn stuck in the V of her jacket. "I didn't mean to scare you."

"It's not you. I'm in my own little world."

Yeah, she was. It sucked that her world included that ass. "Are you going with Kyle tonight? If he has no place to go, he can come with us to the house." Ryan cringed. What the hell was that? Invite the enemy? He could hear the sounds of whips snapping in his mind… or maybe it was coming from the surround sound in the theater. Either way the message was clear. He was whipped.

Sad.

"He has an English paper due Monday. He's going to finish that and then we'll go out tomorrow."

"Really. Does he have another English class? I'm in his English class on Monday, Wednesday and Friday and we don't have an assignment due."

"He probably does. He's an English major." She clutched the popcorn and walked into the theatre. He grabbed the drinks and followed, not buying the crap that fell out of McDougal's mouth. But how could he make Karina see?

~§~

Ryan pulled his keys from his pocket as the group left the Science Center.

The one he thought was named Aimee faced the group loitering on the sidewalk. "So, where are we going?"

"Psi Rho. Who's in?" Gabi smiled.

Everyone nodded, except for Megan. "I think I'm heading home," she said through clenched teeth. She looked kind of green to Ryan.

"You don't look well," Gabi said. "Did you eat something wrong?"

"It's the popcorn." Megan cringed. "Popcorn makes me sick."

"Okay, let's get you home." Karina moved toward Megan.

"Stay here. Have fun. I'm going straight to bed." Megan turned and staggered toward their dorm.

"You're not walking alone." Karina took her arm and turned to Ryan. "We'll meet up with you guys."

Danny and Keith started toward Ryan's car.

"We'll drive you home, Megan. You don't look well enough to walk." Ryan spun the keys on his finger, praying she wasn't sick enough to defile his car. Cleaning used popcorn out of the interior was not how he wanted the night to go. Not at all. But he couldn't let her walk. It wouldn't be right.

"It's not on your way. Why don't you all go and I'll just head home." Megan swallowed hard, pressing a hand to her stomach, but thankfully nothing came out.

Please God, don't punish my car for doing the right thing. "It's only a block or two out of the way." Ryan ushered everyone toward the parking lot. Megan followed the group, but turned to Ryan.

"Should I stick my head out the window? Just in case." She might have to, just so they could fit all eight of them.

"No. It'll be fine." He rested a hand on her arm. Green clammy skin. Red puffy eyes. Sympathy filled his heart for her... enough that he couldn't even worry about his possibly ruined car interior. He needed to get her home. She shuffled forward, her arm wrapped around her stomach.

"Karina and Megan are in the front seat," Ryan yelled to Danny, who was trying to pull Gabi into the front. There was no way he was driving even two blocks with the sick Megan smashed in the back. Danny snarled at him and squished into the back seat. He grinned as the women piled on top of him.

Karina snuck up behind Ryan and grabbed his arm.

"What's up?" he asked.

"Nothing... It's just... That was nice of you to offer Megan a ride to the dorm."

"It's nothing. Anyway, Brent told me not to come home without pretty girls. He said, and I quote, 'it's already a sausage-fest.'"

Karina rolled her eyes. "And they say chivalry is dead."

He laughed. He loved her sense of humor. Loved the way her eyes sparkled as she put him in his place. Loved everything about her.

Shit.

~»ΨP«~

Chapter Thirteen

Karina

THEY DROPPED OFF the ailing Megan at the dorm, and Karina helped poor Elphaba to her room. Karina had this overwhelming urge to ask how the Munchkins were, and when she was going to the Emerald City next, but controlled herself. She didn't think the green-skinned Megan needed her teasing any more than she needed Karina to hover.

Not that she'd stop hovering— until Megan was safely in bed. Karina had known her own bouts with sick-inducing foods and understood what it was like to need one's bed.

"What about your roommate?" Karina asked.

"She went home for the weekend, thank goodness. The last thing I need is her glaring and nastiness."

"Are you girls okay?" Nica, the floor's Resident Assistant, popped out of her room, rollers in her multicolored hair. Bright green today. How appropriate.

"We went to see the movie over at the Science Center and Megan ate popcorn. It made her sick."

Megan leaned against the wall and aimed her key at the door. "I'm fine. I just need to sleep. My stomach needs to digest." Metal scratched against metal as her key failed to connect. "Go downstairs before they leave without you," she told Karina.

Nica lifted her hand to Megan's forehead. "You look absolutely wicked. Come on, I'll take care of you. Karina, go catch your ride."

"In a second. They'll wait." Karina took the key, easily sliding the it in the door. She walked Megan into her room, dropping her onto the bed. *Are you sure?* Karina mouthed to Nica, who nodded and dashed back to her room.

"Go. Unless you want to watch me sleep, go have fun." Megan's eyes closed. "I do expect a full report tomorrow."

"I have some antacid, magnesium salts… or would you like some warm milk?" Nica walked in with a medicine cabinet's worth of remedies.

"Nica, I'm fine. I just need to lie down." Curling into a ball, Megan groaned as Nica covered her with blankets.

"Well, you ladies have this under control." Karina hurried out of the room, hit the stairs, and burst out the front door.

"Get lost?" Ryan asked when she threw open the car door.

"No. I ran into some pirates trying to steal my booty." *Smart ass.* She climbed in the front seat, sitting on Gabi's lap. The four in the back looked coz, now that Gabi was up front. It was like one those mini-cars at the circus. Just when you thought there weren't any more clowns in the car, they fit another one inside.

"Wow." His teeth sparkled in the overhead light. "That one was way too easy. I'm not going to touch that comment. Megan okay?"

"Yeah, the RA is taking care of her. She was pushing the antacid on Megan when I left."

He pulled away from the curb and drove the mile toward the frat houses, speeding past the warm glow of the campus lights and groups of milling college students. Curbs and sidewalks disappeared. The widely-spaced street lamps cast an eerie glow over the large houses bordered by dense woods on the grass-lined road.

Ryan pulled into a small clearing and parked in a lot next to a large brick house. Light poured from the open windows onto the street as loud music reverberated from inside.

They all filed out of the car and wound their way along the concrete path that led to the house, scuffing through the litter of auburn and gold leaves— oh, and cigarette butts and smashed beer cans too— until they came to a porch stretched across the front of a large nondescript, red-brick house.

From watching movies and TV shows depicting fraternities and their living arrangements, Karina had built up a good picture of the Psi Rho house in her head. This was not it. The building resembled a basic apartment building, big and boxy, although the front porch at the front looked new and nice. But still, it was nothing like the white-columned beautifully landscaped examples on the silver screen.

The interior warmth beckoned as the crisp September air bit at Karina's ears and cheeks. Ryan opened the front door of the house, and Karina stepped onto the white tile floor of the jam-packed room. Lights flickered. Bodies gyrated.

The loud music enveloped her, vibrated in her head and chest. The smell of Lysol and beer wafted through the smoky air. The faux dance floor was packed with bodies swaying to the beats pulsating up through her feet. Between light flickers Karina could see pieces of the house. Beyond the dance floor was a small room lined with kegs. To the right was another room with pool and Ping-Pong tables.

"Hey, Ryan." A good-looking guy with reddish-brown hair sauntered over and handed him a beer. His eyes leered. His mouth sneered. His pores oozed smarmy arrogance. "I see you brought friends."

"You told me don't come home without them." He gestured to the group next to him. "This is Karina, Gabi, Aimee and Denise. Everyone, this is Brent."

Karina and the others all made greeting noises—Karina wasn't all that sure she was happy to meet Brent, not with the way he was looking them over.

"I'm glad you all came." Brent ogled Gabi's skinny jeans, his eyes landing on her impressively sculpted chest. Karina really needed to get her a set of those. "We have beer pong and pool here on the first floor. I hear they're playing quarters upstairs. However, last time I checked they were playing strip quarters, so enter at your own risk." Licking his lips, Brent's finally raised his eyes to Gabi's face.

"I've never heard of strip quarters." Aimee laughed.

"They'll play strip anything around here. You should go check it out. Just follow the stairs through that door." Brent pointed to a door beyond the dancing students and elbowed Keith. "I hear Bianca's up there."

"I'm in." Keith grabbed Ryan's beer. "Anyone want to join me? Gabi? Aimee? Karina?"

"No. Thanks." Gabi said for all of them. The other three just shook their heads.

Keith flew across the room and up the stairs. Alone. Not that he seemed all that sad no one wanted to head up there with him.

"Would you like to play a little beer pong? I promise it won't be strip beer pong, unless you want to." Brent arched his eyebrows at Gabi. Gabi had another admirer. Surprise.

"Sure, Karina and I will play." Gabi batted her eyelashes.

Karina had no idea what Gabi's fluttering eyelids had gotten her into now. Beer pong? What the heck? She followed Brent to the Ping-Pong tables. Why did Ryan and the guys go to the Mehnk to play pool when they had this setup here? She'd have to ask him later. She wasn't about to start screaming over the thumping bass of hard rock.

"Why don't you watch these guys play? We'll get drinks." Brent punched Ryan's arm and started for the keg.

"Is it light? I can't drink light beer." Gabi sat on a bar stool near the side of the room. Karina tried to keep a smile on her face, but compared to Gabi... compared to Gabi she was a toddler exploring her first bouncy house. Everything was so different than things back home. Before the incident, Karina had a lot of friends. They'd have parties, but nothing like this. There would be alcohol or pot, but she would try her best to stay away from it. Of course, the one time she let loose... She didn't need to think about that right now.

Here, she was surrounded by people who had a preference in alcohol. She nursed a few beers back home, but she never drank enough of the stuff to form an opinion to actually have a preference. She was so sheltered.

A hearty laugh escaped from Brent's mouth. "No watered-down crap here. We don't serve light."

"Good." Gabi smiled as the guys walked toward the bar.

Karina watched the beer pong game currently underway. Ten plastic cups filled with beer were lined up in a triangle at either end of the table. The man closest to Karina grabbed a Ping-Pong ball, dribbled it on the table and tossed it toward the cups at the opposite end.

A scream of success came from the onlookers as the ball sailed into one of the awaiting cups. A blond giant who looked vaguely familiar picked up the cup and tossed back the contents. He placed the empty cup at the side of the table.

"SKI!" they all yelled as the guy who Karina now remembered from their first game of pool tossed a Ping-Pong ball at the opposing array of cups. With a bounce, the ball landed in a cup. The crowd went nuts as he wrapped his arms around a beautiful woman. And she was a woman, definitely not a college student—tawny skin, long straight black hair, and knowledge in her eyes. There was no way she was a student.

This looked fun. This was what she thought a college party would be like. Over the past few weeks Karina and her friends had tried to hit a few frat parties here and there, but the parties were usually closed early due to sorority or fraternity functions, and by the time they opened up, the curfew had cut things short.

Of course, she could have gone to a college party with her brother or sister, but no matter how many times she'd begged them to take her to one of their parties, they didn't want their little sister hanging around.

But tonight— tonight she was a college student at a college party. She was going to have fun.

She watched Ryan's frat brothers throw a Ping-Pong ball across the table. Back and forth. Back and forth. It didn't take long to figure out the mechanics of the game. Not exactly difficult. She watched the one they called Ski down another full red Solo cup of beer. It was probably a good thing it was uncomplicated. After a few of those cups, who could handle anything that required complex processes or thinking?

Within minutes Brent and Ryan returned with cups and a couple pitchers of beer and the table became available. "Why don't you play on my team?" Brent eyed Gabi as he took the Ping-Pong ball from Ski.

"Okay." She reached over and wrapped her fingers around the little white ball.

"You want to play?" Ryan set up the cups and half-filled each one with beer.

"I guess." Karina's eyes grew wide as Gabi laced the ball through her fingers. She was so screwed. Gabi was a multitalented sports phenom. Karina, not so much.

Ryan leaned over and brushed her cheek with his, the warmth of his breath tickling her neck. The smell of sandalwood overwhelmed her. "Don't worry. I'm pretty good at this. Anyway, the worst thing that happens is we lose and drink too much. I'll make sure you get home safe."

Thump. Thump. Thump. Karina's heart strummed in her chest. She hoped Ryan couldn't hear it. He shouldn't take her breath away. He was a friend. Nothing more. Maybe her speeding heart rate was due to her reintroduction into the world of alcohol. The last time didn't really go so well.

He pulled away and Karina tilted her head toward him. She mumbled a breathless okay and turned toward the table, where Gabi and Brent were taking practice shots.

"You ready to lose, junior?" Brent pointed at Ryan.

"Bring it on, old man. You win one game of basketball and you have delusions of grandeur."

"Basketball and golf... I seem to remember a lost game of golf two weeks ago." Brent laughed and sank the ball into the cup in front of Ryan. Beer splashed on Ryan's Ritter T-shirt.

"Nice shot." Ryan said and tipped the glass back to his lips.

Ryan tossed the ball across the table and into a cup. The smack talk and gratuitous alcohol consumption continued as Gabi and Ryan sank shot after shot, and the group drank beer after beer. Time sped. Despite the fact that Ryan drank most of the cups in front of them, Karina's vision got wonky. Well, it was either wonky vision or there had been an earthquake shaking the house.

She grabbed the table and closed her eyes and waited and listened and concentrated. Head spinning? Yes. Stomach swirling? Yes. Floor moving? No. No earthquake. It was wonky-vision. Laughter bubbled. Wonky-vision. Like Wonka Vision... ooh, chocolate. She moved her hands to her empty pockets. No chocolate. Gabi. Maybe Gabi had chocolate.

She walked over to her friend and wrapped an arm around her shoulder. "You're a good friend."

"You are too."

"I have a question..."

"Okay." Gabi smiled as she raised a lit cigarette to her lips.

"I forget."

"Why don't you go over to your side of the table and think about it."

"You're so smart." Karina ran a hand down Gabi's thick, dark hair—so pretty—and then did it again. "So soft," she whispered as Ryan wrapped an arm around her waist, pulling her away from Gabi and toward him. A ball flew across the table and landed in a cup on their side.

"Oh, shit." She glared at the cup of beer with the ball bobbing up and down. Karina grabbed the cup and hopped, landing her butt on the table. The cup bobbled, spilling beer on her lap as she swished her hips back and forth, getting comfortable.

When she started the game, she wasn't a fan of beer. But now...? She tilted the cup to get the last drop of golden goodness. Who knew this crap could taste so good? She licked her lips and slammed the empty cup to the table.

"Um....Karina. You might want to get down. The table's a bit wet."

Oops. She kicked out her legs and fell to the ground. Spinning. When did the room start spinning. Damn earthquake. She tripped, almost spilling over, but Ryan and the ping pong table broke her fall.

"Whoa. This is mildly familiar," he whispered.

She leaned into the strong arm around her waist, the heat from his body seeping into her side. She looked into his hazel eyes with their streaks of green. He was so freaking hot.

"I think it's time to get you home."

She licked her lips and pictured his mouth on hers, his hands roaming up and down her body. *Whoo*. She turned away. Even drunk, she knew this line of thought was wrong. All wrong.

She had... Kermit. And Kermit was a good guy. Her type kinda guy.

Sweet, cute Kermit. Wait. No, that's not his name.

Kyle. Yeah that's him. She looked into the smiling face of... not Kyle. Ryan. *Swoon*. Ryan still looked good enough to kiss.

Yep, it was definitely time to go home.

~»ΨP«~

Chapter Fourteen

Ryan

RYAN LET KARINA lean on his shoulder as he finished the last beer in the beer pong triangle. Yeah, he let her.

"Do you need help? I think Darnell is designated driver tonight. He could give the girls a ride home." Brent wiped down the table and got a new set of plastic cups for the next game.

"Isn't he playing strip quarters upstairs?" one of the guys asked.

"Damn Sophomores." Lining up the cups, Brent grabbed a lit cigarette from Gabi and inhaled. "Can't trust them to do shit right."

"Don't worry about it. I think I can handle getting them home." Ryan adjusted his arm around Karina's waist. She squirmed to break his hold, but every time he tried to let go, she'd tilt forward. He didn't want her to fall. Yeah. That was his story.

"Well, I hope you stop by again," Brent said as he eyed Gabi through a wave of smoke. Ryan could practically see him undress her with his eyes. What an ass.

Ryan and Karina headed for the exit. Karina stopped as they made their way through the crowd.

"Hey, Denithe. You're Denithe." Karina patted Denise's long brown hair.

Ryan pulled her back. Denise was straddling Danny and didn't appear to want to be interrupted.

"We're gonna go," Karina said. Okay— slurred.

Denise stopped exploring the inside of Danny's mouth with her tongue and looked at Karina. "I think I'm going to stick around for a little while."

Gabi walked up. "Where's Aimee?"

"Aimee's upstairs. We'll walk home together. See you tomorrow." Denise gasped as Danny nuzzled her neck. She turned her face to his and inhaled his tonsils.

"Denithe, we have to go." Karina poked at Denise's shoulder.

"She's going to stay." Gabi laughed as they watched Denise and Danny, hands flying up and down each other's bodies. They were minutes away from X-rated.

Ryan had thought Danny had a huge crush on Gabi. The way he followed her around, it was so obvious. He must have given that up. Although, given the way he slept around, he could still have a thing for her. It was amazing how he could obviously have a thing for one girl while sticking his thing in any number of other ones. Despite Ryan's rant to Karina the other night, it was definitely not his style.

"Fine. Bye-bye, Denithe." Karina leaned her head against Ryan's shoulder. He couldn't deny the warmth creeping down his spine and landing uncomfortably in his lap. It would be perfect if she was this close and sober, but he didn't want her like this. "I'm thleepy."

"Then let's get you home." Ryan said into her mango-scented hair. He rested his lips on the soft strands. He wanted to kiss her head. He wanted to wrap his arms around her. He wanted... But it didn't matter what he wanted. She wanted Douchebag.

"You're hot, but you know that," Karina said as Ryan led her out the front door of the house.

He shook his head. "No more drinking for you."

"Gabi. He's hot. Right?"

Gabi laughed and punched his arm. "Definitely do-able, but so is that Brett guy. So spill, Ryan, is he a good guy? Or is he a huge dick?"

"Depends on the definition of good guy. Now both of you need to keep it down. People are trying to sleep," he whispered as the leaves crinkled beneath their feet. The McMansion they passed was dark and quiet. The old couple must be sleeping. The frat didn't need to wake them up again. They didn't need another visit from the cops. He couldn't understand why they'd bought the house last year. Who bought a house next to a frat house and expected quiet? Insane.

"Okay." Karina rested her index finger against her lips and tip-toed along the walkway. "Shhh...be vewry vewry quwiet, we're punting wabbit..." Karina managed an awkward kick, laughing, but then a frown passed over her face. "Poor bunny wabbit. Oh shith."

"What's the matter?" Ryan asked hesitantly, making sure they were far enough away from the silent monstrosity.

"No key. Oh no, no key," Karina mumbled.

Gabi somehow understood. "No key. Shit. You're right. We don't have a key for our dorm yet. Freshman shouldn't be getting their keys till next week. I have my phone. I'll call someone to open the door." Gabi pulled her phone from her back jeans pocket.

"Isn't everyone out tonight? Who are you going to call?" Ryan asked.

"Ghostbusters," Karina sang, dancing with Gabi. "Dah-dah, dah-dah, dahdahdah...Who you gotta call? Those bastards."

An oldie but a goodie...if Karina wasn't hell-bent on destroying the song lyrics. Ryan shook his head. Why had he thought that he could handle getting these two home?

"No answer." Gabi shoved the phone back into her pocket. There was less and less singing as they walked the sidewalk-free streets back to the softly lit campus. Gabi got a cigarette and lighter out of her purse and lit up.

"I didn't know you smoke," Ryan said.

"Only when I drink." The tip blazed as she inhaled. "Or when I'm having a shit day. Thankfully this is a drinking smoke."

"It's not good for you."

"Neither is drinking." She took another drag of nicotine. Smoke circled the three of them as they walked the dark streets.

"Well, at least you both seemed to have had a good time." Ryan turned to Gabi. "Of course, make sure you remind her of how much fun she had. She might not remember."

"Oh yeah. I'll remind her." Gabi got her phone out and sifted through her contacts again as they came to Dickinson hall. "Hopefully Savannah has made it home now."

Ryan adjusted his grasp on Karina. She leaned on his shoulder and slowly—so slowly—so damn seductively drew figure eights on his chest. It might not have been seductive to her, but he could feel his jeans tighten around his growing interest. It took every ounce of restraint he had to keep his lips from hers.

"Savannah's on the way down." Gabi giggled. "And she has someone with her."

After five short minutes of Karina's touch, Savannah appeared at the glass doors of the lunchroom with a tall, disheveled man in tow. His black hair stood at different angles, adding to his six foot five height. The man had to duck to fit through the doorframe. When Savannah and her boy-toy reached the entrance light, Ryan recognized the Ritter tight end.

Savannah introduced Peter as he leaned down to kiss her cheek.

"Hey, Kent. What's up?"

"Not much, Leventis. I saw the football game last week, you guys are looking good, despite the fact that Jennings can't get the ball in the end zone to save his life."

"Yeah. Thank God for the running game. How's Psi Rho?"

"Same shit."

"Well, you guys can catch up, but we need to get Karina upstairs." Gabi glanced at her lit cell phone.

"Oh yeah, it's getting late." Peter jingled the keys in his pocket. "See ya."

"Bye." Savannah waved and eyed Karina, probably figuring the best way to extract her from Ryan's arms.

"Heading back to Psi Rho?" Peter called back to Ryan, jingling his keys again. "I can give you a lift."

"Yeah."

Karina's hand had stopped circling, but her head still leaned on his chest. He wanted to keep her nestled there for a while longer. Just a few minutes. But Gabi was right, she needed to get upstairs. The beer was going to hit her stomach hard, and she should be lying down when the beer attacked.

Savannah wrapped her arm around Karina's waist and Ryan let go, dragging his fingers along her back. He watched her trip toward the door, almost bringing Savannah down with her. Before Ryan could jump over and help, Gabi readjusted her grip on Karina and the three of them disappeared up the back stairs.

Ryan headed to Peter's car, his side already feeling the frigid air where Karina had been. He could get used to that. Too bad that wasn't his future. Not with McDougal in the picture.

~»ΨР«~

Chapter Fifteen

Karina

GIVEN THE PROXIMITY of Indiana to Lake Michigan, late September could be very dark and dreary. Normally this was a bone of contention, however this morning Karina welcomed the darkness. In fact, if the splattering of light that had escaped the cloud cover could disappear that would be even better.

Karina pried her eyes open and glanced around the room. Savannah, thankfully, was nowhere to be found. Although Karina loved her roommate, she couldn't handle a lecture on her clothes, sleep schedule, or overconsumption of alcohol. She couldn't handle a lecture on anything today. No one needed to tell her she overdid it. Her stomach and head were screeching loud enough to make that point.

She sat on the edge of her bed, nausea swirling in her stomach, crawling up her throat. She leaned her head into her hands. *Please, go away. I'll never drink that much again,* she pleaded with her body.

She could just fall back asleep and try to make the day disappear. But she wanted to make sure Gabi was home safe. She could only remember bits and pieces of the night before and she swore that Gabi walked her home, but she wasn't sure.

Thirst clawed at her throat. She stood on wobbling legs and walked across the twirling floor. She somehow made it to the refrigerator and got a bottle of water. She snarled as she brought the cool liquid to her lips. Never had a simple bottle of water repulsed her so much. Even the thought of taking a drink made her queasy.

She headed out of her room and shuffled down the hall. Once she saw Gabi was home and fine, she was going back to bed. Today was going to be a day of nothing. No homework. No exertion. Nothing.

"Wow, you look worse than I did last night." Megan had her shampoo and towel in her hands as she passed Karina on her way to the bathroom.

"Why are you yelling?" Karina's temples throbbed as each word sliced a dagger in her head. She leaned against the cool wall. That felt good. Nice.

Megan laughed, but quickly cut it to a quiet chuckle when Karina glared. "I have some leftover antacid if you think that will help."

"Probably not." Karina slid her body along the wall, soaking up what little chill could be gained as she coasted to Gabi's room. Megan said a quiet good-bye—*Thank you Megan*—as Karina made it to Gabi's unlocked door.

"You up?" Karina groaned as she opened the door to find Gabi slumped on her bed. The pitch black room was a relief. Gabi didn't have a busybody roommate to throw open the blinds at dawn's early light. Must be nice.

"Unfortunately," Gabi moaned. "I haven't quite made it out of bed, though. I didn't think I drank that much, but apparently I did."

"I feel like death," Karina said and lay down on the empty bed across the room from Gabi. "Do you want some water? I could get you a bottle."

"No thanks. I may never eat or drink again."

"Amen," Karina said, closing her eyes, "but water is supposed to help with hangovers." Despite the spinning, her head sighed in relief as she sank further into the bed.

Silence. Golden, glittery silence. She could stay like this all day. Please, God, let me stay like this all day.

As her mind drifted, a knock resonated from the door as it opened a crack. Denise popped her cropped light-brown head into the room. The glow from the hallway crept into their sanctuary.

"Hi, girls. You awake?" She beamed. Practically glowed. If the girl had a dimmer switch, Karina would have offered to crank it down. "Did you have fun last night? You two seemed to get along pretty well with those frat boys."

"Yeah, it was fun." Gabi rolled to her feet and grabbed a bottled water from the mini fridge. She held it out to Denise, who was still leaning against the open door.

"Thanks." Denise took the bottle and Gabi got one for herself before she dropped back onto her bed.

"So, are you going to see that guy again?" Denise twisted the bottle open.

"Brent? I don't know. I'm sure we'll see each other around." Gabi shrugged.

"How can you be so nonchalant? I couldn't be that way with my guy," Denise said coyly as she played with the wrapper on the water bottle. The crinkle and rip of paper sliced through the air. Was there a megaphone attached to her fingers? Why was that *crinkle, crinkle, crinkle* so loud?

"Your guy? I didn't know you had a guy."

"I do. Your friend Danny. He's so hot. We had so much fun last night. I think I'm in love."

Crinkle. Rip. Crinkle. Rip.

"Please stop that with the water bottle," Gabi said through clenched teeth.

"Oh, sorry." Denise snatched her hand back, eyes widening and lips trembling.

Crap. Karina needed to offer a distraction before the poor girl started to cry. "Danny. That's great. When are you going to see him again?" she asked.

"I'm not sure. I was so excited I forgot to get his phone number. Do you have it, by any chance?"

Karina turned her blurry eyes to Gabi. Was giving her friend the number the right move? It didn't feel right. It wasn't their number to give. Wouldn't he have given her the number if he'd wanted to?

"No, sorry. We generally just call Ryan or Keith," Gabi said, lying through her teeth. Karina knew he'd called her a dozen times over the past few weeks. Heck, she'd even called him when Keith hadn't answered his phone a few weeks ago.

Gabi had brought up Danny's crush last night, but there was no need. Most of them knew about his infatuation with the Latina goddess. It was obvious, though, that he wasn't sitting at home pining for her. Unless pining included planting his seed in any undergrad he could find. Huge red flag in Karina's book. Obviously a huge red flag to Gabi, too, since she hadn't started anything with the whorish heartbreaker.

"Oh. No problem. I'm sure I'll catch him at the gym. Do you want to head over there after lunch?" Denise offered, apparently missing their green pallor and Karina's immovable body sprawled on the bed. Food—not happening. Exercise when not being chased by ravenous zombies—nope. Hell, she doubted she'd leave the bed for ravenous zombies. *Brain in a smattering of beer, nummy.*

Gag. No more brain thoughts or food thoughts. Just no more thoughts.

"Another time. I'm not feeling much like eating or exercising." Gabi grimaced.

"No problem. I'll see you both later," Denise said as she bounded out of the room, closing the evil door and eliminating any shred of light.

Karina and Gabi sat in silence, neither one wanting to interrupt the beautiful quiet. Karina couldn't help it. She couldn't let this go. "She loves him."

"Apparently, but do we really think he loves her?"

"Maybe... But it was only one night and he didn't give her his number," Karina said. She wasn't best friends with the girl, but she hated watching anyone get their heart stomped. "Should we tell her?"

"Tell her what? We don't know what he's thinking. He might be just as smitten."

"Smitten?" Karina lifted her head and looked at Gabi. Big mistake. Blue streaks zipped past her eyes. Her stomach jumped to her throat.

Never again. Never drinking again.

"I'll talk to him next time I see him," Gabi said. "Do you want to watch some idiot box? There might still be some Saturday morning cartoons on."

"Sure."

The harsh light of the television filled the room. When all else failed, watching sponges that lived in pineapples always kept a girl's mind off the pain and misery she so rightly deserved.

~§~

Saturday was lazy and focused on recuperation. Sunday was crazy and focused on preparation. Karina had so much to do before her date with Kyle. What should she wear? Pants or skirt? Sweater or blouse? What should she do with her hair? Up or down? All very important, life-altering questions.

She called the cavalry in for reinforcements. She enlisted Gabi and Savannah to assist in concocting the perfect fourth date outfit, something that still said casual but also "I like you, we should get busy."

They chose Karina's dark blue jeans and Gabi's red blouse, despite Savannah's million arguments on why a skirt would make a better impression. Savannah ran a curling iron through Karina's hair and applied a light layer of make-up.

Karina checked her reflection in the mirror and smiled. Savannah might be a dress-Nazi but she had some crazy talent when it came to making a woman look good. She ran a hand through the soft curls.

"Stop it." Savannah wrapped the cord around the curling iron. "You're ruining my masterpiece."

"Masterpiece? Extreme much?" Gabi raised her eyebrows at Savannah. "Anyway, this is the big date according to *Cosmo*. Date four. If all goes right, Kyle will be messing up her hair tonight." Gabi pinched a curl and inspected Karina's hair. "It could use a little less poof."

"There is no poof." Savannah walked over to Karina and slapped Gabi's hand away. She ran a hand down the curls, fixing the hypothetical atrocities Gabi had inflicted on them.

"My hair is fine." Karina pulled away. She was starting to feel a bit of sympathy for her stepfather. He complained day and night because Karina and her mother nit-picked and snipped. She never understood how annoying that could actually be until dealing with her roommate and Gabi.

Karina checked the clock. She was early but she didn't care. Anything was better than listening to her friends bicker. It wasn't helping her gurgling stomach. Nerves had hijacked her abdomen and were slowly staking a claim on her temples.

She could do this. Kyle was a great guy. No matter what happened in the past, her future was Kyle. She could feel it. Well, if she looked past the nervous stomach and growing headache. "I'm gonna head out," she told Savannah and Gabi.

Gabi just waved, but Savannah said, "I'm heading out with Peter, so won't be home till late."

Karina entered the front hallway to find Kyle standing in the foyer, reading the pamphlets and posters lining the wall. His newly-washed blond hair hung to the light blue collar of his shirt. His jeans hugged his narrow hips. He looked good.

"Hey." Karina waved. "You're early."

"I finished my homework, and I was excited to see you." He leaned down and kissed her on the lips. "Keep love in your heart. A life without it is like a sunless garden when the flowers are dead."

"That's beautiful."

"Oscar Wilde. He had a way with words."

So do you... "Ready for dinner?" Karina wrapped her hand around his. Warmth travelled up her arm as he caressed her palm. Together, they sauntered into the cafe and ordered their meals. "I got this." Kyle handed over his card for Karina's dinner.

A smile washed over her entire body. He actually paid for her meal. They must be official now. Dating. She wanted to break into a happy-dance, but that would end badly. She settled for a quick shuffle of joy as she sat at one of the tables.

Kyle asked, "So what did you end up doing this weekend?"

"We went over to Psi Rho Friday night and stayed in yesterday. How about you?" She ran a knife through her plate of spaghetti, cutting the baby meatballs and pasta into bite-size clumps.

"Psi Rho? I heard they're barbarians over there. All they do is drink and act stupid."

"They're okay guys. We had a good time." She hoped he wouldn't ask her to elaborate on her Friday night. She couldn't remember one of the frat brothers drinking and acting stupid. Mostly, because she was the one doing the drinking and acting stupid and ultimately forgetting most of the night. Not her proudest moment. Not her worst, though. Junior year...

No. She wasn't going there. Not now.

"Well, that's good, I guess." Kyle turned his focus to the spaghetti on his plate. They sat in an uncomfortable silence until he asked, "So, what are you reading right now?"

"I don't have a lot of time to read for pleasure, but I just finished a Janet Evanovich novel."

"Really? How did you like the book?" He spun his fork in the pasta.

"I loved it." She laid her fork down, excitement stirring. She tended to get a bit animated when she discussed the romances jamming her tablet, and no one wanted to hear about the books she read. But Kyle was as big a dork about books as she was. Someone to finally understand her addiction. "I just started her Stephanie Plum series. It's amazing. I can't decide which guy she should end up with... Ranger or Joe. It's the big question."

Kyle stopped his fork mid-twirl and stared at Karina. "Really? I'm surprised you'd like something like that."

"Yeah. She's one of the authors I actually get excited about." She picked up her fork and continued eating the over-cooked ropes in tomato sauce. Normally, the food wasn't this bad. Everyone had an off night, chefs included.

"You just don't seem the type to like that kind of book."

"Why? What kind of book is that?" Karina asked, not sure if she should be annoyed.

A contemplative look swept over Kyle's face, and then he smiled. "Nothing. It's not important. How are your classes?"

"They're going good." She put her napkin over her plate. Between the mediocre food and the nerves dancing in her belly, she was done with dinner. Tonight was definitely going to be the night. She wanted to take their relationship to the next level. He was great, smart, perfect. She was excited. Nervous. He seemed so calm. Didn't he know this was the big date?

"It's good, not well."

"Excuse me?"

"Proper English... never mind." He smiled and tossed his napkin down. "Are you done eating? I would love to see that music collection you've been taunting me with since our first date." He placed a warm hand on her cheek.

"Sure. Savannah's out tonight, we'll have the room to ourselves."

They tilted their trays of garbage into the trash and headed toward Karina's room, passing Gabi and Megan on the stairs.

"Hi, girls. This is Kyle. Kyle, these are my friends Gabi and Megan."

"Nice to meet you." Kyle smiled, his green eyes sparkling.

"You too. We're heading down to have dinner." Gabi pulled Megan down the steps, a smirk lining her lips. "We'll catch up with you later."

Kyle and Karina walked the fifty feet to her room. It felt like a mile and an inch at the same time. The corridor stretched on and on and on, giving her mind way too much time to think about what she was about to do. Sleeping with Kyle. She reached the door to her room. Already.

Ready? Was she ready? She thought so, but this was a big step. He was the one. So... why was she so nervous? She opened the door to her room and followed Kyle inside.

He turned to her side of the room, and stared at the few picture frames lining her wall. "Parents?"

"Parents, sister Kathy, and brother Mike." She walked to her speaker dock and inserted her tablet. She hit play on her classical playlist; Tchaikovsky billowed from the speaker. "This is one of my favorites." She moved to her bed and sat, nerves popping. Foot bouncing, up and down, the sole of her shoe tapping on the tiled floor. She turned to where Kyle stood. When a small smile tickled his lips, desire pooled in her belly.

Kyle awkwardly sat down next to her and grabbed her hand, his eyes never leaving hers. Sparks sizzled down her spine, lighting up her insides like a pinball game stuck on tilt. He leaned over, the smell of citrus and musk floating from his skin.

He lifted his other hand to her face, leaving satiny tingles that ran a trail down her cheek to her awaiting mouth. She wrapped her lips around his finger, slowly pulling in and out. In and out. Her tongue massaging the soft surface.

Fire blazed in his eyes before he threw his head back. A moan flew from his lips. She'd seen this on TV, but apparently guys liked it more than she thought.

"I love being with you, Karina," he whispered as he moved his hand to her cheek. He loved being with her. He was amazing, sensitive and all hers. Their eyes locked as he leaned into her, placing his lips on hers. His kiss was soft, supple, sweet. He ran his hand down her side, grazing the side of her breast.

Good Lord. Her breath came in shaky gasps. Her hand slid down his tight, muscular back as he helped her lay on the bed. His body covered hers.

"I want you." He begged with his words, with his deliciously roaming hands, with the bulge he pressed toward her center. "I want to be in you. Feel you. Love you."

"Yes." She squeaked as he unzipped her jeans. His hand finding that hot, wet center aching for him. *He wants to love me.* This perfect moment. Mouth groaning. Body writhing. Hips swaying. This was the perfect moment with the perfect guy.

He stood up and pulled off her shoes, followed by her jeans and thong. He licked his pink, succulent lips as he watched her remove her sweater. His own jeans dropped to the floor, and then he removed his shirt. His chest heaved as he stared at her mostly naked body.

"Let me." He unhinged the last barrier between them. "What greater thing is there for two human souls, than to feel that they are joined for life—to strengthen each other... George Eliot"

His hot, hungry mouth found her puckered nipples. Teeth grazed swollen flesh. Her back arched. Fingers sliding into his hair, she pulled his mouth closer. *Nibble. Suck. Lick.* Fuck.

He pulled away and got a condom from his jeans pocket. He ripped the package and slid on the latex shield. Her thighs quivered as he angled himself, pushing the tip inside of her. He stilled. "You're a virgin."

"Yes." Really—he asked her this now?

"Are you sure we should do this?" He pulled out, a pained cringe on his face.

"Please, don't stop. I want you," she begged.

That was all the invitation he needed. He slowly guided his shaft inside her, moving slow and steady. *Fuck.* Red fucking pain shot past her eyes as he pushed deeper. Agony. Ecstasy. Anguish. Euphoria.

Her body slowly opened to the hard intrusion. In. Out. Each slow, punishing stroke easing the tension as her body accepted him. All of him. Rocking back and forth to the rhythm of the music, her body rode the line between pleasure and pain.

The sound of her roommate's key in the lock pulled her from the edge. Shit. She forgot the damn scrunchie.

The door flew open and Savannah bounced in. "Oh, God," Savannah stuttered and covered her eyes. "I'm so sorry. I'm leaving." She turned and ran into the door jamb. "Shit." She uncovered her eyes and walked out the door.

With one last thrust, Kyle's face contorted and a groan escaped. He rested his head on her shoulder, panting a little. "That was amazing." He kissed her cheek and lifted himself up, lying next to her frustrated body. His breathing slowed as he gestured to the closed door. "Roommate?"

"Uh-huh." She ran her fingers down his stomach, her buzzing body clamoring for release.

He wrapped his hand around her fingers and brought them to his lips. "I should go." He jumped to his feet and grabbed his clothes, making quick work of returning his jeans and shirt to his satiated body.

"You can stay a little while." Karina grabbed her blanket and threw it over her exposed body. Tears stung her eyes. Tears of humiliation, frustration...

He tucked in his shirt and tossed the underused condom into the garbage can. "I should go. It's not fair to lock your roommate out of her room." He kissed Karina on the forehead. "I'll call you."

Karina stared in frustration at the closed door after he left, her blood boiling with lust. Her head spinning from need. She now understood all those jokes about cold showers. Unfortunately, she didn't see the humor. Hell, she could barely see at all. Arousal had hijacked any and all regularly scheduled bodily functions. Eyes blurred. Ears rang. Breathing gasping.

Did girls get blue balls?

She pulled on a pair of sweats and a T-shirt and headed to the refrigerator for some caffeine. She tilted the bottle back. Soda bubbles hammered at her unsuspecting sinuses. She lowered the bottle to the top of the fridge and bent over as bubbles burnt the delicate lining of her nostrils. She stayed like that until her gasps eased into soft pants.

She glanced at the garbage can, and the rubber sat coiled, glistening on the floor—right next to the can. Couldn't he at least hit the trash bag? Missed shot with the dick snot. She grinned. At least her sense of humor was still intact.

She reached down to grab the slippery remnant of her maiden voyage. Apparently her trip didn't lead to the Caribbean, but it sure had felt cursed. All she needed was a black pearl for the analogy to be complete. Cursed might be a bit harsh, though. After all, the beginning and middle had been good.

Her nose and mouth crinkled as the upper tippy-tippy-tops of her fingers pinched the used condom. *Gross. Gross. Gross.* Her outstretched arm locked as she leaned over the basket, dropping the offensive object into the can. Two points.

"Well, I'm glad one of us had time to finish. Next time, we both will," she promised herself and dropped to her bed. She was sure, one day when they were an old married couple sitting on their back porch watching the grandkids play in the back yard, she'd laugh about this with Kyle. Their first time. Her first time.

Unfortunately, today was not that day.

Chapter Sixteen

Ryan

CRAP WEEK. RYAN was having a crap week. Between a nuisance-worthy business plan that was due Friday and another set of paraline drawings of a lamp, he didn't have time to scratch an itch. He needed this set of drawings to be exact, since next week he'd be building the darn table lamp based on the drawing. Everything needed to be perfect.

The cramped room he shared with Danny and Ski was split into two halves by a partial wall. One side held their beds, the other side—after they banished the three desks to the basement—had a walnut table, a couch, entertainment center and a mini-fridge. They all had laptops, and right now Ryan's was set up at the table.

The business plan wasn't all that difficult. It just required him to put all the information together into a semi-coherent presentation. Both assignments sucked and were keeping him from enjoying the last glimpses of the autumn sun. Soon winter white would cover the Midwest and the sun would go into deep-freeze hibernation. Not even the sun wanted to peek its flaming plasma head out in five below.

On top of all the homework, he hadn't seen Karina all week. Well, he'd seen her, but she'd been distant, barely smiled. Something was going on, but she wasn't talking. Not to him, anyway. He would go so far as to say she was avoiding him. Why? He had no clue.

He grabbed his cell phone when it rang and glanced at the screen. Speaking of avoidance... *Crap*. One more reason his week was crap.

His father had called three times during the week. He had no idea what the old man wanted, but last year his father called once—the whole year. Three times in one week didn't look promising. After the first call, Ryan had texted his sisters to make sure there was nothing urgent or his mom wasn't having any issues. Apparently, mom was fine, and his father wasn't trying to reach anyone else. In other words, his father wanted him. Just him. Not good.

He twisted his neck when the phone rang again, and a loud crack slid down his spine. He hit ignore and tried to focus on the drawing. He had way too much work to stop now. His father and the lecture on whatever disappointing atrocity Ryan had performed would have to wait. Somewhere between *when hell froze over* and *never* would be the ideal time for that conversation.

How many of those warm-fuzzy lectures had he lived through growing up? Well, at least until his mom became sick, and then Ryan became the perfect son... Well, he tried, but apparently even then he couldn't live up to requirements of the Kent name.

The door flew open and took his attention off his mounting parental issues.

Ski walked in and yanked the Xbox controllers off the wooden TV stand. His cousin Joe followed behind the giant and stood by the couch.

"Sit dere." Ski's trademark Polish accent and rolled Rs made it even more of a command. His large hand smacked the couch as he turned on the TV. Joe's worried eyes stayed on Ryan. He actually looked guilty. Joe moved up a few notches in Ryan's mind.

"Ski, I'm studying." Ryan shook the drawings, hoping his buddy would take the hint.

"So, study." Ski stared at the menu options as his large thumbs slid over the buttons.

Apparently not. "Go to the lounge or Darnell's room." Ryan said with little conviction. The *Call of Duty* operation being set up on the screen looked a hell of a lot more fun than the crap he was doing.

"Darnell is studying." Ski pressed a button on the remote and the gunfire on the screen echoed through the room.

"I'm studying, asshole."

"You study too much." Ski pointed at the cowering freshman. "Down, Joe."

Ryan almost laughed at Ski. The two of them had the same conversation over the summer, except Ski was the one who studied too much. Now that he had a girlfriend, his study habits had cooled. It helped he had a photographic memory. Ryan did not.

Joe sat on the couch and took the video game controller from his cousin's outstretched hand. Brent walked through the open door, snatching a bottle of beer from the mini-fridge. He turned to Ryan. "Want one?"

Ryan slammed his book closed. There was no way he was getting anything else done. He liked living in the frat, most days. Some days, though, were a pain in the ass. "Sure. Why not."

"About time you put that shit away." Ski motioned to Joe. "This is my cousin Joe."

"Joe, are you going to be a doctor, too?" Brent sat on the floor, watching them

"It's the family profession. So, yeah. Although, I'm not a genius like Andrzej here."

"Andrzej?" Brent looked confused. Apparently, he forgot Ski had a real parental-given name.

"Sorry— Ski," Joe said.

"Where's your accent?" Ryan pulled a chair from the table and set it next to the couch. He sat and took a pull from the bottle in his hand.

"He got the accent, I got the good looks." Joe dropped a Moab. The massive bomb cratered the ground, scattering around mini-Ski's feet.

"Bite me, Joey. I got it all, little man, and keep that shit away from me." His arms drifted sideways as he moved into his latest knife attack. The virtual Russians didn't stand a chance.

Explosions, gunfire and grunts filled the air as Ryan leaned back, watching the show. Ski tossed a grenade, landing on Joe's character's head.

"Dammit." Joe's character fell to the ground. "What the fuck, Andrzej?"

"Oops."

"I'm gonna kick your ass." Joe leapt from the couch and stood in front of Ski. No one got in Ski's face. He was six five of pure muscle. Everyone ran from the linebacker. But here and now, this five ten freshman who couldn't be more than a hundred fifty pounds soaking wet was in his grille.

This should be good. Ryan brought the beer bottle to his lips, but stopped. He should make sure he could help the little guy if Ski went ballistic. The big man had pounded opponents for less. Of course, the fact that Ryan wasn't much bigger than Joe didn't exactly make a two-on-one scenario a fair fight. They'd be annihilated.

"Move, Joe." Ski hit pause and stood. "It was an accident."

"Yeah right. Dick." Joe pushed the muscled monster, and although Ski shouldn't have budged, he toppled onto the couch behind him.

"Sorry, cousin." Ski jumped to his feet and wrapped his arms around Joe.

"Fine." Joe huffed. "But don't pull that shit again."

"Are we done with all this touchy-feely crap? I got next." Brent put his beer on the floor and inched to the couch. He grabbed the controller and took the seat Joe left open.

"Want a drink, Joe?" Ryan asked, since no one else had offered.

"Soda?"

"I got some in my room," Brent yelled over the video game noise. "Hey, grab my Xbox controllers so we can all play. I owe Ryan an ass whipping."

"Where's your room?" Joe asked Brent.

"Come on." Ryan set his bottle on the table. "I'll show you."

Ryan walked out the door, Joe on his heels. They headed down the scuffed wooden floors, frat alumni pictures lining the newly painted walls. A crew had come in and fixed a bunch of problems within the house before school began. They fixed and painted and made the place habitable. Ski was stuck in the house all summer watching the changes, but he got his girlfriend Samantha out of the deal, so the big man wasn't complaining.

"You gonna pledge Psi Rho?" Ryan asked little-Ski.

"That's the plan. Andrzej... Ski would have a fit if I pledged somewhere else."

"How come you haven't been around the frat?" Ryan led him down the back stairwell to the second floor. They walked past a few doors, and Ryan opened Brent's small single room. Benefit of being the president— your own space.

"Classes. Homework. I wanted to get a grip on school before I came up here."

"That I can understand. The school piece of the college experience is a bitch." Ryan opened the refrigerator door. "Lemon-lime or cola?"

"Cola's fine."

Ryan tossed a can to Joe.

"Thanks." Joe tapped the lid and pulled the tab. "So, have you seen

Savannah?" The mock-casual way he said her name was almost painful to watch. Hell. Ryan knew that one all too well. The right woman walking away had a way of destroying the best of men.

"Yeah, at the gym…" Ryan didn't think he should mention the talk at the library. He had a feeling that was confidential, and since she chose to ditch Joe against his advice, she obviously had her personal reasons.

"Is she okay?" Joe cringed.

"Fine."

"Good." Joe rubbed his fingers along the can, his eyes glued on the uninteresting condensation dripping down the sides and landing on the floor. "I haven't seen her in a few weeks. We had a fight and then nothing."

"Do you want some free advice?"

"Sure."

"Take it slow. Next time you see her, just take it slow." Poor sap. Ryan had been there. Sometimes he felt like he was there, now. Karina seemed to know all the right buttons to push to make his life miserable. It sucked. And the way she was blowing him off... Hell, he should just give up on the whole thing before he started looking as bad as this guy.

~»ΨΡ«~

Chapter Seventeen

Karina

KARINA SAT IN her room pretending to watch a movie, her mind in a fog. She hadn't heard from Kyle. Not once. All the technology available, and not a single call, text, chat or email. She'd checked, pulling out her phone every five minutes. She'd even had Gabi call her cell phone, just to make sure the damn non-ringing contraption was still working.

She tossed her cell phone on the bed. She really needed to chill. Kyle had a life. After all, he'd said he had a paper due this week. When she had a paper due, she was a basket case. She needed to give him time. He'd call when he was done with his assignments. Patience was a virtue...

Ah, screw virtue.

"What did I do wrong?" Karina fell back on her bed and flipped a pillow over her head, making sure not to cover the spoon and raw cookie dough in her other hand.

"You didn't do anything wrong." Savannah huffed and yanked the pillow away. "I'm sure he has a good reason for not calling. That paper was probably more important than he let on—"

"—and if not, he's a dumb-ass." Gabi grabbed the tube of cookie dough from Karina and dipped her spoon in the package.

"Easy for you to say, you're not the one who was a victim of a bump and run." Karina scowled at the pilfered sugar. That package of salmonella was the difference between hunting down Kyle and sitting at home... Well, sitting at home pining. But pining was better than making an ass out of herself and tracking him down.

Gabi and Savannah shared a look as they giggled.

"What?" Karina yanked the dough from Gabi's hand. Traitors didn't deserve any of her cookie dough. "Is my grief amusing to you?"

"No, you've just painted an interesting picture. We're just imagining Kyle bumping and running." Gabi dropped her spoon as she burst into laughter.

Savannah laughter bubbled up. "I don't need an imagination. You seem to forget I got to witness said bump and run."

"Was it good for you?" Gabi asked, rolling on the floor howling like a hyena.

"I'm afraid not, how about you Karina? You seemed to be enjoying yourself."

"It was fine." Karina blushed and held back a laugh. "Now stop it. We don't talk about your sex life."

"Yours is more fun than mine at the moment." Gabi smiled and pushed Karina on the shoulder. "Let's go to the gym."

"Volleyball fixes everything. You can imagine the ball's Kyle's face." Savannah picked up a volleyball and tossed it to Karina as Gabi turned off the movie streaming to Savannah's computer. Karina tapped the ball away before it hit her and tied up her package of dough. They might be able to distract her from her crappy life for a few hours, but eventually she'd be back here and if there was still no word from Kyle...

Crap. Crap. Crap. How did she get herself in this situation again? Thinking a guy would stick around. What was wrong with her?

~§~

By Thursday, Karina's preoccupation with the lack of phone call had messed with her classes. An easy assignment had come back with an F. F! She didn't get Fs. Even at the apex of the incident, her grades hadn't fallen that low.

But she just couldn't stop. Couldn't stop overanalyzing. Had she misread something? Of course not— What part of having sex was confusing? What part of "I love being with you" did she misunderstand? Why hadn't he made any attempt to contact her?

"Hello... Hello... Anyone home?" Ryan asked as he waved his hands in front of Karina's face.

The lunchroom came back into focus. Her study session with Ryan and she couldn't get Kyle out of her head.

"Sorry. I'm a little distracted."

"Do you want to talk about it?" Ryan spun his pen between his fingers.

"No. Let's get back to the German paper."

"Okay, but I'm here if you need to talk." He turned the page on his open textbook. "So, you keep switching tenses in this paper. This whole paragraph is in the present and then you switch to future tense..."

He watched her. She could feel his eyes staring holes into her resolve. Every word he spoke mumbled in her mind. He sounded like the *Peanuts* gang teacher... *Waa, waa waa waa...*

"...and this part is written in Spanish...and this part is written in Greek..."

"Huh?" She looked at her homework. Did he say Greek and Spanish? Her mind really had been blurry the past few days. How had she mixed up the languages? How? She knew how. Her mind was one-track. One single track playing over and over again. All she could think about was Kyle.

Dammit.

She'd become a chick-lit stereotype. Pretty soon she'd be whining about jumpers and curry buffets. It was her mom's favorite movie, so they'd watched it together over and over and over again. And now she was on her way to being an obsessive man-hungry singleton. She should just change her name to Bridget. Get it over with.

"That was a test. You're staring off into space again."

Yes. She was staring off into space… again. She had all these thoughts swimming in her head and no one to share them with. It was just so embarrassing, the whole situation. The girls didn't think so, but they were obviously being nice. Weren't they? Maybe she needed another opinion. An unbiased opinion. Maybe she needed a man's perspective. Maybe she was making this into more than it was.

"It's Kyle." The words left her mouth before she could truly think it through. The damn "maybes" got the best of her.

"Is everything okay?"

"I'm sorry. I don't want to bother you." Embarrassment crawled up Karina's face as she pulled her assignment back. "I'll deal with this later."

"Why can't you just tell me?"

She didn't want to share her fuck-up, and every day it felt more and more like a major, crazy fuck-up. She felt like such a fool.

What would he think about her? After all, who slept with a guy after the fourth date, anyway? No matter what Gabi had read in Cosmo.

She'd had plenty of time to think about those four dates. Dissect them. And it didn't look good. They'd talked superficially, but how well did she know Kyle? He might be out telling the campus all about their sexcapade, her name in magic marker in every men's bathroom. *For a good time with happy ending, call Karina. She only needs four dates and you only have to buy her dinner once.*

Ugh. She wrinkled her nose and tried to ignore her burning cheeks. Ryan was too good a friend to read about her mistake on the college-crapper TMZ. She needed to get at least part of the story out there. "Fine." She huffed. "I kind of slept with Kyle on Sunday and I haven't heard from him since."

"Kind of?"

"I tell you I slept with Kyle and haven't heard from him since and that's what you focus on?"

"Sorry." He dropped his pen into the crease of his book. "He's a jackass. You deserve so much better."

Wasn't that the standard line when I guy broke your heart? *You're too good for him.* But that didn't explain why he's not good enough, yet still managed to be the one to walk away without a backward glance. "Thanks."

"You don't seem to believe me." His eyebrows arched in frustration.

"Not that I walk around quoting *Pretty Woman* all the time, but it's easier to believe the bad stuff." She dropped her eyes to the paper in front of her.

"So which one of us is supposed to be the hooker in this scenario?"

"Eww. I think that's me." She lifted her head and tried to smile. "Not good."

Ryan placed his hand over hers. "He's a fool. I hope you know you are way too good for him."

"I'm glad you think so." She smiled.

"I know so. You should know."

"Normally, I would. I guess this whole thing threw me off."

The warmth of his hand on hers and the intensity of his stare made her turn away. She closed her eyes and exhaled. She shouldn't be doing this. She had a boyfriend. Maybe.

Ryan was a player who believed guys should sow their wild oats. He wasn't her type. She couldn't go through this again. She couldn't handle striking out again. And not just striking out, striking out with Ryan. It would hurt too much.

"I-I, uh, have a one o'clock," she stammered and picked up the garbage from the lunch she barely ate. She hurried toward the exit before turning back to Ryan. "See you in German."

~§~

Thursday after German, Karina found herself staring at her phone. It was time to get serious about finding Kyle. She'd waited for him to make the first move. She needed to initiate something, anything.

She found his number in her contacts and hit the little phone icon. The ring back tone went *tink-tink* in her ear while her stomach did a slow roll. She heard a click followed by Kyle's voice asking her to leave a message. A message. What was the message she wanted to leave? Nonchalant? Worried? Angry? She should have thought about that before she dialed the number.

BEEP! Time's up.

"Um... Hi Kyle, um...this is Karina. I wanted to see how you were doing. Um. Call me when you get a chance." She jabbed the end button. Shit. She forgot to leave her phone number. Maybe he hadn't called because he forgot her number. Should she call again? Maybe leave her number, just in case?

She sat back and covered her face with a pillow. "Aghhhhhh..." What a complete disaster. She couldn't call him again, but maybe she could text him. That would work.

She entered her phone number onto the screen and sent that to Kyle.

Nothing. No vibration. No ring tone. No text tone. Nothing.

After staring at the phone on and off for a few hours, she decided to call again. She dialed the number and flinched at the now familiar ring back tone.

"Kyle's phone," a male voice said—not Kyle.

"Hi. Is Kyle there?" she said keeping her voice cool, moderate. This was no biggie. Maybe, if she said that enough, she'd believe it.

"Corrine? He's on his way."

Corrine? Who the heck was Corrine? Her stomach knotted. On his way. To where? "Uh... No. This is Karina."

"Oh, sorry. I must have misheard the name...when Kyle told me all about you. He just ran out to grab a quick dinner with friends before he got back to homework. I'll tell him you called."

"Thanks."

She closed the phone. Corrine? It sounded like Karina. Right? Innocent mistake. Her name did tend to get butchered. Karen, Karine, Carrie...Corrine.

She was being ridiculous. Worrying about nothing. He was busy. That was what she got for dating an English major. They had a lot of writing and reading to get through.

She smiled and turned on her laptop. Speaking of homework, she had quite a bit to get done, herself. She opened her English book and pulled some research she'd done earlier in the week. Hopefully, she'd been rational enough to grab adequate information to write the damn thing.

One hour. Two hours. Three hours. Her homework for tomorrow was done, she'd even started on next week's assignments. She checked the clock—midnight. Too late to call. She opened her email program. Email seemed so impersonal after such an intimate encounter, but desperation nipped at her throat.

Hey whats up? I wanted to make sure you got my message. I should've called earlier but I haven't had time to breathe, let alone talk. Its been so crazy here. I'd love to go out some time this week. Give me a call when you get a chance.

Karina

The next morning, she checked her email before she grabbed her gym gear. No response. Not that she expected a response this early in the morning, but she hoped. As she locked her door, Gabi walked out of her room toward the bathroom.

"Hey. You look like shit." Gabi adjusted her robe, almost dropping the mesh bag of shower stuff. "You weren't up all night, were you?"

"Thanks and yes." Karina rolled her eyes. Did she really need to know how crappy she looked? Did her friend need to remind her?

"Are you going to class? Let's go to the mall. Brent lent me his car."

"Brent? Fratboy Brent? What does one have to do to have fratboy Brent lend you his car?" Karina laughed.

"...nothing I didn't thoroughly enjoy." Gabi glowed. She actually glowed.

Karina wanted to be happy for Gabi. She *was* happy for her friend. Look at her—that genuine smile, the connection she obviously had with fratboy Brent. The guy lent her his car, for goodness sake.

Karina didn't remember her own smile being that intense after her night with Kyle. She never had that glow. Yet she'd spent the week waiting by the phone... "I'll go. Screw the gym and Friday classes. Screw it all." Karina threw up her arms.

"Can you give me fifteen minutes? I have to wash the sweet scent of sex off my body."

"Ick. Thanks for the visual." Karina walked toward the elevator.

"Don't you dare leave."

"I'm grabbing breakfast before we go."

"Fine. But don't blow me off."

"Gabi. Really? Shopping or sitting through the boring yammering of classes?" Karina moved her hands up and down, weighing the options. "It's so hard to choose. Now take your shower and meet me downstairs. You stink."

Karina pinched her fingers over her nose as Gabi ducked into the bathroom. The gym bag slipped down Karina's shoulder. Well, she wouldn't be needing that. She opened her bedroom door and dropped the bag on the floor. She grabbed her purse and tablet and headed downstairs. This was just what she needed, a day away from campus. A day of just the girls. A day to laugh and just be silly. A day to be herself again.

A little while later, Karina sat at a table eating her egg sandwich and tater tots and reading her latest e-book escape. She should have thought of doing this at the beginning of the week. Nothing like a predestined romance to keep a mind and heart busy.

"Good morning. Reading anything good?" Savannah sat down across the table.

"I only read good things. You should try reading a book some time. You might like it."

"I read for school. That's quite enough for me."

"Aren't you an English major?"

"Elementary Education with a focus on English. Big difference."

"You're still going to have to read. You know, papers, homework, the books you assign."

"I'll be working with grade-schoolers. How long can their papers possibly be?" Savannah stole a potato from Karina's plate. "And I'm not completely sold on English. I'm exploring my options. Anyway, they're small, they only know short words."

"You've thought this through."

"Yeah. Haven't you?" Savannah stole another tot. "These are awesome. Didn't you think about it before deciding to be a lawyer?"

"Yeah."

"Why a lawyer? Didn't Shakespeare say, 'Let's kill all the lawyers'?" Savannah sipped her coffee. At least she brought her own drink.

"Yeah, but that was more a statement on the lawyers' importance to Democracy."

"Really?"

"Have you read any books? Any at all?" Karina hit the button on the tablet.

"Blah, blah, blah. So is that why you want to be a lawyer?"

"I just... I just want to help people."

"Hey, bitches. You ready to shop, Kar?" Gabi walked toward the table, her tight blue jeans and midriff length sweater hugging her curves. Her dark hair hung in waves around her naturally olive face, held back by her sunglasses.

Karina looked at the track pant and T-shirt combination she was sporting. It was okay, right? Provided the vagrant look was now in style. "I should change." She put her napkin and silverware on her plate.

"Why? You look good. We're just going to run around the mall."

"Fine. You're coming with us right, Sav?" Karina stood.

"Where?"

"We're ditching classes and hitting the mall." Gabi dropped her sunglasses over her eyes.

"Shall we be riding your broomstick?" Savannah snagged one last tot off the plate.

"Nice. I offer a day away from this prison and you offer a witch joke." Gabi pulled keys from her pocket and jingled them in front of Savannah's face. "Anyway, my broom's in the shop, I thought we'd take the Jeep."

"Where'd you get a car?"

"Brent." Gabi swung the key ring around her finger.

Savannah's eyes widened as her lips started to form words.

"Not one word. We're dating. He lent me his car so I didn't have to walk home this morning. Let's go. Do you hear that?" Gabi cocked her head.

"Hear what? The sound of the psychiatrist coming to take you away?"

Gabi raised her middle finger. "The sound of the mall calling our name. Hurry up. Oh, and turn off your cell phones. This is a distraction-free excursion."

"But what if Kyle calls?"

"Distraction. He can wait."

The three of them walked out of the dorm and headed into the October sun, Karina's phone silenced in her pocket.

~§~

Gabi, Savannah and Karina were all laughing as they walked into the dorm. The cookie cutter mall was just as expected. The name-brand clothing stores and the accessory stores were the same ones Karina had back home in Illinois. Even though there were no surprises, it was so nice to get away and have girl time.

She'd never admit it to Gabi, but the phone-free couple of hours was just what she needed. She actually forgot about the email she sent last night... Well, technically it was this morning. She turned on her phone as the girls rode up the elevator.

"Couldn't wait five more minutes, huh?"

"Did I check my phone while we were in the car? No. Did I check my phone at the mall? No. So, bite me." They exited the elevator as the cell phone blinked on and Karina's email chimed to signal an incoming message.

"I got mail." Karina clicked on the envelope, Gabi and Savannah affixed to her back. "It's him."

She opened the email labeled *Kyle McDougal* and read the response. Twice. The second time because she didn't believe her own eyes.

"That sonofabitch." Leave it to Gabi to say the words on Karina's mind.

"That has to be a joke." Savannah's eye were wide.

Gabi shook her head. "I'm not laughing."

"Neither am I." Karina looked at the email again.

Hey[.] ~~whats~~ What's up? I wanted to make sure you ~~got~~ received my message. I should've called earlier, but I haven't had time to breathe, let alone talk. ~~Its~~ It's been so crazy here. I'd love to go out some time this week. Give me a call when you get a chance.

Karina

Karina: It was nice spending time with you, but I believe our relationship has run its course. I'll always have fond memories.

Kyle

P.S. You might want to pay attention in English class. Your grammar is atrocious.

Gabi made a rude sound. "Did he *grade* your email?"

"He didn't actually grade it. He just pointed out the grammar issues," Savannah said.

"I don't give a fuck if there's actually a letter grade on the damn thing," Gabi snarled. "He corrected her email. What kind of sick-fuck does that?"

An RA from the third floor stormed out of Nica's room. "Language. Watch your language, girls."

Karina stared at the tiny screen. Really? Really. She put her heart—and her body—out there and got nothing. Well, she did get free grammar advice. Body. Grammar advice. Body. Grammar advice. Didn't seem like a fair trade. Gabi was right. What kind of sick fuck did that?

"Karina, honey, don't cry."

She looked over at Gabi, and realized the whole room was blurry. When had she started crying? And why?

"Honey, let's go upstairs and get ready. Let's go get our drink on at the frat."

"I'm really not in the mood tonight." Karina was really proud of how steady her voice was. "I have homework and I just want to stay here."

"Fine. I'll call Brent and tell him we'll come by tomorrow night instead. Who's bringing the cookie dough?"

Karina patted her shoulder. "Gabi, go out. You've been looking forward to seeing him all day. I'll be fine. I just want to spend some time alone, do a bit of homework and watch TV."

"I'm not leaving you alone," Gabi argued. "We all stay in or we all go out."

"I'm not going to that awful frat." Savannah's lips curled.

"Really?" Gabi glared at Savannah as she took Karina's phone and turned it off.

"Oh, all right. I'll go, but I won't have any fun." Savannah grabbed Karina's phone from Gabi. "You'll get this back tomorrow."

"Why can't I keep my phone?" Karina almost wailed. Almost.

"If I have to go to that beer-soaked hovel, you are not going to obsessively read this garbage," Savannah said in a prim voice.

"I'm not obsessing."

"Oh, please," Gabi snapped. "Your eyes haven't left that bullshit email since you opened it. We're going out to give those eyes some delicious hard bodies to focus on. You will forget that stick-figure horrible excuse for a man when we're done with you."

~§~

Karina stood next to Savannah in the corner watching Ryan, Megan, Gabi and Brent play beer pong. She wasn't in the mood to play. She wasn't in the mood to be there. She sipped the beer in her hand and cringed. Warm. Ugh. She probably should have dumped the brew a half-hour ago, but that would require moving. She liked her little piece of obscurity. No one seemed to notice she existed. Which was how she wanted it.

"How are you feeling?" Savannah inched up to Karina's hiding spot.

"Fine." Goodbye moment of obscurity.

Joe slid up to Savannah—the man looked downright miserable. This breakup was not treating him well. If you could even call it a breakup.

Savannah didn't seem to be handling it much better. Sure, there had been a scrunchie on the door a few nights, but something was off. She wasn't acting like a woman who was having a good time with the men of Ritter University. She seemed—sad, unsettled.

"Hi, Savannah," Joe shouted over the wailing guitars as he offered her a plastic cup. The black shirt he wore was buttoned halfway up, exposing a tight blue T-shirt. His long blond hair was tied back from his square jaw, and the dimple on his chin deepened as his lips attempted a smile.

"Thanks." Savannah took the plastic cup of beer and took a sip.

"How have you been?"

"Fine. You?" Her response was flat. Karina could tell Savannah was trying to seem uninterested, but she was failing miserably. When would this girl realize she and Joe were great together?

"Good. Can we talk? Outside."

Savannah stared at her drink, maybe looking for the answer there. Unfortunately, the answers were never in a cup of beer. Karina learned that the hard way.

Joe sighed. "I just want to be friends. That's all. No more passes. I've taken the hint. But I like hanging around with you. So, friends?"

Savannah nodded and they walked out the door, leaving Karina alone in the corner watching her friends play game after game of beer pong. They'd stopped asking if she wanted to play. Which was nice. She didn't feel like pretending to have fun.

By the time Savannah texted from their dorm room to say she was home, Karina was done. All of her friends were having fun. They didn't need her. She headed toward the bar and dumped her almost full beer into the trash.

Danny stood by the bar rail, a new freshman hanging on his every word. His finger slid down her forearm. Poor Megan. Why she fell for this moron— Who knew? Of course, who was she to judge? Karina was a moron magnet, too.

"Karina. What's happening?" A tipsy smile spread across Danny's stupid face.

"Nothing. I'm going home."

"Oh, do you want me to walk you? I can grab Ryan…" He turned to the Ping-Pong tables.

"Don't bother. I'll see you next week." She smiled and pushed through the throng of people to the front door. The evening was crisp, but it felt nice after the jam-packed body heat in the frat.

A beautiful golden brown and red blanket covered the yards leading to the campus. *Crunch, crunch, crunch.* Her feet on the dried leaves was a therapeutic sound, the sound of moving forward. The loud music and vibrant lights of the fraternity faded away. *Crunch, crunch, crunch.* Darkness and relative silence soothed her angst-ridden brain.

A small 1930's cottage sat on the side of the street, out of place next to the newer suburban monstrosities. But the evergreen shrubs and fall flowers painted a scene worthy of Thomas Kinkade. A six-foot trellis arched over the end of the sidewalk leading to the house. Small white flowers twined through the wooden bars, and Karina caught the faint scent of vanilla.

What was that—? She spun around to face the empty street. Maybe she should have taken Danny up on that escort to the dorm. The pretty street took on an ominous feel as she continued back toward the dorm. She made herself walk calmly, one foot in front of the other, her head swiveling back and forth as she took in her surroundings.

"Karina."

She stopped at the sound of a familiar deep voice and saw Ryan jogging up behind her.

"Where are you going? I think there's a law about leaving a full beer behind."

"The way I'm feeling, I just don't think drinking is a good idea." She kicked the ground, scattering pebbles on the pavement. "I figured I'd finish that German paper. My tutor is a slave driver."

"As your tutor, I'm impressed with your fortitude. As your friend, I advise you to take the night off. Even the president gets a night at or two at Camp David."

"I've been blowing off way to much lately."

"So, you're more important than the president?"

"Shut up." She laughed. Genuinely laughed. It felt good. "Why don't you make yourself useful and walk me home?"

"My pleasure." He fell in behind her as she headed down the street, silent in between the *crunch, crunch, crunch* of the leaves. "You really like him, don't you?"

"Who?"

"Kyle."

"Yes. No. I don't know. I mean, I thought I did, but looking back, we didn't have that much in common," she stammered.

"If you don't like him, why are you so upset?"

"It's not important." Why she liked him was her business. No one else's. Never mind she'd been trying to figure out why for a few days. But when she did figure it out, she wasn't going to share it with anyone. Well, maybe she would, because then she wouldn't feel so damn stupid.

Her feet sped up. She just needed to get to her dorm and drop into bed, end this Freddie Kruger-inspired day. Ooh... he could fix this crap day. Who had time to dwell on feelings when there was a well-manicured psychopath roaming the city?

"I'm sorry. I didn't mean to push," Ryan said, and slowed down. She turned to him. The hurt in his eyes—she knew she was shutting him out. But she didn't know how to stop it.

They made their way through the last of the trees to the campus. Well-manicured lawns and sidewalks crisscrossing the open spaces. Benches along the campus sidewalk. She stopped walking and sat down. Conflicted emotions wrapped around her heart. What should she tell him? Would he think less of her?

She looked into his eyes. The hurt and sadness cut deep. Her stomach spiraled in a tornado of shame, pain and distress. Her mind volleyed back and forth. What to share? What to hold back?

Ryan sat next to her, his eyes following her every move. He reached out and squeezed her hand.

She looked down. "You didn't push. I'm sorry." His thumb drew circles on her hand, each stroke a defibrillator to her numb nerve endings. "At first I was so upset I—lost him, then— I don't know." She stared at their intertwined hands. "I guess I was more upset that I was such an idiot."

"You're not an idiot. If anything, he's the idiot."

She pulled away and stood, not sure why she was smiling. If he only knew. Maybe he could know. Maybe she could tell him—about Kyle, about Craig, about Robby—about everything.

She watched the light from the streetlamp dance across his features. Concern. Confusion. Trust. All those emotions were brawling for dominance on his gorgeous face. Could he handle the truth? The whole truth, not the caffeine-free, sugarless version. The factual version that painted her as a naive, insecure woman. Maybe...

"Kyle was the first guy I slept with," she blurted.

"What?" Ryan's eyes opened wide.

"I was a virgin."

"What about other boyfriends?"

Tell him. Tell him. Tell him. The sentence starts... First there was Craig... Then there was Robby... Dammit. She couldn't. "No one important." She didn't even have to lie to say that. They weren't important.

"Hey, sexy." Parker and entourage walked up, interrupting Karina's confessional.

"Hey, Parker. Bianca, you made it." Ryan stood, and Parker wrapped her lecherous tentacles around his neck.

"I wouldn't miss it, darling." Parker kept her grimy hands on Ryan's shoulder and turned to her friends. "Ry and I have been friends for years.

Our parents have us practically walking down the aisle."

The women giggled and tossed their hair. All of them at once, like a bad musical. Karina could see the jealousy oozing out of Parker's minions. Not a good look. Of course, it was probably a good thing that Karina didn't have a mirror handy. Green wasn't a particularly pleasant shade on her, either.

Ryan inched away from Parker's demonic grip. "Party's at the house, ladies."

"Aren't you coming?"

"No. I've had enough for one night."

Parker's eyes flashed red before she reined it in. If looks could disintegrate, Karina would be one big pile of ash. "No problem. We'll see you around." She shook her hips as she walked down the darkened street to the frat house. Her tight blue dress clung to the curvature of her endowments. Didn't anyone ever tell her that Jessica Rabbit was a cartoon, not a role model?

"Where were we? Oh yes, you were telling me about the men in your life." His attention was back on Karina, like they'd never been interrupted. Karina couldn't take her eyes off Jessica Rabbit's...whatever, yet he didn't look up once.

"Nothing to tell. I have a habit of attracting assholes." Tears stung her eyes.

"Good news. We're not all assholes." He closed the distance between them and gently skimmed her hair behind her ear. "You must have picked some bad ones."

Of course she did. She always seemed to pick the bad ones. It was her gift. Her curse. She just wanted to find someone who loved her. A gasp lodged in her throat. Dammit. She didn't want to cry. *Stop crying*.

His arms wrapped around her waist, drawing her into his chest as the tears continued to fall down her cheeks. She tried to pull away. "I'm sorry. I'm ruining your shirt."

"I have others." His arms held her tighter with every attempt to extricate herself. If he wasn't concerned about saltwater destroying his clothes, she wouldn't worry about it.

Her body relaxed as she stilled, listening to the *thrump-thrump* of his heart. Her tear ducts dried, her heart warming as his lips rested on the top of her head. She liked being in his arms.

"How are you feeling?" he said into her hair, his soft breath tickling the skin on her head.

She wanted to say, *sad, embarrassed, mortified, excited, cared for, happy*. Could one person feel all that at once? She settled on, "I'm better. Thanks for listening to my baggage." Not that she'd even scratched the surface.

"No problem," he said as his hand slid up and down her back. She felt the rise and fall of his chest, the rhythmic movement calming her mind, body, soul.

"I should get home." She leaned back and his arms let her go. He wrapped his hand around hers as they continued their trip to Dickinson Hall. The cool wind stirred the leaves, blowing her hair across her face.

"You can't let an experience with one guy ruin your future relationships. Maybe you just haven't found the right one yet."

"Maybe." She wanted to agree but deep down she wanted... Shit. She wanted Ryan to be the right guy. Why couldn't he be the one?

"You'll find him." He squeezed her hand, and sparks slid up her arm. "Goodnight, Karina."

"Goodnight, Ryan." She turned to him, her hand still in his. Despite the darkness, her eyes locked on his. Dark pools of glistening heat. Her breathing quickened. Heart raced. Body burned.

He ran a feather-light hand down the side of her face, stopping at her lips. A soft sigh escaped her mouth. He placed a finger under her chin, raising her face to his. His lips glided over hers. Starting soft. Growing eager.

Her toes curled. Heat travelled up her body. Never before had she felt this...chaotic want. Passion.

He moved back, face flushed. "We shouldn't do this."

Hurt and anger welled in her throat, sending fire to the back of her eyes. Rejected twice in one day. One might have been an ass, and she should be thanking God for his disinterest. But Ryan. No. He was a good guy. She should have known he wouldn't be interested in her.

"Of course. I'll see you later." She turned and ran to the building, Ryan's pleas following behind her. She didn't want to hear how that was a mistake. The best kiss she'd ever had, and he regretted it. He'd pulled away like it meant nothing.

She ran to her room and changed into pajamas, careful to not wake Savannah. Her phone vibrated, sitting all alone on her desk, Ryan's name emblazoned on the screen. She shut it off and tossed it back on the desk. Tears streamed down her face as she gasped. She wrapped herself in blankets and curled up on her bed.

She wanted a do-over. Today. Yesterday. Life.

Chapter Eighteen

Ryan

RYAN SAT IN class, thumb rubbing against the pages of his book. Waiting. Watching every student in his German class walk through that damn door. Except Karina. The one person he wanted to see—needed to see—was nowhere to be found. He'd tried calling her all weekend, but either she was screening her calls or her phone was broken. He would like to think her avoidance was due to a technological glitch, but he wasn't stupid. She was hiding from him. At least, that's what it felt like.

Well, she couldn't hide forever. The woman had to come to class eventually. And once she was sitting in the seat next to his, he'd make sure she heard his apology.

He'd felt like crap all weekend. He hated the way he left things with her. The whole situation sucked. He'd tried to do the right thing and it bit him in the cheeks. He didn't want to take advantage of her. If they started something now, it would be a rebound thing. A fling to help her get over douchebag, so she could find a real relationship down the line. He didn't want to be the rebound. Well, he didn't think he wanted to be the rebound. The more he learned about Karina, the more he wanted her any way he could get her.

As the teacher began her ramble in German, Karina dashed through the door, sitting in a desk across the room. So that was how she wanted to play it.

He watched her pull out her book and a pad of paper. She got a pen from the backpack she dropped to the floor. As the teacher babbled, she wrote and wrote, her head bent over that damned pad. What she was writing? Who knew? The teacher's monologue on her weekend, though decidedly better than rehashing verb tenses, was not journal-worthy material. Although the part where her cat yacked up a piece of string from her daughter's hair-care products was mildly interesting.

Professor Vierow turned to the board and began writing the usual punishment in red dry-erase marker. Verbs and tenses found their way onto the white surface. Karina dropped her pen onto the desk and shook her wrist. He wanted to announce a medical warning for Karina's benefit... *Fake writing can lead to carpal tunnel.*

She pressed the top of her hand, stretching the muscles, and turned her head in Ryan's direction. A Razzie-worthy smile crossed her lips. He almost couldn't call it a smile. It looked more like a pained cringe. The only thing that lent any truth to the smile theory was the poor excuse for a wave she included before she turned back to the paper on the desk.

Shit.

This was worse than he thought. He needed to fix this immediately. Well, immediately was a bit overzealous. He wasn't about to make a fool of himself in the middle of class. But, as soon as the class was over, he'd make his plea. He just had to make it to the end of this snoozefest.

Karina scribbled intensely.

Verbs were conjugated.

Ryan dropped his head to his hands.

Would this class ever end?

Ryan's foot bounced as the hour dwindled down to minutes, to seconds, until the class finally ended and Professor Vierow sent them on their way. He closed his book, but before he even stood, he saw that Karina's seat was empty and she was nowhere to be found.

He made his way to the door and searched the faces of the students wandering the halls. Her tied-back hair dashed down the hall and out the front door. The undergrads pouring out of the other classrooms impeded his quick route to Karina. Dammit. He stared at the congestion. He wasn't going to run after her.

"Hey, stranger." Savannah bounced into his line of sight.

"How's it going?"

"Good. Was that my roommate?" She waved at the door where Karina just vanished.

"Yep."

"So, anything you want to tell me?" She put her fists on her hips.

"She told you."

"Yeah. What the heck happened? Have you lost your mind?"

He shook his head. "I wouldn't believe everything you hear."

"So, you didn't kiss her and then push her away."

"It wasn't exactly like that." He ran a hand over his face, remembering the feel of her lips, the feel of her in his arms, the look on her face as he pulled away. "Shit, maybe it was."

"Why? I thought you liked her." Savannah adjusted her pink backpack on her shoulder.

"I just didn't want to be the rebound guy. That's all."

A smile found its way to her face, an annoying, all-knowing smile. "So what's the plan?"

"I got nothing." He watched as the students emptied into the classrooms until only a few stragglers lingered in the hallway. "Do you have a class now?"

"No, but I'm meeting Megan in the foreign language lab in a few minutes. Have you tried talking to her?"

"To Megan?"

That got him an eye roll and an annoyed stare. Apparently, she didn't find his deflection funny. But honestly, he was sick of thinking about how to get back in Karina's good graces. He wanted to think about things he could control—school, frat business—anything not relating to a woman. "No. I haven't talked to her. She won't even stop long enough to listen."

"Well—I can help with that. We're heading to the Mehnk tonight to play pool for Megan's birthday. I think you need to drop by around seven."

"I'll be there."

"I'll see you then." She turned and walked toward the language lab.

"Hey, Sav. Thanks." He finally had a plan. Once Karina understood what happened Friday night, there was no way she'd be mad.

~»ΨΡ«~

Chapter Nineteen

Karina

KARINA LAUGHED AS Megan's pool cue skidded across the green felt. Balls flew as the stick rolled and spun.

"I totally suck at this." Megan groaned and backed away from the carnage on the table, tugging her short black skirt back into place. Karina wouldn't have thought it, but Megan's pink sweater looked amazing with her red curls and freckled nose.

Karina grabbed the cue while Gabi spun the balls back to their previous positions. Well, as close as they could manage without a picture. "You're doing fine," Gabi told Megan. "Maybe we just need to get a gorgeous man to teach you the finer points of ball handling."

"Could you possibly get your mind out of the gutter?" Savannah plucked a nacho from one of the plates sitting on the high-top table.

Gabi lifted the runaway eight ball from the floor. "I was talking about these balls. I think your mind is in that gutter. Not mine."

"All right, ladies." Aimee pointed her cue stick at Gabi. "My turn. Now drop the ball and no one gets hurt."

Gabi positioned the ball on the table and stepped back. "Practicing for the police force, copper?"

"Affirmative." Aimee's jet black hair hung in her light brown eyes as she bent to take a shot.

"Why did you come to college if you're just going to go to the police academy?" Denise asked from where she was helping Savannah put a dent in the mound of chips slathered with cheese and meat.

"A degree is a requirement if you want to move up, nowadays. It took my dad twenty-three years to make sergeant because he didn't have a degree, but my brother is already a sergeant after eight years."

"Keeping it in the family, huh?" Karina smiled as she sat at the table. If there was one thing she knew about, it was following in the old man's footsteps. Granted, she hoped to be a lawyer without the sanctimonious unfeeling assholism that seemed to plague her father.

"It is the family business." Aimee walked around the table. A moment later, another ball fell victim to their resident pool shark.

"We'll if that doesn't work out, have you thought about a career in hustling pool?" Karina was joking, but the woman truly had some mad skills.

"Ooh, ooh, like that movie with the salad-dressing guy," Nica said as she sipped her soda. "He played a pretty good game of pool and looked hot doing it."

"Never saw it." Aimee bent down and lined up another shot.

"But he's hot." Nica's eyes were glazed in a dreamy trance.

"He's old." Gabi rolled her eyes.

"He's the ultimate DILF." Nica grabbed a cheese stick from the plate in front of her. Karina didn't exactly think he fit the Dad-I'd-Like-to-Fuck bill, but to each their own.

"Sorry, not a DILF. Now, Bradley Cooper..." Gabi leaned against the table and sipped her drink. Soda, not beer—Karina checked.

Aimee sank another ball. "Is he a dad?"

"Does it matter? I'd still like to swap bodily fluids with the man." Gabi's eyes rolled.

"Maybe he's a BILF or a GILF." Karina giggled.

"Huh?"

Karina's cheeks reddened as all six girls stared at her. "You know, Bradley-I'd-Like-to-Fuck or Guy-I'd-Like-to-Fuck... There's also SILF—stud muffin. Or would that be SMILF?" Karina asked.

"It's good to know the female think-tank of Ritter University is tackling the tough issues." Parker sauntered up to Karina's table, and a few choice swear words hung unsaid on Karina's lips.

"Hey, Nica," Parker said. "I wanted to tell you, I have that shampoo you wanted. My dad sent a box yesterday." She ran a hand through her golden curls.

"Oh, fab. I can't believe your father owns Sleek and Shine hair care. I love their products. Thanks a bunch, Parker."

"Anything for my favorite RA." Parker rested her hand on the table, leaned in and spoke inches from Karina's ear. "So. I had an epiphany today."

Karina kept her eyes riveted on the mound of cheese sticks. Maybe if she ignored the nuisance harping in her ear, she'd take the hint and go away.

"Aren't you interested in what I might know?"

Or not. "Not really."

"That's surprising, since I have been trying to remember where I saw you. But now I know."

Shit. Shit. Shit. Please, no. She tried to keep her face immobile. This crazy chic was not getting past her defenses.

"I wonder what Ryan would think if he knew what a backstabbing slut you really are."

"I don't know what you think you know." Heat crept up Karina's face as anger closed her throat. Tears pierced her eyes. She refused to cry. She refused to let this bitch get to her.

"Really? We're going to play that game. I'm sure your ex-boyfriend has a lot to say on the topic."

"It's your word against mine," she spit out through clenched teeth. Craig was playing ball for University of Southern California. He wouldn't talk to Parker about any of it. Would he? No. He'd left this crap behind. Just like she wanted to do.

"We'll see." Parker turned her back on them all and walked out the door.

What the fuck was she going to do now? She couldn't run away from it. No matter where she went, it wouldn't just die.

"Hey, beautiful ladies." Danny walked over to the table and dove into the nachos.

Savannah slapped his hand. "Go away, chip-klepto."

Danny laughed as he stuffed the pilfered food into his mouth, and stepped up to the pool table. "What are we celebrating?"

"Megan's birthday."

"Happy birthday, Gingersnap." Danny wrapped his arms around Megan and dropped a kiss on her forehead.

"Thanks." Her eyes closed as a goofy grin curved her lips.

"Who's got next?" Danny pulled away, stealing Gabi's soda and taking a gulp.

"Dammit, Danny. You will be buying me another drink."

He tilted the cup back and slammed the empty vessel on the table. "YOLO. Thanks for the hookup. I'll get you another one. Megs, want to come with?"

"Sure." Megan grabbed Gabi's empty cup to get a refill

"Finish this game," Danny said. "Megan and I will play the winner when I get back. Kent, what do you want to drink?"

Karina's heart stopped as her eyes flew up, locking on Ryan's face. His eyes were fixed on her. The one person she didn't want to see. The one person she couldn't handle. Not tonight. Not like this. She needed time to figure out a plan. Parker knew about Craig. Crap.

"Nothing." He walked around behind Karina and watched Aimee sink the eight ball in the corner pocket. As her friends high-fived and reset the table, warm breath tickled the back of Karina's neck. "Can we talk?"

Karina turned around to face him. Big mistake. His delicious—yes, delicious—lips were inches from hers. She remembered the taste of his tongue, the feel of his lips. The way they'd fit together perfectly as his hands had roamed her back and she'd prayed they'd find their way to her front. Her lady parts puckered with just the memory.

Then he'd pushed her away. She didn't want to talk to him. She didn't want to hear how she wasn't his type or how it was a mistake. She was so tired of mistakes. Making them. Being them. Her mom liked to say that adversity made you stronger. Her tattered heart couldn't take much more strength.

"Karina?" He held out his hand to her.

"Fine." She ignored the gesture and slid off the wooden chair, following Ryan out of the cacophony of the game room and up the stairs to the relative quiet of the atrium. Low-voiced conversations surrounded them. Couples kissing. Couples fighting. She had a feeling she knew which category they were about to join.

"Are we going to talk about this?" Ryan asked.

"There's nothing to talk about." She crossed her arms her over her chest, one last bastion of defense.

"We'll, I think there is." He bent his head, his eyes barely meeting hers.

Karina's stomach took a dive. *Don't say it. Don't say it.*

"I'm sorry."

She clenched her jaw. Why couldn't he say it was magical? *Let's do it again.* Why couldn't he say life started to have meaning the moment their lips touched? Oh, yeah because this was reality, not some romantic fantasy world. With an effort, she pried her molars apart. "Sorry for what?"

"For what happened the other night."

"What every girl wants to hear." She brought her hands to her heart, sarcasm dripping from every word. Every action. Every thought.

His shoulders slumped and his voice was soft, brittle. "What do you want from me?"

"Nothing at all. You've made it perfectly clear where we stand." For the second time tonight tears threatened to fall, but this time she wasn't so sure she could stop them. She had to get away. She headed toward the exit. *Please don't try and stop me.* Please don't let him see me cry. It was bad enough she'd let her guard down for him. After all the crap she'd endured, she knew better. At least, she should have known better.

Anyway, now she had bigger problems.

Parker. What did she know? Once Parker tossed her nuggets of dirt to the gossip-hounds, no one would ever speak to Karina again. But maybe that was for the best. Apparently she didn't know how to pick a good guy out from all the bad.

She stomped her way to the dorm, moonlight cutting through the pre-rain haze. Maybe it was good to finally have the truth out there. She hated living a lie. It gave her a new respect for Craig. It couldn't have been easy hiding in the closet all those years.

Yet, he lived the lie—for the football team, for the students, for his parents. And he continued to live the lie, or at least she assumed so. That friendship pretty much fizzled after the lawsuit. That was what she missed the most. His friendship.

Right before she left for college, Craig sent her an email. She still hadn't responded. She wasn't sure they could ever go back to what they had after what he'd done.

A fresh wave of moisture left her eyes as she opened the door to the dorm room. She looked around the room—she needed to change clothes, brush her teeth and brush the hairspray from her hair. She turned to the mirror hanging over the sink. Red-rimmed eyes surrounded by pale skin met her miserable stare.

Fuck it.

She laid down on her soft, welcoming sheets and closed her eyes. Sleep could give her a reprieve. She'd deal with the fallout tomorrow.

~»ΨΡ«~

Chapter Twenty

Ryan

RYAN TRUDGED BACK to the frat, the cool wind slicing through his sweatshirt. He kept his hands jammed deep in his pockets as he nodded to the occasional groups of coeds milling about, getting the campus ready for the weekend's activities.

Women drove him nuts. Well, not all women. Just one.

He ran over the events in his mind again. He kissed her. She got upset and wouldn't talk to him. He apologized. Where the fuck was the disconnect?

You've made it perfectly clear where we stand. Good thing she got that memo, because he had no idea where they stood. How did he subscribe to that loop?

He knew where he wanted them to stand, but him walking home and her wherever she was, was not it. This wasn't even close to how he saw the night ending.

At the house, most of the brothers were planning for the homecoming festivities this weekend. Psi Rho welcomed alumni with a float in the homecoming parade on Saturday morning , before the pep rally and football game. Sunday would be an all-day Psi Rho golf outing, followed by the capstone of the weekend, the alumni dinner.

This year Ryan was in charge of planning the golf outing. He'd finished that task two weeks ago, so all that was left was to get a final tally of golfers after the alumni registration ended on Wednesday.

Even though he didn't have much to do this weekend, he didn't have time to worry about Karina. He knew he'd have a helluva time getting her off his mind, though. He could always have a drink to forget, or head out by the garage where a group of frat brothers worked on the homecoming float. Great choices—pathetically sulking with a bottle of booze for company, or dealing with all the bullshit inherent with hanging out with his guys. Both options sucked.

He walked up the stairs to his room, opened the door and threw his keys on the table.

"Forget how to answer a phone?"

Who the...? Crap. His father stood next to the couch, his tailored suit miraculously wrinkle-free despite his folded arms.

"It's funny, I checked with your mother and I am still paying for that cell phone you ignore."

"I've been busy. You are the one who insisted I spend more time on my studies."

"Taking extra management courses, then?" His father checked his cell phone. He drove over an hour and he couldn't pull his eyes away from his true love—the office.

"Taking what I need to graduate." Ryan removed his sweatshirt and laid it across the chair near the table.

"Things have certainly changed since I went to Ritter. I didn't realize you needed architecture courses for the college of business."

Crap. This wasn't how he wanted his father finding out. He was hoping his father would never find out. But he should have known he would eventually come across the info. Not that it mattered at this point. It was an elective. It didn't matter. It's not like he changed his major.

"By your silence, I assume you didn't think I'd find out."

"There's nothing to find out. It's an elective. I didn't realize I had to run my electives past you. I'm thinking of taking sociology next term, should I submit a requisition now?"

Red crawled up his father's face. Ryan could almost see the few remaining brown strands of his father's hair change to gray. Thank goodness male pattern baldness didn't run in his family or his father's hair would be falling out. "That attitude. If it wasn't for that attitude..." He walked around the couch and stood in front of Ryan.

"What? If not for the attitude, I'd be what—the perfect son? If I'd just shut up and do as I'm told."

"Well, you'd be more successful." His father pulled out a wooden chair and sat, narrowing his eyes. "You think I'm trying to control your life for my own advantage. I'm making certain you don't make thoughtless mistakes. Like wasting time on frivolous classes. They will do nothing for your future."

"How benevolent of you."

"Well, someone has to watch out for you. You are incapable of keeping your own best interest at the forefront of your decisions. Your mother worries about you."

"Well, I worry about her." Anger zinged through Ryan's veins. Whenever his father didn't get his way, he'd just bring out Mom and manipulate Ryan through a well-played guilt-trip.

"You should. She's fighting hard."

"I thought she was still in remission."

"She is, and I'd like to keep it that way. Too much stress messes with our stabilization plan."

Stabilization? Seriously? Ryan couldn't argue if his father was going to use his mother's health. There was no way he'd mess with her recovery...stabilization...whatever. He sat in the chair across from his father. "Look, I'm doing what you want. I'm getting the degree you've preordained. I'm just taking a class that sparks my interest. No one needs to worry or ruin the stabilization plan."

His father pushed the chair back and stood up. "I'll make a deal with you. You can do this architecture thing as an elective, if you start taking your responsibility to your family seriously. As you know, I am running for president of the country club. Doug Breckinridge will be running for vice president, and we'd like our children to be more involved. A strong family presence looks good to the club."

Ryan sat there, almost welcoming the numbness because he knew what his father would say next.

"You will join the club's Men's Golf Association, and I expect you to bring Parker there when you come. She's joining the social events committee and will need to be on hand to assist. Since she cannot have a car this year, you will be responsible for making sure she gets to her meetings."

Ahh...the real reason for the multiple phone calls and the unexpected visit. Ryan knew his father wanted something. He always did. It would be a miracle for his father to visit to impart some fatherly love. "Can't you just buy her an exception? A new wing or a building. Let her bring her own car."

"Yes. But I want you to participate. Actively."

"And I can stay in my architecture class?"

"This year. You have one semester to get this nonsense out of your system." Ryan's father ran a hand down the side of his arm, straightening his sleeve. "You know, son, I'd like for you to join us willingly, get involved in the family interests. It's a shame I must resort to this…this ugliness to get you to participate."

"As long as I can continue with my class, I'll be there. And I'll bring Parker." He rolled his eyes. Spending a weekend or two a month golfing wasn't exactly punishment. And even though he might run into the old man, it probably wouldn't be that often. After all, the man worked weekends, holidays, birthdays…you name it.

"By the way, you seem to get angry when I don't share every little piece of information, so I wanted to tell you, your mother is seeing the specialist next week."

"Why?"

"They want to run a few tests. Apparently, there were some troubling results on her last scan."

"I'll be there." Shit. Not again. "When is it?"

"Monday morning we're going straight to the doctor after homecoming weekend."

"You're still coming?"

"She wants to be here. So, we'll be here."

"I'll follow you home." Ryan felt the fear encircle his heart. The worry. The dread. The angst of waiting for doctors, waiting for test results and watching her fight. Again.

"I don't know why you'd want to sit in that hospital waiting room, but fine. We'll be leaving at six AM on Monday morning." His father pulled his cell phone from his pocket and had it to his ear before his foot crossed the room's threshold.

"Good talk." Ryan sighed.

Chauffeuring Parker around might be annoying. But really, how bad could it be?

Chapter Twenty-One

Karina

KARINA SAT AT a table in the Grand Hall of the Mehnk building, affixing name stickers to plastic badges. How she got conned into helping with the Homecoming festivities, she had no idea. One day she was happily sulking in her room, the next she was sitting at black crepe-covered tables, volunteering for Homecoming weekend.

"Shit." Gabi shook her hand wildly, a sticker flapping from her fingers. She pulled the sticker from one hand, immediately getting it stuck to the other. She shook that hand violently, the sticker waving in the air. "Why are we doing this?" She stuck the sticker to the table and pulled her hands away. Savannah grabbed the nametag and attached it to a badge.

"Because Megan is our friend and she asked us." Karina pulled out another page of stickers.

"She owes us." Gabi huffed and wrestled with another sticker-badge combination.

Megan bounced up to the table, her fingers wrapped around a vase of red roses. She put it down in the center of the black-topped table and turned to her commander, whose pen was frantically marking up a piece of paper on a clipboard. "Of course, Bianca. We should be done with the badges in a half-hour."

Bianca looked like her head was going to explode, but maybe that was Karina. "We need a few more volunteers to help pass out badges and welcome the alumni and their children during the pre-dinner reception. If you can ask around, that would be great." Bianca stared at her clipboard for a moment and then ran across the room, her burgundy dress billowing as she wandered away. Somebody else who drank Savannah's Style-Requirements Kool-Aid.

"Hey ladies. How are the badges coming?" Megan smiled until she saw Gabi shake her fingers, another sticker flying across the table.

"Fine, honey." Savannah caught the wayward sticker and affixed it to a badge. "Don't pay any attention to angry-eyes over there. Bless her heart. She can't operate sticky things."

"Bite me, blondie." Gabi rubbed glue remnants from her fingers.

Megan glued her own smile back on. "So, ladies, who's available to help hand out badges and welcome the alumni tonight?"

"Sorry, my father's an alumni and we're going to the dinner together." Gabi didn't remove her eyes from her tacky fingers.

"I have a non-date with Joe." Savannah lifted a hand and shook her head when Gabi stared at her. Apparently, there would be no discussion on Savannah's non-date with Joe.

"Karina? Come on, you have to stay. Someone has to see that slideshow I've put together."

Crap. Karina's mind went into overdrive, but she had no date. She had no special dinner to attend. She had no excuse. "Of course I'll help."

"Help what?" Parker wandered her swinging man-hypnotizing hips up to the table. She picked up a badge, her red finger nails scraping along the plastic surface. "These are nice."

"I did it myself," Karina snarked as her shoulders swiveled around in pageant-mom fashion. Gabi and Savannah laughed. Megan smiled and shook her head.

The man-hypnotizer stared at Karina, her brow arched. "You designed this?"

"Uh, no. I just put the sticker on the plastic." Obviously, the ice queen was immune to the altered pitch and the body language of a joke.

"Destined for greatness, aren't you?" Parker rolled her eyes and dropped the tag on the table.

Karina's heart raced as she watched the frigid devil spawn, her giant lion claws running through her bleach-blonde hair. Maybe she'd accidentally stab herself with those nails. Ah...daydreams...

Parker rambled on and on while she and Megan talked about the design of the badges, how the fancy script for the names accented the red and black glitter of the Ritter Battle Trooper, the school mascot. Megan did an excellent job, even if it was a little too sparkly for Karina's taste. But apparently Parker couldn't seem to stop gushing. Even though she was being nice, there was something evil about the blonde demonette, something that urged Karina to gird her loins.

"Karina? Earth to Karina," the ice queen barked.

"Sorry?" Shit. Had she said all that out loud? She looked around to see that her friends had boxed up the nametags and were carrying them into the front hall.

Parker stood with her hand on her attitude-ridden hip. "Let me guess—naming your imaginary children with Ryan."

What the hell was she talking about?

"I saw you two that night, you know. It was weirdest thing. A friend was driving me home, and we pulled up to the dorm and walked into the most disturbing sight. You throwing yourself at Ryan, your face glued to his. Pathetic."

The school had a no violence policy. Karina couldn't help but wonder how tightly they clung to that little rule. Because more than anything she wanted to haul off and beat the crap out of the demonette ice queen.

"He pulled away so violently. It was so hard to watch."

One punch. How Karina would love to land just one punch. Two, tops. She'd never punched anyone before, but she'd watched her brother do it. How hard could it be? You made a fist and swung. She'd been practicing for this moment for three months on the volleyball court, and she didn't even know it.

There could always be a first time for kicking frigid butt...if it didn't lead to expulsion.

No expulsion. She'd done that before. Bought the shirt. Hid it in her closet. Not doing that again. But that didn't mean she had to sit back and take it. "Which night was that? Oh yeah, that was the night you put your arm around him and he pushed you away, right? But he does that so often, that really doesn't tell me which night that was, though." The words tumbled out of her mouth before her brain could stop them.

"We have a delicate relationship. What kind do you have?" Parker flipped her hair back. "Oh yeah, you don't. He finally realized he's way too good for you and dumped you."

That might have hurt, if her and Ryan had actually been dating. But no, they hadn't even broke that threshold... But Parker's nasty joke-handicapped butt didn't need to know that. "Is there a point to your story? I mean, it's just a suggestion, but a point goes a long way when telling a story."

"Enjoy this time while it lasts. You'll get what you deserve."

"Is that a threat?"

"I don't have to threaten." Parker swung around and walked across the room. Guys stopped and watched her walk by. Too bad the inside didn't match the outside. Her face and body were gorgeous, but she was just so...so...mean.

~»ΨΡ«~

Chapter Twenty-Two

Ryan

RYAN STOOD IN front of the mirror and tied his red striped tie. His only homage to the school colors. Well, he was wearing a black suit, but that wasn't because it was his school color. It was the only color suit his mom would buy.

Not that he cared.

He would have been fine going to the party in jeans, but then his mom would've had a fit. She was all about dressing up and socializing with the local elite. Learning about others, telling them about her children—she lived for that crap.

A few years ago he would have fought the whole monkey-suit and social obligation. But it made his mom happy, and her happiness had become so fragile, so infrequent... He would do anything to keep that smile on her face.

His frat brother Darnell knocked on the frame of the open door. His dark skin appeared even darker against the white suit he wore. "Dude, your parents are downstairs. Danny is entertaining them."

"Shit, why didn't you stay with them and send Danny up?" Ryan shoved his dress shoes on. Danny was inappropriate and vulgar. Great friend and roommate, but not great at keeping the parents appeased.

"Because this way was funnier." Darnell adjusted his own tie. "It's your parents, not mine."

"Both your parents coming tonight?" Ryan stuck one of his Ritter University cufflinks through his shirt cuff and then did up the other one.

"Yeah, and they're both bringing their spouses. This should be an interesting night."

"They're both professionals. I'm sure they can behave like adults."

"Yes. My cardiothoracic-surgeon mom and my Neuroradiologist dad do sound impressive. But get the two in a room and they become reality show contenders. You heard about my high school graduation. She threw coleslaw in his face. It was, umm, interesting. She gave the old man a black eye."

"With coleslaw?"

"The bowl. She threw the slaw while it was still in the bowl." Darnell laughed. "It's funny now, but then—all my friends were there. My family was there. The pastor from our church asked if I wanted one-on-one counseling. A few months later my mom won an award for some scientific breakthrough she discovered. She's brilliant, but get her in the same room as my dad..."

"Sort of like getting my father and me into the same room." Ryan pulled his overnight bag from the table. He wanted his bag ready to go for tomorrow. He might miss a few days of school, but nothing was going to stop him from getting to that doctor's appointment.

His father had tried to block him out of the first round of chemo and treatments by not telling him about the appointments and downplaying her illness. But Ryan didn't fall for it. He'd managed to be front and center for most of them, thanks to Parker and his sisters.

"Oh yeah, dude, you should get downstairs. When I left Danny, he was telling your parents about that little trick his old girlfriend use to do with that golf ball."

"Shit." Ryan shoved his wallet in his pants and blew past Darnell, a laugh rolling from his friend's chest. "You might have started the conversation out with that."

He ran down the stairs to rescue his parents and started toward his mom, her laughter floating straight to his heart and lodging there. She looked so fragile in the peach dress that hung loose around her body. She never gained the weight she lost during the height of her illness. But right now it didn't matter. Her smile dazzled. Her eyes sparkled.

His father stood beside her, his arm wrapped around her waist, his face overtaken by a grin. He'd never seen the old man so happy. He seemed to be basking in the joy radiating from his wife's healing body.

"...so his caddy stared at the bag and said, 'But none of these are made from wood'." Laughter erupted from the small group. Danny was sharing stories, but nothing like Darnell had alluded to. The caddy who didn't know what club to give a golfer when asked to hand over a wood was not exactly the X-rated tale he expected. "Mr. Sheldon grabbed the titanium driver from the bag, but he was so frustrated he sliced the shot." More laughter erupted. "A pro golfer almost lost today because of a virgin...a trainee caddy."

Ryan walked the last few steps to his parents. Danny was doing a great job of entertaining them, but the way he rubbed the back of his neck and moved from foot to foot told Ryan he wanted out. Ryan could understand that feeling.

"Hi, Mom."

"Oh, Ryan. We were just talking to your roommate. He was sharing a fun story about one of the Psi Rho alumni, Jack Sheldon."

"He's always been an interesting man," Ryan's father added. "But those pro golfers usually are."

"Will you be at the homecoming party tonight?" his mother asked Danny.

"Nope, not a legacy, but you have a wonderful time. I have to work, and then I have a mountain of homework to do."

Ryan nodded to Danny as he walked away. Homework. Right. If any of Danny's classes included fondling some girl's assets, then he would be going after extra credit tonight. Otherwise, homework was the furthest thing from Ryan's roommate's sex-aholic mind.

"Ready?" Ryan's father led the way out the door, while his mom slipped her arm through Ryan's.

Her small hands wrapped around his arm. "I've missed you." She leaned her head on his shoulder, and he adjusted the overnight bag on his other shoulder.

"Me too." His head dropped to the top of hers. It was nice to have her on campus again. He honestly wasn't sure that he would ever see her here after last year.

They piled into his father's car and drove up to the Mehnk. The building was lit up, sparky lights lining the four support poles for the entrance overhang. A line of cars waited for the student-valet parking at the entrance.

The line moved quickly, and Ryan and his family slid out of the car, walking the red carpet into the brightly lit building. Every tree in the foyer was covered in black and red lights. Suits and elegant dresses crowded the room. The murmur and laughter of old friends filled the remaining empty space. Ryan and his parents walked across the tiled atrium floor and made their way to the Grand Hall.

A familiar wave of blond hair hung down past bare shoulders, with a black strapless dress hugging her body, curving in all the right places. The material stopped in the right places too.

Long muscular legs.

Soft, milky shoulders.

Karina… Dammit.

His eyes wouldn't move. Couldn't move. His mind was going places—places best left alone until he was actually alone. He watched her lean over the table, innocently helping Edward Schultz arrange his lanyard over his ninety-four-year-old neck.

Of course, all he could see as she altruistically helped the elderly man was her heaving chest, her dress squishing all of that alabaster goodness. The round hostages rose as she laughed at something Edward said. Karina glided around the table and rested her hands on the handles of the wheel chair. When she lifted her head, she met Ryan's eyes. Shock. Sadness. Hurt. All three emotions passed through her eyes before she turned away and wheeled the old man into the bustling dining hall.

He wanted to wrap his arms around her. He wanted to talk to her.

His father handed him his nametag and followed Karina into the room, breaking right as she broke left. He watched Karina walk up to the front of the room.

He missed her. Bad.

Shit.

He needed to talk to her. At some point tonight, he needed to find himself back in her good graces.

Chapter Twenty-Three

Karina

DESPITE PINCHED TOES from a borrowed pair of Savannah's ridiculously high heels, Karina helped Mr. Schultz to his table. The man was hilarious and adorable. He'd asked her to marry him, twice. He wanted to know why she wasn't a model. A model. Of course, that might have been due to his poor eyesight. He did try to put a pen on his face until Karina pointed out his glasses. But that didn't matter. He said she should be a model after he put the specs on his face.

She needed the compliment. She was taking it.

"Thank you, honey. Are you sure you don't want to sit and eat with an old man?"

"Sorry, Mr. Schultz. I have to get back to work. Can I get you a drink?"

"Only if you'll share one with me." He rested his wrinkled hand on hers.

"Sorry. I need to get back. There's a line at the front table."

"Well then, I'll have to find another pretty girl to help me out. But none will hold a candle to you."

"You smooth talker. I'll send over a waiter, Mr. Schultz." She squeezed his hand before pulling away. On her way to the door, Karina stopped at one of the work-study waiters, donned in black shirt and pants. "Can you please see if Mr. Schultz needs anything to drink? He's at the head table." The undergrad nodded, grabbed a tray and headed for the table.

Karina made her way back to her post without looking once at Ryan. Not one look. She was the poster-child for restraint. The tracking device that must have been implanted in Ryan's perfect body was begging her to look at him. But somehow she fought it and kept her eyes fixed to the black and white floor.

She kept herself busy, smiling as she handed the next group of alumni and their children their name badges before waving them on into the main hall.

"Paula and Parker Breckenridge," a familiar, nasally voice said from in front of the table.

Karina kept her eyes down as she found Parker's name. She lifted her head, a forced smile stuck on her face. She recited the words she'd uttered over and over to the numerous patrons who'd approached her table. "Welcome to the Alumni and Family Reception. Your table number is on your name tag. Please visit the open bar, the alumni slideshow will begin shortly."

Parker and her creator walked to the door, whispering together. Apparently, that nasty little tone was hereditary. "That's the one I was talking about."

Karina rolled her eyes and handed out another set of name tags until the well-dressed alumni and their progeny were all identified and herded into the large room for a long night of festivities and food.

Speaking of which—her stomach gurgled and popped. Food sounded like a great idea. And the smell wafting from the hall... She breathed in the scent of garlic and shrimp. *Num.*

"Karina, they're about to show my slideshow. Come on." Megan grabbed her clipboard from the table and dragged Karina into the hall. She cringed as the torture devices on her feet crushed her innocent toes. She slipped out of the foot-afflicters and stood very still behind the occupied chairs. Maybe if she didn't move, no one would notice her lowered stature and lack of shoes.

On the large screen, the introduction slide showed a picture of the school chapel. A senior manned the laptop, waiting for the perfect moment to start Megan's masterpiece. The slide show that kept Megan locked in her room for the past two weeks. The slide show that kept her from socializing with anyone and everyone. Karina couldn't wait to see it. Megan deserved this moment after all her hard work.

Men and women found their tables as the lights lowered and Billy Joel sang about remembering the good times. Pictures flew across the screen. Younger versions of the people here tonight lined the screen, all of them smiling, laughing, hugging. The pictures were perfect, each faded transition incredible. The music worked flawlessly—loud crescendos paired with bright, active shots, while quiet melodies set the mood for familiar friends in muted poses.

As the final bars of the music rolled on, Karina choked up. What a beautiful show. Definitely worth all of the time Megan spent on it. "Megan this is amazing," she whispered.

As the notes slowed and hung in the air, a final picture popped onto the screen. Except it wasn't a picture. It was a video, and it didn't fade like the others. It just stayed on the screen...

No.

And played.

No.

A girl dancing in nothing but a high school scarf…

No. Heat crawled up Karina's neck. *No. Please, no.*

He'd taken down the video. He'd *promised.*

Up on the big screen, her body writhed as she raised the scarf above her chilled breasts. Yes, she and everyone in the hall could tell the room had been cold…dear God.

Her feet dangled as her bare legs straddled the statue of the Redeemer High School mascot. Her body swayed back and forth, and even though the metal lion hid her from waist to thighs, it still left *a lot* to the imagination. She puckered her lips into a kiss as she threw her leg over the lion, dismounting and then pulling the scarf through her legs. *Oh no, not through the legs.* She swiveled her hips against the length of orange and blue, her recently-shaved assets bare to the wind. Naked.

Totally naked, she ran her hands through her hair, pulling the soft wisps away from her face. Her unobstructed face. Unobstructed. Nothing stood in the way of her features. She was completely recognizable.

Most of the partygoers stared at the final video and then looked at each other with arched brows and wrinkled noses. Unfortunately, a few recognized the starlet, if their soft gasps and open mouths when they turned and found her frozen at the back of the hall.

Red crept up Karina's neck and nausea wrapped around her throat. Breath sputtered as fire lit the back of her eyes.

Megan ran to the computer and disconnected the cable. She raised her hands, frantically signaling to some unknown student worker to turn the lights on. "Hello everyone. The DJ is going to start some music as dinner is served. Thank you."

Megan flew back to Karina's side as soft music flowed and waitstaff began to bustle between the tables. "It'll be okay." Megan pulled on her hand, but Karina didn't move.

She wanted to move. She wanted to run. She should have run. But her feet remained planted where they stood. Denial. Disgust. Derision. The three stages of mortification.

Karina turned to the room full of people, most of them oblivious to her innermost destruction. Most. She swiveled her head to the left, where blonde hair bobbed up and down in synch with a throaty laugh. There was no question where that video originated. Evil skank. The big question was how she got it. But that wasn't a question she'd get answered tonight.

There was only one person she wanted to see…but didn't want to see. Fear of rejection, contempt, repulsion—Ryan's potential loathing couldn't match the miasma of shame filling her heart. Maybe, just maybe he wouldn't think less of her. Maybe he'd see past the one mistake she'd never been able to hide from.

How could he? She couldn't.

Despite everything, she couldn't help but twist her head to the right. No matter how hard she tried to stop her head from turning, it angled and looked for Ryan. He sat in his chair, eyes wide. His lip curled, and even from here she saw his eyes harden.

Well, surprise, surprise. There went that fantasy. She'd been afraid she lost him before, but that video was the straw that broke the lion's back.

Gabi walked up to Karina and laid a hand on her arm. "Honey, let's go home."

"Your dinner?" Karina felt the words leave her lips but wasn't quite sure what she was talking about. All she saw was that video. Her naked body.

"My dad's talking the old days with his friends. It was so boring listening to the same stories told over and over again and pretending I hadn't heard them a million times. He doesn't need me. You do." Gabi slid her arm through Karina's and turned to Megan. "I'll take her home."

"I'll be right behind you." Megan removed the walkie-talkie from her pocket.

"Don't you have work to do here?"

"I've devoted the past two months to this night. They'll just have to get along without me." Megan walked over to Bianca and dumped the electronic device and clipboard into her arms. Sympathy washed across Bianca's face—or was it pity?

Karina hated pity, it ranked up there with contempt.

Megan sped back across the room and grabbed Karina's other arm. "Let's go home, girls."

Gabi whipped out her cell phone. "Sav, you busy? We need you *now*. Grab cookie dough and" —she pulled away from the phone— "what else?"

"Potato chips," Megan added. "And soda."

Karina didn't add anything. She didn't care. She had a feeling she was the entertainment for tonight's garbage food consumption marathon. And she was not at all excited about the prospect.

Her old life was creeping into the new. Every sordid detail laid out for the world to see. Every bad decision.

Maybe it was time to cut her losses, pack her stuff and head back home.

~§~

Karina walked across the night-chilled grass of the quad in silence, high-heeled death shoes in hand. No one spoke. They probably didn't know what to say. Hell, she didn't know what to say, and how many times had she talked about this subject over the past year and a half? She should be an expert at this point, teaching seminars and crap.

Savannah was cutting her non-date short and meeting them at the dorm. On the one hand, Karina hated that her mistake was non-date-canceling excitement. On the other, she wanted to say this once and be done.

Who was she kidding? It would *never* be done.

All the people on campus would look at her like Ryan did. Angry.

Disgusted.

They trudged into the brightly lit dorm and hiked up the stairs to the second floor. Every step she took was one step closer to the inquisition.

Would her friends understand? What if they didn't? Could she live through four more years of being pariah number one? Could she handle the name-calling, the snubs, the attitudes?

Savannah stood in the open doorway to their room, wearing flannel pajamas covered in pink hearts. It looked like Savannah had been home for hours, which didn't make any sense since Joe had thrown down the no-sex ultimatum. Karina couldn't really blame him, with Savannah's no-dating ultimatum. The whole thing was a mess, and if Karina didn't have her own shit to deal with, she'd be all over her roommate to start talking..

"What the heck happened at that dinner?" Savannah's hand flew to her hips.

"Karina, honey, why don't you put on pajamas and we'll all meet back in your room." Gabi glared at Savannah.

Karina was upset but not blind. They were treating her like a child, but she didn't care. Not now. "Okay."

Savannah sat on her bed and watched Karina pull off her dress and replace it with a black t-shirt and sweatpants. Her body stayed still while her gaze followed Karina around the room. That was a common reaction. Everyone staring at Karina like she was the headliner in the freak show. *Let's stare at her, to make sure she doesn't do anything else stupid. Or if she does, make sure we get to see it...or have a phone handy to capture it.*

Karina sat on her own bed, dragging a pillow onto her lap. "You know you can call Joe back if you guys were busy. It's no big deal."

"Please, we were watching a movie on my laptop. It's not like anything good was happening." Savannah picked at her red slipper socks, but her eyes stayed fixed on her roommate.

Within seconds, the other two had wandered in carrying bags of chips, soda and various sugared treats. Karina had lived with these girls for months and never had they appeared so quickly in sleep clothes. There were usually bathroom breaks and last minute phone calls to return, notes on doors to address and make-up to remove. The last time the four of them went to dinner and met in Gabi's room to watch a movie it took over an hour to get everyone wrangled back together.

Tonight? Four minutes—ops.

"So, can someone tell me what the heck is going on?" Savannah sat on her bed, knees bent and her ankles crossed, in perfect lotus position. Megan wrapped her nightie around her legs and dropped to the floor as Gabi opened a bag of chips and sat next to her.

Silence.

How to begin...

"Well...there was a video..." Gabi said at the same time Muse sang on Karina's phone about the madness of love. Karina loved that ringtone, but she was in no mood to talk to whoever was on the other side of that tune.

Megan picked up the vibrating cell phone and held it out toward Karina, who grabbed the annoyance and checked the screen. Ryan. She couldn't handle a lecture tonight. She couldn't handle his attitude or his disappointment. She glared at the screen and pushed down the off button.

"Don't you want to answer that?" Megan asked.

"No." Karina tossed the now-silent irritation onto her desk. "I don't want to talk to anyone outside this room right now. So, anyway, where were we? Oh yeah, there was a video of me at the end of the slideshow tonight."

"I didn't put that in there." Megan protested, eyes wide. "I know it looks bad since I did the slide show, but I swear I knew nothing about that."

"We know that." Gabi leaned over and rested a hand on Megan's shoulder. "We know that, right?" She cocked her head at Karina.

"Of course, we know that." Karina didn't think Megan had anything to do with this nightmare. She had a feeling she knew the demonette that held the distinction.

She found the tag on her pillowcase and wound the bit of smooth material around her finger. She watched her finger turn an interesting shade of purple as the blood flow halted with every pull on the fabric. She unwrapped the vise. Her finger tingled. She wrapped it up again. Wrapped. Unwrapped. Wrapped. Unwrapped. Back and forth the material flowed between her fingers. "So, should I start from the beginning?"

A resounding "yes" round-robbined from the group. She didn't think she'd get off easy and give them the short version. Nope. So, from the beginning...

"Okay. So, um, the summer between sophomore and junior year of high school, I worked at the local movie theatre and became friends with Craig, the quarterback of our football team. I went to a Christian school and football was one of the sports we rocked—"

Gabi held up a hand. "Wait, when we first met, you said you went to Hemingway High School. Isn't that a public school?"

"I did, after I left Redeemer." Karina unwound the tag from her finger and tossed the pillow on the floor. Neurotic finger suffocation was not the answer here. "Redeemer was a big football school, so Craig was like a god on campus." Deep breath.

"He'd never given me a second glance. We had gone to school for like eight years without one single word. No hi. No bye. Nothing. Then, all of the sudden we're besties, talking and laughing. He listened and hung on every word. I thought he liked me. He even gave me one of his game jerseys in front of the whole school after a game. Everyone was so jealous." Karina shook her head to remove the memory. Those looks of jealousy turned to revulsion before Karina could utter the word cheese.

"We were dating as junior year started. We met families, friends...but never got past second base."

"Second base?" Megan's eyebrows arched.

"Hand up the shirt, playing with the girls." Gabi honked her own breasts. "Four months and only to second. Tragic."

Despite everything, Karina found herself smiling. "Yeah. Tell me about it. That's as far as we got and he rarely felt the girls. They wanted to be felt, so I asked him why he didn't try anything on me. You, know, why no sex? I was so worried he wasn't interested in me, and we'd just be over. But instead, he said I wasn't adventurous enough. The women he'd been with before were more, more—experienced, audacious, hot..."

"Jerk." Savannah slapped her bed.

"Maybe...probably, but I was so happy it was something I could fix."

"Fix. Why?" Megan laid a hand on Karina's knee.

"Because...because I loved him... I thought I did, anyway. So, after Vanessa Bentley's party that night, where I had a few too many to drink, I grabbed a friend and we took the video of me on the lion—the school mascot. We saved it to my phone. I thought it would be romantic. Okay, not romantic, but hot. I thought he'd see it and go nuts. You know, break down my door and take me. So, then I sent it to Craig." Karina went to the fridge and got a soda.

"Sent?" Megan asked.

"Texted." Karina cringed as she plopped back down on her bed. "I figured he'd see the whole thing as adventurous."

"Did he?"

"I don't know. He posted it to YouTube, and all the guys were passing around the link. The school found out, the pic was taken down, and I was expelled."

"Crap." Gabi covered her mouth with her hand.

"Wait. It gets worse." Karina tipped back her soda, letting the bubble-infused liquid gurgled down her throat.

Gabi blinked. "How could it get worse?"

"While I was expelled, Craig got nothing. Nothing. Heaven forbid Craig miss any football, and heaven forbid he miss school. That would destroy all hope for a state championship." Karina set down the can so nobody could see she was shaking.

"My dad's a lawyer, and he got all pissed off when Craig wasn't punished. So dear old dad threatened to sue the school for discrimination, and Craig for disseminating child pornography, and everyone who opened the file with a felony pornography charge. He promised to call every TV station in the country. So, two weeks before the state championships, they brought the entire male population of the high school into the office, one by one, and asked who had seen the video. Craig was expelled. The rest were all suspended and removed from every after school program in which they participated. Craig was gone and over half the guys were kicked off the football team and suspended. We—I mean they—lost the championship."

"Your boyfriend betrayed you. You were expelled. Who cares about some stupid football game?" Gabi threw her arms above her head.

"Everyone at my high school." Karina found some imaginary lint to play with. "My brother swears they never would have won, anyway. He hated Craig. He must have been out the day they gave everyone Craig's fan-club button, so he was a bit biased. But now we'll never know. And it was all my fault. Everyone blamed me. If I wasn't such a tease. If I wasn't such a slut..." Tears welled in Karina's eyes. She could still smell the scent of rotten eggs covering the front of her home. The flaming bag of crap on her doorstep. The time and money to have her parent's car fixed after some moron keyed the paint, and drew inappropriate pictures and swear words on the hood and doors.

"Assholes. You are none of those things." Gabi slapped the floor.

"Craig's a jerk." Savannah broke out her definition of a swear word.

"Actually, we saw each other at the mall a few months after the whole mess. He apologized for posting the video."

"Too late, creep." Gabi's scowl spoke volumes.

Karina looked around the room. Her friends, true friends were nothing like the people she hung out with back home. These friends said all the right things, didn't blame her and didn't think she was a cheap slut. A slut. How ironic. She must have been the only virgin slut in her high school. What a load of crap. "No, well, yeah it was too late, but apparently he got the text while he was out with a few of the guys. They told him he was gay if he didn't post it."

"So, because his manhood was called into question, he threw you to the lions." Gabi crossed her arms in defiance.

Karina wasn't sure if the pun was intended, but it did make her smile again. Well, as much as she could smile today. "Um, he was actually hiding in the closet. So it hit a bit too close to home. He was kind of gay and didn't want anyone to know about it."

"Kind of?" Savannah smiled and shook her head.

"Officially, he went farther with Tad from summer camp than he went with me."

"No shit?"

"Shit. He didn't want anyone to know and they were unrelenting, so..."

"Wow."

"His parents still don't know. At least, they didn't know as of the end of the summer."

"If Craig was fine with it, then why was everyone so mad?" Megan slid her hand back in the bag of chips.

"In their eyes, it was my fault—I took away Craig's future and lost them state."

"No, Craig did," Gabi snarled.

"I wish you lived in my town, they didn't see it that way. Well, except my brother, my mom and my stepdad. My father and my sister can't even look at me anymore. I'm an embarrassment."

Gabi hopped across the aisle between the beds and flopped onto the bed. She rested a hand on Karina's arm. "Oh, honey, parents suck."

"It was rough, but that's why I was so happy to come here. Start over. I guess that idea's shot to hell."

"Why?"

"Because all anyone will see is a slut who makes porn. Girls will be disgusted. Guys will think I'm easy. That's what happened at my new school. After I was expelled, I went to public school. Hemingway High. Things were fine, at first. Then someone found out about the video. This guy Robby started being real nice and we went out a few times. He seemed nice, thoughtful. We went to the park and to school events. It was great. Then he took me out to dinner. Apparently buying the fifteen-dollar franchise restaurant special, in his mind, meant he'd paid for my body or something. He wouldn't take no for an answer. So, I kicked him in the balls and ran. The next day he told everyone I slept with him, and behind closed doors he called me a tease and a slut."

"How does one become a tease *and* a slut? Don't they contradict?" Gabi asked the question Karina had wondered for over year. Not that she'd ever get an answer.

"I don't know. I have a gift. I was the virgin-tease-slut. But now I'll have to live through all of that again."

"The rumor might not even get around campus. It was mostly old people there tonight. The rumor mill is good, but not that good." Megan reached for Karina's hand and squeezed.

"Anyway, fuck 'em." Gabi turned to Savannah. "Do you feel disgusted or think she's easy?"

"No."

"You?" Gabi pointed at Megan.

"Not even a little."

"So, that's unanimous." Gabi wrapped an arm around Karina's shoulder. Savannah and Megan joined in for a group hug.

"I love you guys." Karina smiled. A real smile. It was so nice to be accepted, no matter what stupid thing she'd done in her past. She'd like to think she would never do another dumb-ass thing, but that seemed unrealistic.

Hell, she'd made enough mistakes over the past few weeks, and she didn't seem to be getting any better. Maybe the mistakes weren't as grandiose these days, but really, on the stupidity scale, how does one top posing naked on the Internet?

~§~

Karina and Savannah sat at a table in the dining hall eating their breakfast. The idea that it was too early for the rumor mill to have gotten hold of her pornographic performance was grossly incorrect. Stares and whispers floated around them.

"Morning, ladies. What's up?" Gabi strolled past the staring spectators, oblivious to the Karina Exhibit.

Karina pasted on a cheery look. "Well, Savannah's dining on yogurt and I'm having tater tots. Oh, and I'm the entertainment for the morning." She could almost see the conflict brewing around her—it was rude to stare, sure, but what if she decided to straddle another mascot or take off her clothing?

So awful.

So fascinating.

"Mind your business." Gabi turned and yelled at the gawking masses. "Nothing to see here."

"Shush." Karina flapped her hands at Gabi. This was not what she wanted. She wanted less attention, not more. She hated the attention, but she hated attention brought to all the attention she hated even more. She thought so, anyway. She wasn't sure what she just thought. Shit. She was no longer making sense, even to herself.

"So, what are we doing today?" Gabi stole a tater tot off Karina's plate.

"Something private." Karina pushed the plate toward Gabi.

"Why?"

"I don't know. I just...I want things to blow over."

"If you don't get out there, it's just going to get worse." Savannah dipped her spoon in her uneaten breakfast.

"Look, I don't want to run into Ryan."

"Why?" Gabi dunked another tot into ketchup and ate it.

"Didn't you see the way he looked at me last night? He was repulsed."

"Ryan?" Savannah stopped stirring her yogurt.

"Yeah. I'm sure that's why Parker did it."

"Well, then he's a jerk." Savannah dipped and spun her spoon into the full cup of yogurt again.

"Parker put the video in Megan's slideshow. Are you sure?" Gabi snatched another tot from the plate.

"Pretty much. She had access since she was on the committee with Megan, and she told me last week she knew my secret. I figured she was just messing with me, like all the times she supposedly was dating Ryan, but apparently not."

"We have to do something." Gabi picked up the last tater tot on Karina's plate.

"There's nothing to do. I'm sure she has nothing scandalous in her past."

"She's failing pre-calculus. She asked Megan for help." Savannah blurted.

"You knew bitcherella was failing calc and you didn't share?"

"I just found out and I didn't think it mattered. We could tell Megan to stop tutoring her. It would be good for Megan to lighten her volunteer load anyway."

"No." Karina shook her head.

"Oh, hell no." Gabi smacked the table. "We are not sitting by and letting her get away with this."

Karina leaned forward. "Gabi. Let it go. I don't want any more attention. You don't know what it's like. This fishbowl." Karina waved a hand at all the spectators. Their eyes widened—what did they think she was going to do? Jump on the table, next? "I just want to let it all drop. Anyway, even though he's a jerk, I don't want Ryan or his mom finding out about this. She's been sick and seems to rely on Parker. It would just cause a bunch of family drama and it's not worth it." Karina looked into

Gabi's chocolate eyes and pleaded. She knew Savannah wouldn't talk all over town, she had her own issues to deal with. "Promise me you won't tell him who put the video out there."

"I promise." Gabi nodded her head. "I don't agree but I promise.

Gabi gestured to Savannah's food. "Are you going to eat that or just fondle it?"

"I'm not hungry." Savannah sighed.

"What's going on?"

"Nothing. I'm heading up." Savannah grabbed the plastic cup of yogurt and tossed it in the garbage before walking out the door.

"Something I said?" Gabi asked.

"Probably, but who knows. Something's going on with her. She'll talk when she's ready."

"Yeah, but will we have to start shoving food down her throat before she's ready to talk?"

~§~

Karina somehow made it to classes on Monday with minimal human interaction. The soft hum of whispers swirled around her, but no one felt the urge to say anything to her face. No condolences. No confrontation.

She could live with that.

She walked back to the dorm, feet light and her shoulders free of the knots from the weekend. Maybe things would be different here. After all, she was surrounded by open-minded college students now, not judgmental ignorant children.

She walked up to her room. Something was wrong. Red, green, blue, and yellow paper lined the outside of the door and wall, screen shots from the video and commentary on each sheet.

Nice tits.

Where's the stripper pole?

How much do you charge?

Go back to your brothel.

Crap. Crap. Crap. Red anger streaked across her eyes, and her fists clenched, tension tightening the muscles in her body. Her mind was in fight or flight mode, and right now she wanted the fight.

"Who did this?" she yelled down the semi-empty hallway. The back-stabbing girls lingering in the hall dropped their heads and shrugged as they scampered like cockroaches back into their rooms.

So done. She was so done with this crap. She ripped paper from the door, wadding the sheets into a ball. "Quit killing trees for this shit."

Nica stomped out of her room. "Is everything okay? What's with the yelling?"

"I'm trying to thank the person who decorated my bedroom door." Karina shoved a piece of paper at the RA.

"Oh no." Nica scowled as she scanned the flyer. "Are you okay?"

"Fine. Great." Karina continued yanking down multicolored paper.

"Who did this?" Nica demanded.

"I just asked that question." Karina choked on a laugh. "Surprisingly, no one came forward."

"This is unacceptable. Why would anyone... How could they... We need to have a floor meeting. Get this stopped." Nica's eyes blazed.

She'd moved from the pity stage to anger. Now Karina just needed to get her to the acceptance stage. There was no way she wanted more attention brought to herself. "Please don't. I don't want a meeting..."

"I can understand that, but we will not have this hatred on my floor. They can't get away with doing this to you."

"I really don't want to sit in a room and have my life discussed in a forum."

"But..."

"Please, Nica. It won't change anything. I just want this to blow over."

"All right. I won't put you through any meetings. But I'm watching the situation. If there is anything you need to tell me, if this escalates, you will come to me."

"I'll try."

"No. This is not an option. At any moment if you don't feel safe or you feel they've taken it further than you can handle, you come to me. No questions. Just do it."

"Sure." Karina felt a small smile pull at her lips. The passion with which Nica harped at her—the anger under the words—there were people who knew this whole thing was ridiculous, who knew Karina and would fight for her. It felt good.

They pulled the remaining papers down and Karina opened her door. Inside, she stuffed the pages into the trashcan, paper hanging out the sides.

"Maybe we should just take this to the garbage chute?" Nica still had a ball of ridiculousness poking out of her arms.

"Yeah. Good idea." Karina wrapped her arms around her pages as Savannah walked into the room.

"What's going on?" She threw her book bag on the bed. Her eyes saucered. "What is this?"

"Welcoming committee. They're excited to have a stripper in their midst." Karina felt the joke fall flat before she said it. But she somehow couldn't stop herself. The words just fell out.

"Not funny." Savannah huffed as she pulled a page from the ball. "My word, this is what all the fuss is about? That picture's not that bad. You look good."

"Thanks."

Savannah and Nica grabbed a handful and they all walked to the garbage chute. With one push, the hate slid down into the trash.

"Karina, you tell me if you run into any more problems." Nica's mom-voice resonated with concern again.

"I will."

The RA walked down the hall to her room, taking one last glance before shutting her door. Karina and Savannah walked back into their room and dropped onto their beds.

"So, really, how are you?" Savannah asked as she stared at the ceiling.

"Fine, but I wish it was Munchies Monday."

"Munchies Monday?"

"Yeah, I made it up. It's Monday and I need a boatload of munchies." Karina laid her arm over her face. Maybe if she blocked the light, the headache building behind her eyes would go to sleep.

"Maybe we should go away. Just get off campus for a while."

"I'm not running away and giving up…"

Muse floated from Karina's cellphone. The number wasn't familiar, but she answered anyway. She should have known better than answer weird numbers. She did know better. Too bad she was distracted by all the BS of the day.

"Hi, Karina," a low tenor voice she didn't want to recognize said. Well, apparently Kyle still had her number. Just awesome. As if today didn't suck enough.

"Hey."

"It's Kyle. I haven't had a chance to call. I've been so busy with classes. I was hoping we could meet for dinner."

"Why?" Had she missed the memo where they were talking to each other again?

"I miss you." Kyle's melodic voice scratched Karina's nerves raw.

"You miss me? I thought our relationship ran its course or some bullshit."

"Don't you miss me?"

"Not really." She said the words before she could stop herself. Harsh, but fortunately true. How could she miss someone who bumped and ran? Despite what people might think after hearing the video rumor, she did have more self-worth than that.

"Ouch. We had some good times and great sex. I guess it meant nothing to you."

Anger simmered in her veins. "Nothing? I tried to talk to you how many times after that night—and you sent me back a corrected email. A corrected email."

"I don't want to be mean, but in my defense you came across as...as boring."

"So now I'm not boring?" Red haze colored her vision. She was boring? She was? He couldn't stop orating about how her books sucked and her video games sucked. Everything she did was wrong. Yeah, let's go back to that. But before she could say a word, he was talking again. Typical. Jerk.

"I just never got a chance to know the real you. I thought we could try it again."

Again. Try what? The poor excuse for a relationship, or the pathetic excuse for her lost virginity? And why? Why try again? It was a disaster. Unless he thought he'd get some street cred for dating the porn star. "If you're talking about that video, that's not the real me."

"Yeah, it is. Everyone is talking about how hot you look."

Well, that made sense—he was looking to brag about his easy girlfriend who looked hot in her nudie video. Double awesome. "Kyle, we had fun, but whatever we had ran its course. Lose my number." She slapped the end button and tossed the phone across the room. "Uncle," Karina yelled at the ceiling, thumping her heels on the bed.

"Give up?" Savannah rolled over to face her.

"Yep. I want it all. Munchies Monday and then let's get the hell out of here. Let's get out of here before I hurt someone. We'll head to my house this weekend."

Savannah didn't even blink. "Road trip to Karina's house in Oak Park. Fun."

Karina didn't know how fun it would be, but anything was better than the freak show she was living on campus.

~§~

On Saturday, Karina sat on the ripped vinyl bench seat of the bus, staring out the dirty window at the farmland creeping past the windows. Despite the lack of traffic, the bus continued its slow crawl down the highway. At this pace, they might get to Oak Park by Christmas.

Not that she was in a huge hurry to see her mom. She missed her stepfather, though. It was funny, when her mom first mentioned marrying Stan, Karina was so mad. She'd always hoped her parents would figure out their shit and get back together. But after all the crap went down and her father bailed, Stan was there. He was her protector. Between her brother Mike and Stan, she felt like she had someone in her corner.

It had meant the world to her. And since then, she'd gotten to know her mother's husband better. He was a good guy, and he put up with her mother. The man should be sainted for that. Karina loved her mom, but she was a control freak. It took a strong man to tolerate her helicoptering.

The bus hit a bump and Karina bounced up. The view outside had changed to buildings and urban sprawl. They were getting closer. Still in Indiana, but edging closer.

Gabi sat across the aisle, headphones on her ears, head bopping up and down to the thumping even Karina could hear. It would be a miracle if she had any hearing left after blasting that much noise directly into her eardrums. Gabi's gym shoe tapped a steady beat on the scuffed black treads of the floor. Her dark brown hair was tied with a blue ribbon that matched her T-shirt and jeans.

Savannah leaned back against the headrest next to Karina, eyes shut and head bopping up and down with the turbulence of the Indiana roads. Savannah's unusual outfit of jeans and sweatshirt were suggested by Gabi. She swore Savannah would want the coverage a non-dress would offer. From the disgust written all over Savannah's face as they boarded the bus, she'd made the right choice.

Megan managed to sneak out of the expedition across state lines by claiming she had a paper due. Karina couldn't blame her, but it would have been nice to have her along.

Not even homework could keep Karina from getting a break from campus. She was bringing any homework she needed to complete with her for the weekend. Nothing could keep her from leaving the fishbowl of a college campus. When she originally applied for Ritter, she was a good girl from a nice Christian high school. After the sexting incident, she thought about applying to a few public institutions—places where judgment was a bit less frequent and intense. However, her mom was so disappointed her daughter wasn't going to Harvard, and somewhat excited about Ritter, Karina didn't have the heart to suggest anywhere else.

Especially after all the heartache from that damn video.

Her parents, who were happily divorced prior to that, lost any semblance of toleration for one another. Battle lines were drawn, with those supporting Karina on one side and those sneering at her amateur burlesque act on the other. Her bio-father and sister fell into the latter group, desperately afraid her whorish ways might rub off on them or something. Stripper Flu was a bitch. It took all of her control not to climb every pole that she walked past. At least, that was how her father and sister treated her.

Savannah kept her eyes shut, her body mimicking sleep. "Are we there yet?"

"Not so much. We're still in Indiana."

"You're kidding." Savannah lifted her head, sleeping pretense over. "Do you get the impression we could get out and run faster than this?"

"Amen."

"Gabi awake?" Savannah turned to look at Gabi's tapping feet as she stared out the window. She grabbed her purse and whipped out her phone and a pair of headphones. "That's a good idea. Why aren't you listening to music?"

Karina picked up her backpack. "You're right. Maybe a podcast would make this trip move a little faster." She fished around her backpack. No phone. She pulled out her wallet and checkbook. No phone. When was the last time she saw it? Yesterday, when she'd stuffed the thing in the drawer, again. She'd been doing that a lot this last week. Crap. She'd never grabbed it.

On the one hand, she couldn't help feeling naked without her phone. And on the other, she wouldn't have to worry about any unwanted phone calls. "I forgot my phone."

"Bummer. Can you be without it for the weekend?"

"I'll have to. I'm not heading back." Karina pulled out the German assignment due next Friday, the one on the early life of Anne Frank. Without Ryan's help, her German homework was going to take much longer. She wasn't going to let her grade fall. She'd never let it happen before, and she refused to let it happen now.

She flipped through the photocopies of the research she'd done online. Good thing she'd printed the things out before she left.

After an hour and a half of the German language and glimpses of the Illinois/Indiana countryside, the bus pulled up to Union Station. Karina, Gabi, and Savannah gathered their bags and walked off the bus into the bright Saturday morning sunlight. Karina forced herself to stay upright. She had this deep urge to bend down and kiss the Illinois soil.

Since no bus, train, or magic carpet went straight from school to the Chicago suburbs, from here they needed to take the elevated train—the L if you were a local—to get to Karina's house. They walked into the station and just made the Blue Line train headed toward Oak Park.

Yet another set of vinyl seats, this time in the back of a train. The car shook and swerved as it started out down the track, building speed. Lights flickered on and off as the car made its way from the station. Sunlight streamed through the smudged glass, lighting the handful of patrons sitting in the car.

Savannah's eyes widened as a seemingly homeless man sat a few seats back and across the aisle. He leaned possessively over a three-by-two-foot trunk, beady eyes nervously glancing over the green seats. The screwdriver in his hand jiggled at the lock on the box.

Ahh...the interesting people of Chicago. Karina smiled as Savannah stared at the locksmith down the aisle. Chicago must be an interesting place for someone normally surrounded by farms and cows.

Heck, Chicago was an interesting place to those who lived ten miles away.

~§~

Karina, Gabi, and Savannah got off the train at the Oak Park exit and walked the Saturday morning streets of Oak Park. Bare trees and leaf-infested sidewalks ran along the one-way roads lined with parked cars. Bungalows, Colonials, and Victorians stood side-by-side, ten feet between each house.

Crunch. Crunch. Crunch. Red, brown and yellow leaves crinkled under their feet. Dogs barked in the fenced backyards. The sound of horns and the purr of tires on pavement wafted over from the major streets surrounding their five-square-block of village solitude.

Home. Karina missed home. Even though it sometimes felt like a pain-in-the-butt existence after the expulsion, she could still remember this town as the place she grew up. The place where her parents laughed when their three kids planted flowers for their anniversary. The place where so many good things happened over the years, despite the bad.

They walked the mile from the train station and came up on the Chicago-style redbrick bungalow Karina had called home for eighteen years. Karina walked down the gangway between her house and the neighbors, opening the wooden gate and heading through the backyard.

They headed up the wooden stairs of the back porch. When she checked the door, the knob turned, so she held it open for her friends and followed them through the door into the white kitchen. She never thought she'd miss the white kitchen.

The rest of the house was warm and cozy, a typical middle class

1950's bungalow. Everything in shades of soft beige and cream, while potted plants and multi-colored foliage gave the interior a calming outdoor feel...except for the kitchen.

The kitchen was white. Just white. No life. No color. Counters, cabinets, appliances. White. It was dirt heaven. Well, if her mother would ever allow dirt in her home. Hell, Karina would welcome the color that dirt added, but her mother loved her kitchen scoured and color-challenged.

"This is nice," Savannah cooed. "I love the decorations."

Karina laughed. "Decorations? It's white." Leave it to Savannah to love her mother's crazy lifeless kitchen.

"It's beautiful. Pristine." Savannah ran a hand over the white counters.

"Who cares about the kitchen? Where's a drink?" Gabi dropped her trendy pink backpack on the floor.

"Soda's in the fridge." Karina motioned to the refrigerator and slid past Gabi to open the door. The cool air tickled Karina's face as she grabbed two sodas and bottled water. She tossed the water to Savannah and handed one of the sodas to Gabi.

"What up, little sis?" Karina's brother Mike walked into the kitchen, pushing his retro glasses back up his nose, wearing his usual baggy faded black jeans and faded blue V-neck T-shirt. His arms opened wide. "How are you, Reema?"

Her brother's arms wrapped around her in a warm cocoon. The familiar embrace of her best friend, her Gibraltar. This moment was worth the never-ending bus trip and interesting train ride. Being here with her brother, the one who never gave up on her, felt right. Felt like home.

"Reema?" Gabi put her can on the counter.

"Mikey here couldn't say my name when I was born. *Karina* was too hard for his two-year-old mouth, so I became Reema. To him anyway." Karina stepped away from Mike.

"Awww... That's so adorable." Gabi smiled.

"And you are?" Mike walked up to Gabi, a smarmy smile on his face. Of course, it might not have been smarmy, but there were certain things siblings should not share. The "I want you" stare was creepy and disturbing. Karina wanted to scrub her eyes.

"I'm Gabi." Gabi shook his outstretched hand.

"Mike. It's a pleasure." He held her hand a little too long and then ran a hand through his long brown hair.

Oh brother. Karina did not roll her eyes, much as she wanted to. "This is my friend and roommate, Savannah."

"Ah...the roommate. I heard a lot about you before she left for school." He turned back to Gabi. "So how do you know my sister?"

"Same dorm. Same friends. And we hit it off."

"She's likable like that." Mike walked to the fridge and got himself a soda. "What are you doing home, kiddo?"

"Well... First, I need you to sit down and promise not to get mad."

"What happened?" He popped the top, fire already brewing in his hazel eyes. Her protector.

"A girl at school found the video that Craig posted on the internet." Karina paused. She could already see Mike's brow crease and his lips thin. He was going to flip out when she finished the story.

"And..." The metal of the can crinkled and whined as his hand squeezed.

"And she plastered the thing at the end of the Homecoming slide show." Gabi spit the words from her mouth.

"What?"

Karina grabbed the innocent can from his grasp and put it on the kitchen table. "It's not that big of a deal, Mike. I just needed time away from school. You know how things blow out of proportion."

"Why do I get the feeling you're not telling me everything?"

"Because when I tell you everything you flip out and make it worse."

"When?" He dropped to a chair at the table.

"Let's see—remember that blonde chick from Hemingway? You picked me up from school one day and told her that at least your sister could get some. And that guys probably ran the other way when they saw her frigid ass coming."

"What's wrong with that?" Gabi pulled out a chair and sat at the kitchen table.

Mike grinned. "Thank you. Exactly."

"You basically told everyone I put out. Every guy in school was hot for my easy bod after that." Karina sat down across from Mike. "And they knew I was easy because my brother told them I was."

"That's not exactly what I said."

"But that's what they heard. I love you, but please do not get involved in this." Karina grabbed his hand. "I'm okay this time. I swear. I have really great friends, so I don't care."

Gabi huffed. "Well, as one of those friends, I do care. I think we should dye the bitch's hair blue."

"Courtney from high school?" Mike laughed.

"No, Parker." Gabi flipped her hair back. "She needs to pay for messing with you and Ryan for the past few months."

Mike raised his eyebrows. "Ryan?"

"A friend," Karina said quickly. "We were just friends, although I'm not sure he wants to be my friend, now."

"Friend?" Gabi widened her eyes. "I seem to remember you shared a pretty intense kiss. Do you kiss all your friends? 'Cause if you do, I'm still waiting for mine." She leaned over the table and puckered her snarky lips.

"This is getting interesting." Mike took a drink from the can, his eyes never leaving Gabi. "Although, I'd rather it not include my baby sister."

"Shut up, pervert." Karina laughed as Savannah took the last chair at the table.

"So, why aren't you and this guy friends anymore?" Mike leaned back in his chair.

"Mike, are you ready to go?" Karina heard the voice and cringed. She knew that voice. Had loved that voice. Until she heard what a disappointment she was in that deep voice.

"Mike…" Karina's father walked into the room. Karina could tell when he saw her, his mouth stopped moving. "Karina, I didn't know you'd be here."

"I just stopped by the house with my friends to see Mom and Stan."

"That will make her happy." His eyes moved to Gabi and Savannah. "You must be the friends. So nice to meet you."

"You too, Mr. Wolfe." Savannah waved and smiled while Gabi's lips quivered as they curved upward. Gabi's smile was fake, but the fact that she kept her thoughts about Karina's father to herself was sincere.

"Michael, we should go." Karina's father backed up a few feet. "I'll meet you in the car."

She watched him walk out the door, and her heart constricted. There was a time when she was daddy's girl, sharing everything with the only man in her world. They'd talk about everything. Of course, back then the hot topics were tween-TV and cartoons. Now—? Now he couldn't even manage a simple hello.

"Hey, Reema. He'll get over it. Give him time." Mike pushed back from the table and stood.

"It's been over a year. How much time does it take?" Karina held back a tear.

"I don't know. I wish I did." He kissed her forehead. "I'll see you tomorrow."

"Where are you heading?"

"Boat trip." He said. "Dad wants me to mingle with some of the partners in his firm."

"Well, have fun. We're heading to the mall."

"Have fun, ladies." Mike walked out the door, silence hanging in his wake.

"What a mess." Savannah stood and wrapped an arm around Karina.

"I'm fine. Used to it."

"That sucks." Gabi slapped the table.

"Do you want to talk?" Savannah pulled away.

"Or would you rather hit that mall I heard you talking about?" Gabi waved her wallet.

"Um… mall, please." Karina pasted a smile on her face. She was going to show her friends a good time. She needed to stop dwelling on her parents and her schoolmates and any other thing she couldn't control. A trip to the mall was the best distraction.

~»ΨP«~

Chapter Twenty-Four

Ryan

RYAN STEPPED OUT onto the porch and dialed Karina's number for the...well, he didn't know the number of times he called her, but it was an unhealthy amount. Straight to voicemail, dammit. She wasn't taking his calls. Why wasn't she taking his calls? Maybe her phone was stolen.

Who was he kidding? She didn't want to talk to him and he had no clue why. The woman confused the hell out of him. He stared out over the greens of the country club, the trees dancing with the crisp northerly winds. There weren't too many golf games left of the season. Pretty soon the bite of winter would cover everything in white, making it impossible to play. Of course, there was always the indoor range, but to Ryan, the fake computer-generated greens were a cheap imitation.

"Ryan, darling, how was the game?" Parker walked up behind him.

"Fine. How was your meeting?"

"Perfect. They loved my idea for the Member Party. They loved it. Everything will still be black and white like they wanted, but we're adding a dash of color. One maroon flower per vase, and small splashes of maroon throughout the room. I'll also add something to the gift bags. I was thinking chestnuts or a garnet. I'll see what I can find. It's going to be amazing. I can't wait to start."

"That's great, Park." He stared at his silent phone. Damn phone.

"What are you doing out here? Phone do something wrong?"

"What?"

"Well, you're looking at thing like it beat your dog. Let me guess. Karina."

"It's nothing." Frustration wedged in his neck. He ran a hand down his collar, fingers pressing on the knot shooting pain into his head.

"It looks like nothing." She smirked and rolled her eyes. "Maybe she's just not into you. Has a boyfriend back home or something."

"Maybe." He couldn't believe that for a second. He knew Karina. They'd spent hours talking while studying, talking while hanging out. She knew him better than anyone. He thought he knew her the same.

"No more hiding, lovebirds." Paula Breckenridge walked onto the porch, heels clicking on the wood slats. Her hand partially covered her eyes as she grinned.

"There's nothing going on, Mrs. Breckenridge."

"Pity." She dropped her hand to her side. "Always so formal. How many times do I have to tell you, Ryan, call me Paula. Your mother's looking for you, darling."

"Is there a problem?"

"No, she just misses your smiling face." She reached out and patted his cheek as she grabbed her daughter's hand and walked back inside. He followed the duo through the club foyer and into the parlor, where the floor to ceiling windows welcomed the afternoon sunlight. Women dressed in their Sunday best sat and stood around the room, engrossed in conversations.

"Ryan, honey." His mother needed both hands to lift herself from one of the multiple antique chairs. "I was just telling the ladies about the homecoming dinner. I had such a good time with my men." She rested her hand in his.

"It was a wonderful night, Mom." He gently squeezed. His mother was doing so much better, but she still had days where she looked exhausted and fragile. It tore him up seeing her struggle.

"It was a beautiful night. You kids did such a great job. The decorations, the music, the food—it was amazing." Parker's mom squeezed her daughter's shoulder.

"You're absolutely right, Paula." His mother grabbed Parker's hand. "Parker, you and your friends did a wonderful job."

"Although, you might want to rethink utilizing the skills of the student who created that slide show, the final video was…" Mrs. Breckenridge shook her head and huffed.

That damn video. Where the hell had that come from? There's no way Megan put that at the end of her slideshow. She'd been talking about that show for weeks, and she'd never do that to Karina.

Karina. Why the hell had she'd made the video at all? She looked good, sexy as hell, but his family would never understand, never be able to separate her from the woman who made the video. Never understand why she did it. Not that he understood why. She wouldn't talk to him. Ryan's head pounded, putting pressure on his eye sockets.

"Yes, that was a bit disturbing. How incredibly sad. Who would make a video like that?" his mother asked rhetorically. At least he hoped it was rhetorical, because he had no intention of answering it. This conversation made him… sick and nervous. His mother couldn't find out about Karina being in that video. She'd never understand.

"Ryan should know. He's friends with her." Parker smiled as he glared. He knew Parker didn't like Karina but *he* liked her. That should be enough for Parker to back off. She promised she wouldn't do this again. She promised she wouldn't get involved in his love life. Betrayal ran deep.

"Oh, darling, you know her?" his mother asked, worry etched on her brow.

"Yeah, she's in Parker's dorm," he said.

"She's best friends with Gabriella Blanco," Parker said, all casual.

"Oh, there's another troublemaker." Parker's mom sneered. "I never did like that girl."

"I'm not sure about being a troublemaker, but definitely troubled," Ryan's mother said. "That young woman must have a lot of issues if she posed naked like that. I'd hate for anything like that to happen to either of you. You two watch out for each other. Be careful. You're practically relatives. We've been family friends for so long."

"We'll watch each other's backs, Mrs. Kent." Parker told her, squaring her shoulders.

"Mom, we have to get back to school. I have a test tomorrow" —and a few words to share with the car's passenger. Although he suddenly had an urge to drop that passenger at the nearest bus stop.

"Of course, of course." His mom wrapped her arms around his waist, leaning her head on his chest. "Please, drive carefully."

"I will." He stepped back as Parker went in for a hug.

"Bye, Mrs. Kent." She leaned out of the embrace and moved to press a kiss on her mother's cheek. "Bye, Mom."

"We'll see you in two weeks. One last meeting before the party." Parker's mother smiled.

"I'll be here. Right, Ryan?" Parker batted her devious little eyes as he cringed. He wanted to tell her to where to shove it. He couldn't believe she pulled that crap, bringing up Karina's video.

"Of course you'll be here. Ryan will bring you," his mother said.

Ryan walked out of the club with Parker following close behind.

"C'mon," she coaxed. "You're not mad at me, are you? I was just having a little fun."

"Get in the car, Parker." He wasn't having this argument out in the open. Out where his mom could walk up at any moment. He opened his door and slid into the seat.

Parker stood outside, staring at the door. She looked nervous. Smart girl.

Normally, he'd let her get away with the goofy crap she did. They were old friends. Their parents were old friends. He knew the life she'd dealt with all these years. Her mother was a habitually-recovering drug addict, and her father was too busy sticking his thing into every twenty-something female with daddy issues.

It was hard for her to deal with their crap. The sad thing was that nobody ever saw the real part of her life. The Breckenridge's put on a pretty good show.

Compassion crept past his defenses before he could stop it. No. He was not going to let her get away with this. He had to put his foot down. He shoved the key in the ignition and started the car.

Parker stood outside the passenger door, looking back and forth from the club to the car. He rolled down the window on her side. "If you want a ride to school, get in."

She sighed and pulled open the door, sliding into the seat with a muffled thump.

"Forget how to open the door?" He shoved the car into drive and pulled out of the parking lot.

"No. Trying to decide if listening to you whine is worth the ride."

"Why did you do it?" He flew down the side streets to the interstate.

"Do what?"

"Seriously? I hope you're just playing stupid."

"You don't have to get mean." She crossed her arms like a spoiled toddler.

"Parker, why did you bring up Karina?"

"I was just messing with you. I didn't tell them her name." She pouted—he didn't have to look to know that. "Anyway, why does it matter? She's not even taking your calls."

"Now who's mean?"

She stared out the window, pout intact. "Fine. I'm sorry I brought up Karina. Apparently, it was a poor joke."

"Yeah. It was."

"Aren't you going to apologize to me? I apologized to you."

"For what? For being angry that you used my love-life against me? Should I apologize for trusting you?"

"Don't be like that. You can trust me. I wasn't using it against you. Just playing. But you could apologize for being mean."

"I'm not going to apologize, Parker."

"Fine." She stuck her nose in the air, arms still crossed. "Are we done talking about all this?"

"Yeah." He flipped the radio on and turned up the sound, loud enough to prevent talking, but not loud enough to blow out their eardrums. Parker stared out the side window as he watched the road. This suited him just fine.

An hour and a half and he'd be back on campus. An hour and a half and he could track down Karina and get to the bottom of all this.

~»ΨP«~

Chapter Twenty-Five

Karina

KARINA SAT IN the passenger seat of Mike's Ford Taurus as he drove down the tollway on Monday morning. When Mike offered them a ride back to Ritter, Karina jumped at it. No crazy L and no turtle bus.

Although, right now she was questioning the tradeoff. Gabi and Savannah sat in the back seat over-sharing Karina's life and secrets. Not that she had any secrets from Mike... Well, she refused to tell him about how far she'd gone with Kyle. Thankfully, she'd sworn the blabber twins to secrecy on that gem.

"What kind of a creep corrects a love letter?" he yelled. "I'm going to kick his ass."

"Don't even think about it. None of us are going to tell you who he is. It's not worth it." She gave a pained grin out the window. If he only knew the whole story.

"I'll give you the name," Gabi piped from the back seat.

"Don't you dare," Karina told her. "He will literally kick his ass. You have no idea what a total nightmare my brother was when I was younger."

Mike's eyes were fixed on the road as a frown deepened on his face. "Kiddo, I'm sorry I was so protective of you in high school. I just knew guys were assholes and had only one thing on their mind. The one guy I thought was actually different turned out to be the worst one of them all. I should have kicked his ass before he got a chance to put that shit on the Internet." The fire in his hazel eyes grew as he pounded his fist on the steering wheel.

"I don't know, Mikey. I think it's me. Maybe there's something wrong with me. If I was so irresistible, men would sleep with me and fall at my feet, not run the other way. I mean, look at Savannah."

"What do I have to do with anything?" Savannah asked from the backseat.

"Wait, let's get back to sleep with you?" Mike's fingers turned a scary shade of white as he wrapped them around the wheel.

Subject change! Subject change! "It's a figure of speech. Don't blow a gasket." Karina smiled and turned to Savannah. "And you have guys falling at your feet. You have Leland and Joe's adoration."

"I wouldn't go that far. Leland and I haven't talked in over two weeks."

"What?" Two weeks. How did Karina not notice?

"I've been busy. He's been busy. I don't know. It's just not the same anymore."

"Maybe you need some face time." Gabi laid a reassuring hand on Savannah's shoulder.

Shock passed over Savannah's features at Gabi's gesture. "Maybe."

"You should go visit him. How long has it been?" Karina asked.

"Two months." Savannah's attention dropped to her twined fingers. Her head popped up. "You're right, but it's almost Thanksgiving. I can wait."

Wait? Since when? Things with Savannah and Leland were not looking good. No wonder Savannah was eating like a bird.

"I saw the scrunchie on the door last week."

"Ooh, finally giving it up to Joe, huh?" Gabi raised her perfect eyebrows.

"No, we're just friends. Steve and I are going strong."

"Who's Steve? Weren't you with that guy Pete?"

Savannah's eyes squinted in confusion. "Oh yeah. Steve. Pete. I have so many boyfriends. I forget their names." She sighed and turned to stare out the window. "I can't wait to see Leland."

"So, we never did get to finish our conversation from the other day. What's up with you and that Ryan guy?" Mike adjusted his glasses.

"Nothing. We're friends."

"Kissing friends? Why aren't you dating him? Or are you afraid he'll break up with you via post-it? I hear that's the worst."

"I think corrected email is the worst. And we're just friends. He saw the video of me writhing on top of Simba and he looked appalled." Karina sighed. How she had hoped to avoid this conversation.

"Looked appalled? What did he say?"

"He didn't say anything. She's not taking his calls," Gabi blurted.

"You could let me tell the story." Karina glared at her yappy friend in the backseat.

"I could, but you suck at it."

"Anyway" —Karina ignored the peanut-gallery— "I forgot my phone at school, but he hasn't been in class since the video posted."

"But he's called." Mike phrased the statement as a question. Karina wasn't sure she wanted to answer it. She could see the direction the conversation was heading. And it didn't make her look like a Rhodes Scholar.

"Yes."

"Then why aren't you taking his calls?" Mike couldn't let anything just die.

Karina closed her eyes. "Do we have to talk about this?"

"Yes," three traitors screamed at once.

Et tu, Savannah? "Fine. I don't want to hear the disappointment in his voice. I already know I lost him, but if I don't take his calls, there's a smidgen of hope that maybe he'll be able to see past the crappy porn and want to be with me."

"But you won't take his calls to find out." Why did Mike keep talking?

"What if I'm right? What if I lost him?"

"I get it. It would suck to lose him." He stopped behind a long line of cars waiting at the tollbooth.

"Exactly," she agreed.

"So, you ignore him so you don't find out how he really feels. Reema, that is the saddest thing I've ever heard. Are you *trying* to live in a bad TV drama?"

"No."

"Then talk to him. Get it over with." He inched to the automated tollbooth and waited for the iPass to register the toll. The sound of gears shifting floated through the air as the gate rose, allowing the car to pass.

"What if he doesn't want to be with me? Hell, he already said I wasn't his type."

"Then he's an idiot." Mike merged back into traffic, his eyes focused on the road.

"What if he does want to be with me? How will I know if he wants me or Stripper Barbie? I think he likes me. He seems like he does. But then he does things like pull away when we kiss."

"That happened once and you were drunk. He was trying to be chivalrous." Traitor number two twanged from the backseat.

"Chivalrous? He called it a mistake. That's not chivalry, that's being an asshole."

Mike pulled into the parking lot of Dickinson Hall and found a parking spot. He followed Karina into her dorm room, carrying all their bags.

"Thanks for the ride." Gabi took her bag and wrapped her arms around his neck. His eyes closed as his glasses practically hazed over. A smile captured his face. When Gabi pulled away, she waved before she walked out the door.

Savannah gathered her shower bag and a change of clothes. "I'm taking a shower. I still feel dirty from that train ride."

"The train wasn't as bad as the bus." Karina sighed.

"You're right." Savannah picked up her bottle of soap and held it at eye level. "Do you have extra soap?"

"Yeah. Grab it from my stash."

Savannah pawed through Karina's shower caddy, grabbing bottle after bottle. "Ooh, this looks good." She smiled as she read the label on the pilfered products. "Bye, Mike. Thanks for driving. I don't think I could've lived through another public transportation adventure." She practically skipped out the door, a giddy schoolgirl with new toys. The two showers she took in Oak Park apparently hadn't been enough to remove the stench from a train ride two days earlier.

"Nice room." Mike looked at the pictures lining the wall over Karina's bed. A few family shots and a few shots of her friends here at Ritter, that was all she had. He plopped down on Karina's bed, grabbing the heart-shaped pillow he'd bought her for her third birthday from the corner. He pulled on the fringe lining the edges. "You still have this."

"Of course. It came from my favorite brother."

"I'm your only brother."

"You're lucky there's not a lot of competition." She grabbed two bottles of water and gave one to Mike. "We need to do a grocery run. This is all we've got."

"Thanks. It's fine." He twisted open the bottle and tossed back a swig. "I'm thirsty after dealing with all that estrogen."

"Don't be an ass. Want a tour of the campus?" Karina sipped her own water.

"Nah. I've got to head back to school." He tossed the pillow to the bed. "I like your friends."

"Yeah, I found some good ones. Do you want something for the road?"

He drank the last of the water and tossed the plastic bottle into the garbage can. "I'm good. What I really need is for you to put in a good word with Gabi."

"My Gabi? She's seeing someone."

"Okay, but if that doesn't work out..."

"No."

"Come on." He slid his glasses up his nose.

"No. Hit the road, before I hit you."

"The violence..."

Karina led her brother down the flight of stairs and out the front door. Straight into Ryan. "Hey," she said.

"Hey." Ryan's attention moved to Mike. His eyes narrowed and his lips thinned as he stared.

Karina's pain-in-the-butt brother offered Ryan a big smile. "Hi, I'm Mike."

"Ryan."

"Ah, the infamous Ryan."

"Don't you need to go?" Karina grabbed Mike's arm and tried to pull him toward his car before things got out of hand.

"No, but I think we should revisit our last conversation. I really want a good word. Then I'll go."

"No." Karina wondered if kicking her brother's shins would get him moving.

"Mike held out a hand to Ryan. "It's so nice to finally meet you. I heard so much about you—"

Karina grabbed his hand and pushed it down. "Yes. Fine. Good word. You can go now. Thanks for the ride."

"No prob, Reema." He leaned in, pulled her to him and whispered, "This guy is totally hot for you. The jealousy..." He kissed her cheek before strolling to his car, waving over his shoulder.

She stared after him, completely off balance. Hot for her? She wished. All she saw was anger. Would it be inappropriate to run to her room and never look back?

Probably.

~»ΨΡ«~

Chapter Twenty-Six

Ryan

RYAN WATCHED THE new douchebag drive away. Hell, he might not even be new. He could be the old douchebag for all Ryan knew. Maybe Parker was right and Karina had her own Vegas arrangement going on.

Dammit.

He wanted to scream or hit something or scream as he hit something. Although what just happened did make one thing clear... "We'll, now I understand why you couldn't answer my phone calls."

"What?"

Ryan shrugged. "I didn't realize you were playing the same game as Savannah. At least she was up front about it, though." *Now* he could walk away. He wasn't going to be runner-up to another dipshit guy. He couldn't do it. He was done.

"Ryan. That's my *brother*."

He spun around and stared at her. As the icy hot mix running through him dissipated, he actually felt his shoulders relax.

"No games. That's Mike. My brother."

Her brother. That changed things, or did it? "What about my calls? You forget how to answer your phone?" Crap, he was starting to sound like his father.

"No. I...I just didn't know what to say."

"Hello, hey, yo, wazup...all standard responses to a ringing phone." He was being an ass, but he couldn't help himself. Why was she keeping him out? "Any of those would have worked."

"Look, after homecoming, I didn't—I saw the way you looked at me after you saw that video." She waved her hands, not wanting to spell it out. "I get it. It's not my proudest moment."

She might as well be speaking Mandarin for all the sense she wasn't making. "What is it you get?" he asked slowly. "You keep saying that you get it, yet I have no clue what you're getting. I'm not getting it. Could you possibly share it with me?"

"I get that I messed everything up. I don't know how that video was found, but it was a stupid high school mistake and now I get to pay for it for the rest of my college career. I get that you're disgusted with me. Get in line. I'm disgusted with me. My father and sister won't even talk to me. Half the students here look at me like I'm a freak of nature." Tears fell down her face.

Crap. He didn't want her to cry. He wanted to pull her close and tell it would be all right, but she didn't seem to like him at the moment. He watched her drop her face to her hands. He didn't seem to like himself either.

Fuck it.

He wrapped an arm around her waist. He used his thumb to wipe away the tear on her cheek. She didn't pull away.

Good sign.

"I don't even know where to start on that monologue. First, I'm not disgusted with you. I was shocked. That look you saw was shock. I'm sorry your dad and sister won't talk to you, but they're missing out, because talking to you is the highlight of my day. You're not a freak of nature. You made one mistake. We've all made mistakes. Your mistake just happens to have a video to remember it by."

Karina leaned her head on his shoulder, stuttering with laughter through her tears. "Yeah, I should remember to hide from the camera when I make my mistakes."

"True, but it was such a nice video."

"Nice. Really?" She leaned back to look at him, her eyes bright with the last of her tears.

"Hot?" he offered, and she laughed.

She wiped her eyes. "Please, it's hard-core porn. I just want to go back to my life of oblivion."

"I know porn and that was not hard-core. Trust me." He ran a hand down her cheek. Her skin slid softly against his fingers. He slipped his hand under her chin and lifted her face to his. "I don't care about some stupid video. I missed you."

"I missed you, too."

He lowered his mouth to hers. Her lips were soft. Warm. Amazing. He pulled back. He didn't want to move too fast, and everything about that kiss urged him to move fast. He wasn't about to let her get away, because he couldn't control himself. But then she leaned into him. Her lips found his and slowly opened for him. The warmth of her mouth and the slide of her tongue dazed and confused his senses. But not enough to miss that he was enjoying this too much. Way too much. His body was taking unintentional liberties, as every sweep of her tongue coaxed a rise in interest.

They were on the sidewalk of the dorm. They had to stop before he was tempted to carry her in the building. That might conflict with her desire for oblivion and discretion. The sweet taste of her breath lingered on his tongue as he pulled away. "Wow."

"Yeah."

Ryan rediscovered breathing as his heartbeat strummed in his chest. Her flushed cheeks slowly return to normal. He said, "I think we need to do that again. Wednesday night."

"I have a German paper due Friday, but I think I can fit you in." Her lips turned up as her teeth grabbed a hold of her lower lip. How he wanted to run his tongue over that lip.

He turned away. His thoughts were not cooperating with the whole discretion thing. But he hated walking away. He wanted to stay right there in her arms. "I'll pick you up at six."

"I'll be ready."

Ryan started down the stairs leading to the front door of the building, pausing when he felt a touch on his arm that slid down to his hand. Karina. She leaned into him, a smile on her face. She couldn't stay away from him, either. At least he hoped that was why she grabbed his arm.

"So, you know porn, huh?" she whispered in his ear.

"Um...I think I should plead the fifth on that one." He stood, his face inches from her lips. Her breath mingled with his.

"See you Wednesday." She squeezed his hand and walked away. He watched her stagger to the dorm. She turned and waved before she ran in the door.

A sigh blew past his lips.

Was it Wednesday yet?

~»ΨP«~

Chapter Twenty-Seven

Karina

KARINA SLID INTO the front seat of Ryan's car, dropping her purse onto the floor. She had ridden in this very seat many times, but this time was different. This time they were alone and on their way to dinner. Together. A date.

Soft music wafted from the speakers as he shut her door and walked around the car to the driver's side. He got in, his hands sliding familiarly over the leather-covered steering wheel. Given the talent of those lips— she could only imagine how gifted those hands were.

"Karina?"

"Yes." Her attention left his hands and the illicit thoughts that were running rampant in her brain. Bad brain.

"Is Italian all right for dinner?" The grin that overtook his face as he watched her eyes struggle to stay on his face was annoying. She could control herself. Her eyes were just taking in the shirt that fit snugly across his broad chest, and the hands... no she wasn't going there again...and the black wool pants that conformed to his body. Enough. She had control.

Bad brain.

"Italian? Okay?"

"Oh. Uh, yeah," she stuttered.

Ryan started the car and navigated the barren Wednesday-night streets toward the restaurant. Winter had crept over the campus when she wasn't looking, cold wind and frosty rain overtaking the once-bustling sidewalks.

He stopped at a yellow light and leaned over to the passenger side of the car. His seat belt stopped him from getting closer, so she met him half way.

"I've been waiting for this since Monday." He leaned in and touched his lips to hers. The soft, sweet kiss sent shivers down her spine.

Honk.

"Green light," she whispered as she pulled away.

He licked his lips and smiled as he turned back to the road. After a few blocks of Bruno Mars moaning about buying a woman flowers, they came to another red light. Ryan inclined toward Karina again. She couldn't resist the pull of his mouth to hers.

This kiss was hot, hungry. She felt the strength of his lips all the way down to the nail polish on her toes. His hand found the crook of her neck, his thumb massaging circles at the nape. She pulled back to grasp a piece of air, her eyes opening to green speckles spattered across his face.

"Green light." She fought to say the words with what minimal breath remained in her lungs.

He dropped his head and sighed. The smile he wore earlier was still pasted on his face as he drove the remaining blocks to the restaurant. He pulled into the lot of Casciani's Italian Restaurant and parked the car. She reached for her purse and the handle on the door.

"Hold on." He said as he pulled off his seatbelt and leaned across the front seat. "There's no green light to save you now."

He unbuckled her seatbelt and ran a hand down her arm. Goosebumps crawled up her skin, sending tremors to her core. A gentle kiss breezed across her neck. She tilted to allow him easier access.

Feather light lips brushed along the sensitive skin. Heat pooled at her center. This had to stop, they were in the middle of a very public parking lot. But she really didn't want it to stop. Decisions, decisions.

Ryan pulled his lips away and leaned his forehead on hers, making the decision for her. "Hungry?"

"Yes."

He opened his door and slid out. He walked around the hood as Karina stepped out of her side of the car. Cold air bit her cheeks as he reached for her hand and walked her to the front door.

The restaurant was busy for a Wednesday night. Ryan gave his name to the hostess and she led them to a table in the back of the room. The quaint Italian bistro had small cozy tables covered with red tablecloths. White roses in a clear vase surrounded by white candles sat in the center of their table, the flickering flames casting a warm glow over everything.

"I hope this is all right," Ryan said as he held her chair for her.

"This is beautiful." She looked down at her black jeans and blue sweater and couldn't help but cringe.

"Are you sure this is okay? We can leave." Concern furrowed his adorable brow as he sat down across from her.

"No. I just don't think I'm dressed to eat here." She eyed the other women in the building. Dresses were the norm in this fancy-schmancy place. She so did not fit in.

"You look beautiful." He grabbed her hand and squeezed. "But we can leave if you're not comfortable." He watched her with expectant eyes. He was trying so hard. And— he made reservations. No one had ever made reservations for her, and she was considering leaving? Not so much.

"No. I'm starving." She smiled as the waitress handed each of them a menu.

"So what are you having?" he asked over his open menu.

"Fettuccine Alfredo. You?"

"Linguine di Mare. It's my favorite thing here."

"You've been here before?"

"With my parents. This is where my mom and dad met, so she likes to eat here at least once every time she comes up." Ryan nodded, and a waiter appeared and took their orders before scurrying for the kitchen. Ryan grabbed her hand. "I'm glad we did this."

"Me too." She smiled and took a drink of water. The warm touch of his hand as his fingers rubbed the inside of her palm tickled, but she couldn't bring herself to pull away.

"This is cozy." Parker walked up to the table, failing to hide a sneer. If she was even trying to hide it. Evil ice bitch. Karina tried to release Ryan's hand, but he tightened his fingers around hers. Unless she wanted to arm wrestle, she was stuck.

"Parker." Was it Karina's imagination, or did Ryan sound a little cold? "What are you doing here tonight?"

"I'm here with a friend." Parker flipped her hair. "I'm planning on pledging next semester, so I wanted to talk about the changes I'd like to see with one of my future sorority sisters."

"Don't they have to accept you first?" Karina had no idea how sororities worked, but she thought there was some sort audition process. She hadn't bothered looking into it. So far, her parents had put their foot down on Greek life. Karina was there to learn, not hang out at frat parties. Apparently, they had missed the memo that said joining in a sorority was not a prereq for getting into said frat parties.

Parker looked down her pointy little nose at Karina. "*You* would need to go through all of that. I'm a legacy. I don't."

"Being a legacy—I guess that's probably a good thing." *Because no one would accept you based on your personality alone.* She kept the last part to herself and took a sip of water. No need to ruin a perfectly good date because of a backstabbing bitch.

"It is. I really wanted to tell you how fabulous the decorations on your door were last week. My compliments to the designer. I couldn't have done a better job. Great use of—colors."

Maybe one or two nasty thoughts *could* be shared. Just this once.

"Yeah, some people have nothing better to do than decorate other people's doors. I guess they don't go out on dates. Or have any friends. Or maybe, if they spent more time studying, they wouldn't be failing pre-calc."

Fire blazed behind Parker's eyes before she reined it in. "Yes, you're probably right. Ryan, it was good to see you." The infringer swayed back to her buddy and left Ryan and Karina alone.

Ryan watched her go with narrowed eyes. "That was weird. What am I missing?"

"Nothing." Karina's heart raced—she refused to let Parker ruin her night. "I still don't get why you're friends with her."

"She's an old family friend. My mom and her mom are best friends. Parker was the one who told me about my mom's radiation and chemo schedule. My father didn't tell us anything. I don't know if my mom would have made it without her. She took her to the doctor when I couldn't be there, and picked up meds. She was a good friend to my mom. And anyway, I rarely deal with her."

Any anger with Parker fell away. It didn't matter. All that mattered was him and his family. "That must have been so hard watching your mom go through the chemo, the pain."

"It wasn't easy, but now she's been cancer free for over a year. There was a time I never thought I'd say that. But she's a fighter."

"That's nice. It must have made her happy to have you in her corner."

"I think so."

The waiter brought their order, and offered to grind fresh Parmesan onto the plate. Karina's mouth watered.. She dipped her fork into the long strands of fettuccine and spun until she had a manageable bite. She probably should have gotten mostaccioli. At least the round tubes offered less of an opportunity to wear the food.

However, once she put the pasta in her mouth she didn't care. She didn't care if she made a mess. Al dente pasta with a rich creamy sauce. Delicious.

They finished their meals in relative silence. A few questions popped up, but neither wanted to stop eating long enough to give a long drawn-out answer. They finished off their dishes, and the waiter brought the check after Ryan signaled him that they were done.

"So, what would you like to do now?" Karina refolded her cloth napkin and set it on the table next to her empty plate.

"Psi Rho party?"

"Sure." Her nerves sparked. With the exception of classes, she hadn't been out in public for over a week, let alone at a frat party. A party with drunk guys. Awesome. How many of those drunk guys were at the homecoming dinner? How many had seen the video? How many would give her a hard time or a demeaning leer?

Was she making a mistake?

~§~

Karina stood against the redwood-paneled wall of the small second floor lounge as Ryan bounced a quarter on the scarred coffee table in the center of the room. The coin hopped from the table and splashed into the shot glass.

This was the first time Karina had been up here. Apparently, it was the perfect setup for a friendly game of quarters. At least that's what Brent kept saying.

"Drink up, Sinclaire." Ryan sat back on one of the tattered red couches that surrounded the table. A handful of frat brothers stood around the table talking smack, chugging back their plastic cups of beer.

Brent lifted the glass to his lips and threw back the contents. He pulled the quarter from between his teeth. He refilled the shot glass with vodka and set it back on the table.

Karina couldn't help but cringe. Pulling a coin out of your mouth and throwing it into a glass so someone else could put it in their mouth seemed… unsanitary. No washing in between. Ick. She sighed. She was turning into Savannah. It was alcohol, though, right? That killed germs. Maybe.

Brent bounced the quarter straight into the goal. "You're up, Kent."

Ryan tilted the shot to his lips and drank it back. "All right, I'm out."

"Pussy," Brent shouted, pouring more vodka into the glass.

Ryan punched him in the arm. "I need to get Karina home sometime tonight. I need to be sober."

"Wimp," Brent yelled at Ryan before he got up and stood next to Karina, leaning one hand on the wall. When he leaned over her, the overwhelming smell of an obvious cologne bath tickled her nose. "If you're looking for real man, I'd be glad to take Kent's place. I can hold my liquor."

Karina shook her head and smiled. "I'll stick with the lightweight."

Brent laughed and dropped his arm. "He is a lightweight. Dude, she must like you. She said no to me."

"Or maybe she just likes a guy who's not an asshole." Ski saluted Brent with his beer bottle.

"You are one crabby bitch." Brent sat back at the table. "When is Samantha coming home? You need to get some or you might stay that way."

"Shut it, Sinclaire."

"What? A few days without your woman and you're walking around like a sandy vagina. Just wondering when she's coming home to douche your ass."

"Fuck off." Ski walked out of the room, a huge frown on his face.

She'd only met Joe's cousin a couple times, but he did seem down. Sad. Everyone else seemed to understand and was giving him wide berth, except for Brent. Karina really couldn't understand that guy.

Ryan walked up to Karina and wrapped an arm around her. "Brent, back off and go find your own woman. This one's mine."

I'm his. She wanted to squeal like a—okay, like a girl. Thankfully, she kept her mouth silent. The two of them left the lounge and headed down the hall. Karina was surprised how clean the upstairs was kept. The downstairs reeked of beer and the floors were as sticky as a theatre after a kid's movie. But the upstairs by the bedrooms was clean and odor free. Some of the wheat smell wafted up the stairs, but overall the walls were crisp white and the floors were spot free. Well, there were some stains...relatively spot free.

"So. I'm your woman, huh?" She bumped her shoulder into his.

"Yeah."

"Does that make you my man?"

"Absolutely." He turned and pushed her against the nearest door. His lips met hers just as a voice shattered the moment.

"Ryan," some guy slurred as he stumbled toward them, bumping into the pictures lining the walls. "I love you, man."

"Thanks." Ryan grabbed the drunkard before he bumped into his woman. She smiled. She couldn't help it. No matter how barbaric it might have been, she liked the sound of it.

Drunk dude goggled at her. "Hey, you're that chick from the movie. With the cans." He moved his hands to his chest and honked, upending the plastic cup in his right hand. His bloodshot eyes grew to saucers as the amber liquid slid down his shirt.

Speaking of barbaric.

He turned to Ryan and tipped back his cup, looking confused when it was empty. "Nice job, dude."

"Walk away, man." Ryan's eyes narrowed as he put an arm in front of Karina.

"Sorry, dude. I just meant she's hot." His eyes travelled to her chest. Heat slid up her neck and pooled in her cheeks. This was what she didn't want. The notoriety. The embarrassment. And in front of Ryan.

Ryan's arm moved a bit higher, blocking the view. "They're playing quarters in the red room."

"Cool." The nameless drunk stumbled down the hall and into the room they had just left.

Ryan watched the guy walk away, his arms surrounding her. "Where were we?"

"Ryan, I'm sorry." Regret, sadness, defeat all lodged in her throat, encouraging the moisture prickling her eyes, demanding release.

"For what?"

"I'm sorry you have to deal with this." She stepped away from his arms, trying to ignore the salty liquid pooling in her eyes. "It's bad enough I have to deal with all this crap."

"Wait. What crap have you dealt with? What's happened?"

"Nothing important. I just want to give you the chance to walk away if you want." She ran a hand over her face, mopping up the tears on her cheeks. Great first date. Dinner and a counseling session.

"What's nothing important?"

Stupid. Stupid. *Stupid.* She should learn to keep her mouth shut. This was not the way to keep a man interested—sharing the world's views on your boobs and whorish ways. No way out of it now. She shrugged. "Pictures from the video on my door. Suggestions. Compliments." She downplayed the situation, hoping he'd let it drop.

"Like?"

"Nice tits. Go back to your brothel. Where's the stripper pole? Nothing I can't handle."

"Has it stopped?" Muscles bunched underneath his sweater, and she could see he was gritting his teeth.

"No, but I don't care. I've let it go. I just don't want you to get hurt by all of this. This is my problem. Not yours."

"You're my problem…" He grabbed his forehead and pulled in a breath of air. "That didn't come out right. Your problems are my problems."

"Keep digging yourself out of that one." She smiled—he might not have meant it, but she kind of liked being his problem, or maybe it was more his concern.

"I'm sorry." He shook his head.

"Don't be. I like being your concern. I like that you care about me. You're my concern, too."

His hands moved to her sides. "I do care. I want you to tell me if you get any more notes or comments or smoke signals. I could just beat the crap out of whoever put that video in that slide show."

It was the perfect opportunity. Tell him about Parker. Tell him what an awful bitch she was. Tell him how she made Karina's life a living hell.

But she couldn't.

She couldn't start some family fight. She thought of his mother and her best friend. Karina's friends gave her strength through all of this. His mother was sick, or had been. At any moment, she could be again. She must need her friends just as bad, if not more. Anyway, he said he barely saw Parker these days.

"It's not worth it." She laid a hand on his cheek. "But I love that you offered to beat the crap out of them."

He smiled and dropped his lips to hers. Yeah. She could live with notoriety if he kept kissing her like this. She could live through anything, with these lips on hers.

~§~

Karina pulled on a pair of black leggings and an oversized slate-blue sweater. She fluffed her hair for the umpteenth time.

"Your hair's fine." Gabi shoveled a spoonful of ice cream into her open mouth.

"We're going out for dinner."

"So?" Gabi's tongue shot out to lick the spoon clean of any butter pecan goodness.

"You'll spoil your appetite."

"Okay, Mom." Gabi slapped the lid on Ben and Jerry and placed the carton in the freezer. "It's not like we're going to Casciani's for a romantic dinner. We're going to the Mehnk. It's not like even going out." She snatched the bag of chips from the shelf above the fridge and sat back down on Karina's bed.

Karina stared at her friend in awe...and concern.

"What? I haven't eaten all day. Some of us had a bitch of a project due in English. Ten pages on the effect of social media on education. Nap inducing." Gabi popped a chip in her mouth. "It was horrible. Horrible, I tell you." Gabi put the back of her hand to her forehead in mock dramatic fashion.

"All right, Scarlett O'Hara." Karina laughed. Drama much?

"Frankly my dear, I don't give a damn." Savannah walked into the room, Ryan following behind. "All I heard was Scarlett. What don't I give a damn about?"

"Gabi's ten-page paper."

"Suck it up. I had a fifteen-pager." Savannah ran a brush through her hair as Ryan wrapped an arm around Karina.

He felt so good. His warmth. His strength. She leaned her head back and sighed. She could get use to this. He skimmed his lips up her neck.

"You." Gabi pointed at Savannah. "I liked you better when you were all sweet, southern hospitality. And you" —she pointed at Karina and Ryan— "get a room. I'm trying to eat."

"I thought we were going to the Mehnk for dinner." Ryan said the words before Karina could stop him.

It was so nice knowing him.

Gabi's eyes were fixed on Ryan. Karina could almost see her silent prayer for a death-ray to stream from her retinas. Thank goodness no one had perfected that whole if-looks-could-kill thing.

She crunched on another chip as Ryan said, "Never mind."

Smart man. Karina patted his arm as Gabi closed the bag and walked to the food shelf.

"Do we have chocolate?" Gabi picked up boxes and moved bags, now scrounging for sugary snacks.

Ryan leaned down. "Does she live here?"

"One would think," Savannah answered as she put on her socks and shoes.

"I heard that." Gabi came up with a box of chocolate cereal and a bowl.

"You are not eating that now." Savannah yanked the box from Gabi's hands and put it back on the shelf. "What is wrong with you? Are you pregnant?"

"No. Opposite." She sank to Karina's bed. "I'm menstrual."

"And crabby."

"Bite me, blondie."

Savannah laughed. "I deserved that. But you made it all too easy."

Ryan pulled his arm from Karina. "This is getting too...too...never mind. I think I'll go wait in the car with the men." He kissed Karina's nose. "Hurry, before she starts eating furniture."

Once he was out of sight, Karina and the other two broke into laughter.

"You scared him away." Savannah sat on her bed.

Gabi preened. "I know. That was fun."

"That was fun to watch." Savannah turned to Karina. "You know, you two are adorable. It reminds me how it used to be with Leland. Back when...I don't know. When it was about us, and not about showing our parents that we were right."

"You've been apart for two months. I still think it's time to see him.

Absence makes the heart grow fonder unless you let him go and he comes back…or some shit." Gabi opened the mini-fridge as she butchered another saying.

"Thanksgiving is coming up. I'll see him then." Savannah grabbed her purse. "Now, the fine cuisine of the cafeteria is not going to eat itself."

They walked out the door as Gabi snarked, "Are you sure? I swear that stew I ate on Thursday had eyes."

Outside, Brent's Jeep idled at the curb as everyone piled into the car. Since he was driving, that allowed the crabby one to sit in her own seat in the front. Savannah sat in the middle of the backseat, with Joe on her right. That left Karina on Ryan's lap, with a seatbelt pushing them closer and closer. Not that she was complaining. Her roommate on the other hand…

"Why didn't we walk again?" Savannah asked.

"Because we have a frat meeting at Barnacles, and have to be there by ten." Brent rested his hand on Gabi's knee.

"You have a frat meeting at a bar?" Karina couldn't see what they'd accomplish with all the noise of the bar.

"Isn't it Tittie Tuesday?" Joe asked.

"Tittie Tuesday? How sexist." Savannah huffed.

"It's not Tittie Tuesday, dumbass." Brent glared at Joe in the rearview mirror. "It's Traditional Tuesday. Now, if some poor girl with daddy issues accidentally wets her T-shirt, I won't stop her."

"How do you get any work done?" Savannah shook her head.

"Work?"

"The meeting," Savannah said, speaking slowly. "The disguise for your debauchery."

Karina laughed as Ryan's arms tightened around her.

"Disguise?" Brent glared at her in the rearview mirror. "Please, we meet—"

"—in between peep shows and heavy metal songs. So, what? Five minutes?" Gabi rolled her eyes

"At least ten." Brent drove toward the Mehnk.

"Brent, you're killing me here." Ryan buried his face into Karina's shoulder. "I would much rather spend the time with you," he whispered.

"Liar." Karina ran a hand through his hair as he kissed her neck, tingles shooting down her spine. Maybe she could see why he'd want to be with her instead.

The Jeep pulled into the parking lot and the passengers piled out onto the pavement. Gabi threw an arm through Karina's. "You are both so cute." She made a gagging noise. "It's disturbing."

Brent and Joe traded insults.

Savannah laughed at their ridiculousness.

Ryan smiled at Karina.

Karina looked at them all, and happiness swelled inside her. Ryan was amazing and all hers. She would ask someone to pinch her but if this was a dream, she didn't want to wake up. The moment was perfect. Friends. Boyfriend. Her secrets revealed.

Absolutely perfect.

Her smile faltered. Perfect was usually where she messed things up.

Oh, God, please don't let me mess this up.

$$\sim\!\text{»}\Psi\text{P}\text{«}\!\sim$$

Chapter Twenty-Eight

Ryan

RYAN STRUGGLED TO stay on the barstool, bent over trying to catch his breath in between gasping with laughter.

Karaoke night at the Mehnk. It was killing him.

Karina had dragged her feet all the way to the stage, helped along by Savannah and Gabi. She'd started her karaoke debut in a brilliant shade of red, her hands hiding her face. But as the song progressed, she'd moved from head covering to head swinging while Gabi and Savannah shook their hips, dirty dancing on either side of her. Definitely a better show, especially when Karina aimed a line or two at him with a wink.

If it wasn't so damn funny, it would be hotter than hell.

As they bellowed the final verse of "Bust A Move" from their pretty little mouths, the three of them bounced into each other, hands fisted above their heads. Young MC would've been proud.

He loved seeing her like this. Carefree. She hadn't been this laid back in weeks. That damn video. It took away this side of her. The side where she laughed and acted with abandon.

As the parting notes of the song faded, the women stopped their mini mosh-pit and crossed their arms, striking a pose.

The room erupted in applause, Ryan leaving his seat as he clapped and hollered.

The women bowed and made their way through the throngs of well-wishers to the high-top table where the men sat.

Ryan wrapped an arm around Karina. "Nice job. I almost stood up and busted a move."

She put her hands to her cheeks. "Please. That was horrible. I can't dance to save my life, and my singing's worse."

"Yes, but you can bounce and twirl with the best of them."

"Thanks. I think." She picked up her water from the sea of glasses and drank. "I'm heading to the bathroom."

"I have to go, too." Gabi put her own drink on the table.

"Me, too." Savannah grabbed her purse and the three women walked away toward the restroom. He could never understand why women travelled in packs.

Brent turned to Ryan. "Are you going to the kegger on Saturday or are you going to wimp out?"

"I have to take Parker to the club for the final planning session."

"So you're heading back home for the whole weekend again?"

"Yep. But hopefully this will be it." At least that was what he was counting on.

Brent shook his head. "Your old man is going to find another way to suck you into his bullshit. Probably including Parker or the Breckinridge family. Either way, you'll be dealing with her crap."

"Wait." Joe leaned into the table. "You're driving Parker back home?"

"Yeah." Ryan shrugged. What was the big deal?

"Does Karina know?" Joe asked.

"No. Karina's got something against her, and I don't want her to worry."

"I'm not surprised. Parker is the reason—" Whatever Joe was going to say interrupted by the return of the pack.

"Oh my goodness, that bathroom is awful." Gabi sat on Brent's lap. "Does anybody clean that thing?"

"We have to go, ladies. We have business." Brent kissed Gabi and slid her onto her feet. "You ladies don't stay out too late."

"Hey, you're watching wet T-shirts, we're playing skee-ball the rest of the night. We'll be out for a while. It's the championships."

"I think we win," Brent mouthed to Ryan and walked out the door. Ryan wasn't so sure.

Karina threw her arms around Ryan. "Have fun."

"You too." He kissed her lips. "Maybe I should stay here."

"Go." She pushed at his chest.

"I'll text when I'm done. See if you're still playing."

"Okay." She kissed him one last time.

It took every ounce of energy to walk away. But he would make sure he came back here. He was already in the shithouse with the frat for leaving every other weekend for this crap with his father. He couldn't miss the meeting. But that didn't mean he had to stay all night. After a few drinks, they'd never even notice he was gone.

~§~

Ryan walked back into the Mehnk at eleven o'clock. He hadn't quite made it the whole hour at Barnacles. The vast array of talent on the stage there tonight meant he was able to slip out earlier than planned.

He found Karina at the air hockey table with Gabi, just as she'd said she'd be when he texted earlier. Savannah and Joe had left early, so the skee-ball tournament had been cut short.

"Hey, ladies. Who's winning?"

"I am." Karina smiled as Gabi snarled. Karina slapped the disc with the mallet, sinking the puck into the goal. "I won."

"You cheat." Gabi tossed her mallet onto the table.

"Nah… Just motivated."

"Are you ready to go home yet?" Gabi slung her purse onto her shoulder. "I have an accounting test."

"Accounting?" Ryan asked.

Gabi huffed. "My major."

"I thought you'd follow the old man into law."

"No thanks. I'll leave the lawyering to Karina here."

Karina wrapped an arm around Gabi as they walked to Brent's car. "How's Brent getting home if you have his car?" Karina asked.

"Ski's designated driver tonight. He'll make sure they all get home." Ryan laid a hand on Karina's back, leading her to Brent's car.

Ryan pulled up to Dickinson and Gabi threw open the back door. "It's weird. I've never sat in the backseat while the car's been moving. It's a totally different view."

"Really? You've never been in the backseat before?" Ryan's sweet, unsuspecting girlfriend asked. He, unfortunately understood.

Gabi laughed. "I've been back there, just never while the car was moving." She waved to Karina. "And on that happy note, 'bye."

Ryan lifted a hand in goodbye as he tried to shake the X-rated pictures of Gabi and Brent out of his head. He turned to Karina. "So…"

"So, are all the brothers going to be out all night?"

"Most of the night. Did you want to head to the frat for a drink or something? We could watch a movie, play video games."

"Okay."

He slid his hand into hers as he drove the sleepy streets of the campus. Once they were inside Psi Rho, he led her up the stairs to his room. He hoped the barbarians he lived with hadn't left the room a disaster. Last time he tried to bring a woman up here, she'd left in a huff after she sat on a lump of ice cream on one of the chairs. He couldn't blame her.

He held open the door as she walked into the room and looked around.

"Nice. No smelly clothes and empty pizza boxes. I'm impressed."

"Thought I'd be a pig?" He took off his shoes.

"Maybe not you, but put three of you guys together in one room, and you never know." She laughed as she pulled off her gym shoes and sat on the couch.

"Thirsty? We have water, soda, beer."

"No thanks."

He sat next to her on the couch, his arm brushing hers. His body burst to life as she leaned against him. Slowly she rubbed his knee with her hand. He slid his fingers through hers and stopped the painfully slow onslaught of her inquisitive hand. He wanted their first time to be perfect, maybe after the perfect date. Tonight was not it.

He picked up the remote with his other hand. "Want to watch something?"

"Sure." Karina drew her hand from his and ran it down his chest, trailing over the front of his jeans. The jeans that no longer fit as she stroked him. Up and down. Her lips adhered to his. He curved his fingers around her waist and eased her onto her back. His hand explored her body, slipping beneath the sweater she wore.

He deepened the kiss, her tongue sliding along the inside of his lip. Her center pressed against him, the friction sending sparks surging down his body. He wanted her. He wanted all of her.

She lifted his shirt over his head, running her nails up his chest. She was making this incredibly hard to resist. She ran a tongue along the seam of his lips. Why was he resisting again?

For some reason he couldn't remember. She wrapped her hands

around his back and grabbed his ass, pulling him closer. His body was on fire.

"Are you sure about this?" he panted. *Please be sure. Please be sure.*

"Yeah." She groaned as she spun her hips, destroying all thoughts of stopping.

He pulled back and now her hands ran down his chest. Her warm, soft fingers glazed over his stomach, lingering at the snap of his jeans. She felt incredible. His breath labored with every stroke of her hand. She unsnapped his jeans and slid the zipper down. Could she possibly move any slower?

Easing her hand away, he stood and removed his pants, sliding the boxers down with the jeans, the barrier between his body and hers.

He pulled her sweater over her head, and then took care of her front-clasp bra. He slowly bent down and ran his lips down her neck, stopping at the pebbled nipples of her naked breasts. Each nipple growing harder. Harder with every lick and suck of the sensitive skin.

He pulled back and slid her leggings and panties down her legs, her center hot and wet, waiting for him. He spread his hands around her ass, bringing her hips to him. Moans escaped her lips as he lifted her from the couch and carried her to his bed.

He wanted her. This. He placed her gently on the bed, and her legs spread for him. He wanted to fill her. His manhood throbbed at the thought of being inside of her. Of loving her. He was desperate.

She stared at him, her lips swollen and red. Wanting. Waiting. All for him. Her chest rose and fell, her body writhing. So responsive. So hot. She wanted him. He absolutely loved that.

He controlled his breathing as he leaned down between her legs. He ran a tongue along her thigh as it shivered. Chasing the shiver with his lips, gently moving higher until his mouth found her hot, wet center. She tasted so good. Sweet and salty. His tongue circled her, each brush sending a pulse up her quivering body.

"More," she begged.

He had more. He could always give her more. He moved his mouth lower, deeper. Sucking. Licking. Her body bucked with every movement, with every thrust of his tongue.

"Please, Ryan." She pulled his face to hers. "I want you."

He pushed a strand of hair behind her ear as he grabbed a condom from the drawer. He rolled it on and knelt over Karina's hot, amazing body. He lowered his mouth, kissing her frantically, wanting more of her inside of him as her tongue mingled with his.

He pushed inside her, the tight opening enveloping and massaging him. In and out, slowly at first, he felt the pleasure build. Higher and higher. In and out. Her moans rivaled his as they rode the last wave of bliss together.

He leaned on his side, a corny smile pasted to his lips. He could feel the damn thing. He probably should have turned off the lights so she didn't have to see that.

"You are perfect." He ran a hand down the soft, glistening skin of her hip.

"I'm far from it." She smiled, her lips still shiny from his kisses. She might not be perfect, but she was perfect for him.

"I love you." He held his breath. Would she say it back? What if she didn't? *Oh, crap.* What if he ruined everything?

"I love you, too." She snuggled closer and dropped her head to his chest. The soft beat of her heart strummed against his chest.

He could definitely get used to this.

~»ΨP«~

Chapter Twenty-Nine

Karina

KARINA OPENED HER eyes, realizing that the warm, strong arm that covered her chest also pinned her in place. Not that she was complaining.

In fact, she was in heaven. They'd made love once before she fell asleep the first time, followed by middle-of-the-night sexcapades. She was a huge fan of late-night sexcapades. Well, with the right guy.

And Ryan *was* the right guy. After last night, she had no doubts about that whatsoever.

He told her he loved her.

Loved her.

That was huge. Of course, her brother always told her she shouldn't take anything a guy said in bed seriously. Would he still feel the same this morning, or was it just temporary orgasm insanity?

She'd meant it. Holy crap. Her chest constricted, and her heart actually started to ache.

What if he hadn't meant it? Somewhere over the past few months she'd fallen in love with him. It might have been during their months of friendship or the weeks of dating. Either way, she adored him.

Ryan's arm went from warm and comforting to a vise constricting oxygen from entering or leaving her body. She needed to get away.

"What are you thinking?" Ryan moved his arm and ran a hand down the side of her face. "I can practically hear the thoughts running through your head."

"Nothing." It was way too soon in their relationship to share her neuroses. This was the time when everyone pretended they were perfect. No burping, farting or secret *Jersey Shore* addiction revealed. Although, she'd already put her big porn reveal out there and he'd handled it pretty well.

"Nothing?" Ryan nuzzled her ear. "Are you sure?"

"I was trying to figure out how to get up without waking you." That wasn't a complete lie.

"Why would you want to do that?"

"Get up, or not wake you?" Karina wrapped her hand around his arm and pulled him close. Their lips touched, gently.

"Both. We seem to have a lot of fun right here with both of us awake."

A voice she recognized as Danny's yelled, "Shut the hell up," from the other side of the room. Karina couldn't see him with Ryan's body blocking her view.

Ryan ignored Danny and moved in to kiss her lips. "Hungry?" he whispered.

"Sure."

He rolled off the bed and went into the bathroom, coming out with a robe. He helped her put it on so she wouldn't give his roommates a view of her good parts. Not that it mattered; they were passed out and snoring.

She picked her clothes up off the floor and walked into the bathroom. The dirty, grimy bathroom. Not that she was complaining. She turned on the faucet. Water was water and it would get her clean. Well, cleanish.

She looked in the mirror. Her hair was surprisingly flat after their impure playdate. She ran her fingers through her hair, but there wasn't much she could do after that. Opening a cabinet in the corner, she saw a roommate's name on each shelf. She pulled deodorant from Ryan's shelf and used the spray. A *Jersey Shore* shower.

She threw on her clothes from the night before and walked out into the bedroom. The smell of beer and sweat tickled her nose as the roommates snorted their way through sleep.

"How can you sleep through this every night?" she whispered to Ryan, who'd put on a pair of jeans and a T-shirt. He led her out of the bedroom and down the stairs to the kitchen.

"They only snore when they drink." He opened the metal door and held it as she stepped into the large kitchen.

"So, what is that, every night?" Karina looked around with interest— she'd never been in here before. Two stoves on one wall, a giant refrigerator, a large sink surrounded by lots of counter space, tiled walls. And surprisingly clean.

"Yeah." He laughed. "They do drink pretty much every night. Would you like an omelet?" He opened one fridge and pulled out a carton of eggs.

"You're going to cook?"

"I can cook two things. Omelets and meatloaf. I don't have the stuff I need for meatloaf, and it's a little early for a big slab of beef. So I'm thinking omelet." He opened a door next to the refrigerators and walked into what she saw was a pantry. "Or I have cereal." He shook a box of Fruit Loops. "Although I'm not sure how long these have been sitting here."

"An omelet is perfect."

He got the skillet from a cabinet and went back to the fridge. "Cheese?"

"Sure."

Karina watched him whisk and pour, flip and stir. He slid the eggy concoction on a plate and pushed it toward her. Her stomach growled as the scents of egg and cheddar spiraled to her nose. Ryan reached into one of the multitude of drawers lining the sink and handed her a fork.

She dug into her breakfast. "This is huge. I'll never be able to eat this all." That didn't mean she wasn't going to try.

"I'll help." He got a fork of his own and started on the other side of the mound.

"Mmmm, this is fantastic," Karina said after a few mouthfuls.

"Thanks. I have a few hidden talents."

Karina smiled. She'd been introduced to some of those hidden talents last night... Her body ached with every move, but she didn't care. Her mind kept playing a highlight reel of the night before. Totally worth every tug and pull on her overworked muscles.

"When's your first class?" he asked as he took another bite.

"Nine. You?"

"Same."

They finished their breakfast and Ryan took the empty plate to the sink. Karina found a towel hanging on the stove and dried everything after Ryan soaped and rinsed.

"Let's go upstairs and get your coat. I should get you home so you can change." He dried his hands on the towel in her hands.

"Not a bad idea." She stared at her two-day-old outfit. It was bad enough she was doing the walk of shame. She didn't need to live that shame all day long.

They walked out into the cool fall morning. The house was quiet. The street was quiet. She'd never seen the building in the light of day. It was a nice neighborhood. To the right were large homes with Greek letters that hung over the front doors. To the left were the neighborhood homes she'd walked by over and over again.

She followed him to his car and he opened the door. "What are you doing this weekend? Want to go see a movie…one made in this century?"

"I can't this weekend. With Thanksgiving next week, I have some family stuff to deal with."

"Okay. Next weekend?" Her stomach dropped. Not good. She didn't expect an invitation to family stuff, it was way too early for that, but she wouldn't see him while on Thanksgiving vacation. There were only a few days till they left. Déjà vu was starting to settle in her bones.

"Sorry. Thanksgiving stuff."

Of course. Disappointment slithered down her spine. She had to admit, the omelet was a nice touch. Made her feel warm and fuzzy, like he actually cared. Maybe this was how he treated all the unsuspecting females. Tell them he loved them and then walk away. Maybe she'd get another break-up email or text or fucking Facebook post.

So many inappropriate ways to get dumped, so many men willing to do it.

"Well, then I'll see you when we get back to school." She attempted a smile. "You know, I'm sure you have to get ready for class. You don't have to drive me to the dorm."

She turned and headed down the sidewalk. She needed to walk off the nervous energy—the anger. At him. At herself. Mostly at herself. What was the saying? Fool me once, shame on you, fool me twice, shame on me. She'd been fooled over and over again. The shame was all on her.

"Karina. I don't have to come back here. I've changed clothes. Let me give you a ride." He reached out and held her arm, his fingers sliding under the sleeve of her jacket. The warmth from each finger was a dagger in her heart.

"It's okay." She kept her eyes down. She couldn't look into his face.

"Don't go." He lifted her chin until her eyes met his. "I don't want last night to end. I want to keep it going as long as possible."

"It had to end eventually." The words stung the back of her eyes. It always ended. Although, just once in her college career, she'd like it to last longer than a day.

"Can I see you tonight?" He ran his thumb along her jaw. "We can see a movie, dinner…whatever you want."

Confusion ping-ponged in her mind. He wanted to see her again. He wanted to go out again.

"I thought…" She shook her head and smiled. No need to think about what she thought. "Tonight would be great."

He pressed his lips to hers. "Let's get you home."

~»ΨP«~

Chapter Thirty

Ryan

RYAN LIFTED A box of party favors from the trunk of his car. Somehow, not only did he have to show up for the Member party on the Saturday after Thanksgiving, but he also got sucked into helping. He was such a sap.

It did give him time to think, though. He hadn't laughed—truly laughed—since he left the campus for Thanksgiving break. Before that, he spent a few perfect days with Karina doing normal, easy stuff. Going to see a movie, hanging at her dorm and studying. And laughing. A lot.

One week away from Karina. One week of his father's bullshit. One thing had gotten him through this last week—knowing that after this weekend, he'd be back on campus and in Karina's arms. He'd called her, and they'd texted, but it wasn't the same as having her here, with him.

When the country club had a party, they went all out. Which meant the members had to go all out as well. Anything less than a suit and tie was not acceptable. So after he spent a couple hours helping with all the last-minute details, he had to go shower and get dressed in his monkey-suit.

When he returned to the ballroom, dim lights glimmered over the white-covered tables. Parker and her crew had done a great job. She had a gift for throwing a party.

Once the members started arriving, including his and Parker's parents, Ryan strolled around talking to the golf club members and a few old friends. It wasn't a bad night, but he wanted it to be over.

He found his way to the appetizer table and took a mini-quiche. He loved these things. Not that he'd admit that to anyone out loud. They'd take away his man card for that one.

Parker slid up and linked her arm through his. "You looked bored. Could you at least pretend to have fun?" she snapped.

"I'll start pretending to have fun when you start pretending not to be a bitch. Deal?"

"You are incredibly whiny today. Is it that time of the month?"

"What do you want, Park?" He grabbed another mini-quiche. His prize for putting up with Parker nipping at him.

"Your parents wanted me to come get you." She tried to pull him across the room. "If you miss her so much, why didn't you invite her to the party? She lives around here, doesn't she?"

Ryan knew exactly who Parker was referring to. Karina. He should have invited her. He gave Parker a sideways look. "Like I could do that with you telling everyone she was the girl in the video." He pulled his arm away.

"Embarrassed?"

"Shut up."

"I wouldn't have said anything, Ryan. I owe her."

"For what?"

"No reason. I have to get you to your parents. Are you going to be difficult?" She relinked their arms. He gave up the fight and let her tow him over to his parents. He was never going to win. Ryan was surprised he hadn't seen Gabi and her parents. She would have made the evening a little more interesting.

As they walked up to his parents, his mother reached out for him. "Ryan," she said as she grabbed his hand, "was so great through the last round of testing. I wanted you to be here when I tell everyone, the doctor called while we were driving over. My tests are clear."

Ryan's father wrapped his arm around his wife, a smile on his lips. No matter how questionable the man's parenting skills might have been, he did seem to love his wife.

"Karol, that is great." Parker's mom jumped up and down.

"Paula, please." Mr. Breckenridge placed a hand on his wife's shoulder. "You're making a scene."

"Hi, Ryan."

Karina. Did just thinking about her make her appear? If so, she should have appeared long before this. He was smiling when he turned to his parents. His mom stared at Karina. Did his mom recognize her? He wanted to see Karina, wanted her to be here. But...

"Karina, Gabi. What are you doing here?" Parker saved him from his frozen tongue.

"I'm a member. It's a member party." Gabi sighed as she rolled her eyes.

"I'm glad you came." Ryan pulled his arm away from Parker. "Mom, Dad, you know Gabi, and this is Karina, a friend from school."

Karina's smile dropped, only for a second. He never should have let Parker put her arm through his. He'd hate to see her with some moron hanging off her arm. She had every right to be pissed.

"It's so wonderful to meet Ryan's friends." His mother shook Karina's hand.

"Aren't you the one from that video?" Parker's mom smiled as she moved in closer. "You are. You're the girl from the Homecoming video."

Red travelled up Karina's neck, but she didn't back down. She looked Paula straight in the eye. "Yes. It was a mistake from my youth."

"In your youth?" Paula's sputtered laugh was too loud. "How long ago was that video taken, dear?"

"Two years ago, but I learned my lesson." Karina didn't back down. Her chin was held high.

"And what was that, dear?"

Karina looked at Ryan. "Never trust a man."

Ryan stared at her. He didn't know how to fix this, but he hated the anger and hurt in her eyes. She had to know that nothing was going on between Parker and him—didn't she?

"That's a terrible lesson to have to learn." His mom rested a hand on Karina's. "There are some good men out there."

"I'm sure there are, Mrs. Kent. I just have yet to find one." Karina pasted a smile on her face.

"My son is a good man," his mom said. Gotta love Mom.

"Of course, he could probably introduce you to some of his friends," Parker's mom added.

"No, thanks." Karina stepped back. "Please, excuse me."

He watched her walk away, feeling like he missed something. He didn't miss the glare Gabi sent his way before she followed her friend.

"Excuse me." He nodded to his parents.

~»ΨΡ«~

Chapter Thirty-One

Karina

KARINA STALKED THROUGH the country club, past the opulence she had admired when she first walked through the doors, past the ice sculpture that had impressed her so much. The smell of smoked salmon-wrapped caviar and fried shrimp followed her, but even the heavenly smell of overpriced food couldn't take away the hurt in her chest.

She didn't stop till she was outside. Fresh air assaulted her pounding chest. *Thump.* Her heartbeat slammed into her temples. *Thump.* Her eyes forced back the tears that wanted to fall. *Thump.*

...this is Karina, a friend from school.

Friend. *Friend?* Jackass. Jerk.

She leaned against the banister on the porch and let the evening air cool her overheated face. In a moment she'd be too cold, but right now it felt lovely. She closed her eyes, the dull rumble of people enjoying the party invading her quiet moment.

Her moment to close the gaping hole that Ryan left behind.

"Kar?" Gabi sounded like she was right behind her. "Are you all right?"

"No." She wouldn't turn around. She couldn't look at Gabi. She wanted to cry. Needed to cry. But couldn't do it here. Not now. Not in front of Gabi's parents, Ryan's parents, Parker, and all the other people that wouldn't understand. And not in front of Ryan. He didn't deserve her tears.

"Karina. Are you okay?" Ryan. Just what she didn't need.

"Back off, Ryan," Gabi said. "Give her some space."

"Gabi..."

"Ryan, go away," Karina heard herself beg. Dammit. She did not want to beg for anything from this man ever again.

"Karina." He took her by the shoulders and turned her toward him, "I'm not with Parker. She just had her arm through mine for a minute."

"Really? Really?" Anger stirred in her gut. Was he really so dense he thought she was mad about another woman's arm being near him? Clueless. Just fucking clueless.

"There is and never will be anything between us..." He ran his hand down her arm in a soothing manner. However, it wasn't soothing anyone—definitely not her.

She twitched her arm out of reach. "Ryan. Stop. I don't care. Why would I care what you do? I'm just a friend. Right?" She could tell when realization knocked him upside his slow head. How she would have liked to have been the one that did the knocking. "Right, Ryan? I'm your friend. At least that's what you told your parents and all the other people standing around. I generally don't fuck my friends, but I guess that's where we're different. You had no problem fucking me— in more ways than one."

"Karina, let's go." Gabi held up her car keys. They'd driven here separately from Gabi's parents, thank goodness. Although the original reason was so that they could stay out with Ryan. Dumb plan.

"Yeah. I'm done here." Karina started toward the stairs.

"Karina, please." Ryan held out his hand. "Give me a chance to explain—"

"Explain what? Why you said we're just friends? Please—explain that."

Silence surrounded them as Ryan stared at her. Guilt seemed to swim in his eyes. Well, at least he wasn't a complete monster. Just a jerk.

"I thought so. The stripper who poses naked in online videos isn't good enough for the Kent family. I get it." She shook her head and turned toward Gabi. "I'm ready."

They walked down the porch stairs and headed around the building. Gabi had the good sense to keep her away from the happy partiers. They walked through the parking lot, past all the other high-priced cars to Gabi's father's Beemer.

"Karina. Gabi."

Oh great. The worst of the happy partiers.

Karina turned around, her fist balled at her side.. "Here to gloat?" Her blood boiled. She refused to let Parker know she'd won, but she must've figured it out. Why else would she be following them?

"No."

"What do you want?" Karina just wanted to hit her once. Just once.

"I'm sorry."

"You're *sorry*?" Karina's fist flew before she even knew what was happening. The crunch of knuckles on Parker's shoulder hurt, but it also felt so damn good. She raised her fist again. This time she was getting that pretty little face.

"Stop." Parker lifted her hands in surrender, blocking that face. "I deserved that, but please stop."

Well, shit. She couldn't exactly keep hitting a person who knew they deserved it and wasn't willing to fight back. Karina folded her arms and glared. "Where'd you get it?"

"I dated a guy who went to Redeemer High School. We were talking and your name came up. He had a copy." She shrugged. Winced. Good.

"I just wanted to say I'm sorry. I really am. I never meant for things to get so out of hand and I deleted it. Just so you know, I deleted my copy and my friend's copy. He'll be pretty pissed when he finds out." She laughed, a stilted, forced chuckle.

Karina didn't know what to say, so she turned to Gabi. Gabi always knew what to say. However, Gabi had the same confused expression that Karina no doubt had written on her face. Now it was up to Karina to find a word. "Why?"

"You didn't tell Ryan I was the one who put the video in the slideshow, did you?" Parker asked.

Karina blinked. "No. Ryan told me how much his mother relied on you. With her getting better, I didn't want to put any stress on her. She shouldn't suffer for your nastiness."

"Thank you," Parker said, and amazingly, Karina actually believed her. Parker offered Karina a strained smile before turning to narrow her eyes at Gabi. "Don't get too excited, you're still a bitch." The three of them stared at each other until Parker said, "Can I talk to Karina, alone?"

Karina nodded at Gabi, who raised her eyebrows. "I'll go get our coats." Gabi headed back toward the building. Thank goodness she remembered them.

"I'm so sorry about everything I did," Parker said, voice low. "It had nothing to do with you. Or Ryan, not really. I've always wanted to be a part of the Kent family and he was the only way—"

"But from what I hear, they love you," Karina said.

"They do, but I'm not family. You—you don't know what it's like to be alone all the time." Parker ran her hands over her bare arms, probably to fight off the cold. Karina's teeth were on the verge of chattering, too. Without the flow of adrenaline to keep her warm, November could be pretty frickin' cold. Where the hell was Gabi?

"You have your mom and dad."

"Yeah, I guess." Parker attempted a smile.

"I have my own family issues. I get it." Karina watched as Gabi left the building carrying Karina's winter coat. "I should go."

"Yeah." Parker took a step back. "It's just, the Kents have always been there for me." She shook her head and pasted a smile on her gorgeous face. "Anyway, thanks again for not trying to take that away." They stared at each other until Parker took another step back. "You should go before Gabi's head starts spinning around while she vomits pea soup. I'll see you at school."

Karina walked over to a staring Gabi, and stood next to one of her best friends and watched Parker's retreating figure and then the still door. Gabi handed Karina her jacket, but she still hadn't put it on. The cold was shocking, but not nearly as shocking as that little spectacle.

Gabi shook her head like she was coming out of a trance. "What. Was. That."

"Who knows—but let's get out of here before someone else finds us." Karina slid her arms in the coat as she walked toward Gabi's car.

"Do you want to stay at my house tonight?" Gabi asked once they were on their way.

"I'd rather go home." Karina stared out the window as they flew down the suburban streets. "I just need some time alone."

"No problem." Gabi merged onto the freeway to get to Karina's house.

As the miles separated Karina from Ryan, home sounded better and better.

Chapter Thirty-Two

Ryan

RYAN STORMED BACK inside the country club, opening the French door with a little bit too much force. Eyes turned his way. Ryan anchored a smile on his face and walked over to the line of people at the bar.

How could two people who had so much chemistry screw things up so many times?

The stripper who poses naked in online videos isn't good enough for the Kent family. What a line of bullshit. That's not what he meant when he called her a friend. He just wasn't ready to introduce Karina to his mom. That's all. He wanted to wait for the whole video thing to blow over. He wanted to make sure the two most important people in his life met on the best of terms. He didn't want them to be at odds right off, so he tried to protect Karina from a bad first impression. Hell, maybe he was protecting his mom from the bad first impression. Either way, he didn't want Karina to be known as the "girl in the video".

"Miller, bottle."

"You old enough to drink, son?" the bartender asked.

Of course not, dammit. "Fine, a bottle of Coke."

The bartender grabbed a glass and was starting to pour the contents of the glass bottle into the vessel. "Don't bother putting it in a glass. I'll take the bottle." Ryan grabbed the open bottle and downed a gulp. Tonight would have been a good night to get drunk. He walked back to the porch, bumping into Parker. "Sorry."

"Why are you saying sorry to me?" Parker moved to one side. "You didn't screw me over."

"What?"

"It's Karina you owe the apology to, darling."

"It's none of your business, Park."

"No, but I'm your friend and you're messing everything up."

"What do you care?" He tilted back the bottle. "I thought you hated her. Why do you care what I do?"

"You're such a trainwreck. You're...self-destructive."

"Self-destructive? None of this shit was my fault."

"Really? Every time. Every time you get close to having something real with a girl, you sabotage it. Every time."

He took another pull from his soda. Why, oh why couldn't it be a beer? She was so full of shit. "This was a big mess, and I had nothing to do with it."

"So, you didn't call the girl you're sleeping with *just a friend* in front of your parents. That didn't just happen."

Dammit. He hated when she was right. Not that he'd admit it to her. Not that he'd admit anything to her. To anyone. He was so done. He was done with the pretense, the bullshit, all of it.

The stripper who poses naked in online videos isn't good enough for the Kent family.

Shit. Maybe she was right. Not that he thought that. But dear old Dad? He'd never see her as good enough. Hell, Ryan wasn't good enough and he was born with the Kent name. And didn't that just suck. He was so tired. Tired of trying. Tired of failing.

"I'm done." Ryan went out the side door to the little patio overlooking the valet parking area. He rested his foot on the marble ledge lining the patio. Breathe. Just breathe. The air was cool, nipping at his warm face. Anger—nature's heater.

Cars were crammed in the spaces around the building, but the lot was silent except for crickets chirping over the faint sound of the valets talking shit at their station.

"Ryan." His father's voice broke through the semi-silence.

"Dad." Ryan removed his foot from the ledge but didn't turn around. Didn't need to. He could hear the disappointment in his father's voice. No need to verify.

His father walked up and stood next to him. He sipped his glass of cognac as he looked out over the lot. Not saying a word. Just watching. Watching what—who knew? Not a damn thing was happening. All the partygoers were still inside, dancing and laughing. They'd probably stay that way for the better part of the night.

"Are you going to tell me what that was?" his father said finally.

"What, what was?"

"That scene with that...*girl*."

Ryan's hand clenched. He had a feeling that his dad wanted to use another word, and if he did...fuck. Ryan didn't care if the old man was his father. He was going down.

"Nothing that concerns you." Ryan tried to keep his voice and heart rate even. No need to show the controlling bastard he was getting to his son.

"I beg to differ. That scene concerns me. Are you sleeping with her?"

Ryan lifted the Coke to his mouth as he shot a glare at his dad. *None of your business*. He threw back a little more soda.

"I'll take that as a yes." The old man sighed and swished the cognac around the glass. "It's normal to want to—sample the different woman out there, but that experimentation needs to be separate from your future. This club—and Parker—is your future. Don't forget that."

Forget it? He'd love to forget it. This future was not his future. "I will never be with Parker."

"Think, Ryan. You'll need a strong woman who can handle the social requirements and expectations when you take over the company. Look how well Parker did on this party. Look at how she handles herself. Look at her family. And it's safe to say she's nice to look at."

"Dad." Ryan's knuckles whitened as he held onto the bottle for dear life.

"She'll make you a good wife. That girl from that video is a phase."

"She's not a phase." Ryan's anger wrapped around his temples, squeezing like it was a live thing.

"You don't build a life with trash. And that's what she is. Trash. A distraction like that architecture garbage." His father finished his drink and gave Ryan a withering look. "Dammit Ryan, it's time to take your future seriously."

Trash. Garbage. Distraction. Fuck it. "You're right. I need to take my future—*my* future—seriously." Ryan set the half empty soda bottle on the marble with a sharp click and took a step closer to his father. "The future I choose includes Karina, and it includes architecture. I'm switching my major."

"Like hell you are." The old man threw his glass, the sudden crack startling the crickets and the valets into silence. Ryan reminded himself to breathe.

"If you change your major," his father said in a flat tone that was worse than if he yelled, "find another way to pay for school. Because I'm not paying for you to mess around. You want to take the hard way through life? Go ahead, but I won't be a part of it."

"Fine. I don't want your money. I can do it all on my own." Ryan turned to walk away. This conversation was going nowhere.

"How would you know? You've never had to do anything on your own."

"Well, whose fault is that?" Ryan spun on his father. Whose fault was that? He had to share some of that blame. "Maybe you're right. Maybe I don't know if I can make it on my own, but I'm almost twenty years old. It's about time I found out."

"Stupid. You're doing this over some stupid girl."

"This has nothing to do with her. Don't you see? This is about me and my future. And I'm done doing things your way. I'm doing them mine. And if that includes Karina, so be it. But if you want to be in my life, you will never call her 'that girl from the video' or 'trash' again."

Ryan walked away from his father, pulling his keys out of his pocket. His footsteps felt lighter. His shoulders looser. He was doing things his way. And for the first time in a very long time, he felt a smile creep onto his lips. A smile for his future. A smile for himself. Because he owned whatever came next.

And what he wanted next was Karina. Now he just had to figure out how to make that happen.

~»ΨP«~

Chapter Thirty-Three

Karina

THE NEXT DAY, Karina woke up in Oak Park to an empty house. Her brother and sister had already started their trek back to their respective colleges, and her parents were probably at church and brunch. That was usual way they'd spent their Sunday mornings.

Usually however, her mother would have woken her up to visit Jesus, but apparently she'd had a heart and let her daughter sleep. It might have been the tissue shrine erected next to Karina's bed. The large pile had grown and grown as she'd cried herself to sleep last night.

Ryan had hurt her, disavowed her. Their relationship. Hell, if they even had one. Maybe the relationship was just in her head. It didn't feel like it was one-sided, but who knew. It didn't feel like a relationship she had to lie to her parents about, either.

Maybe that's where they were different. She always thought a few differences were good in a relationship. Maybe she was wrong.

She shuffled down the stairs and opened the fridge. A full selection of food lined the glass shelves, yet not one thing looked good. Her eyes watered as she thought about last night. Was she being too hard on Ryan? He seemed so upset after everything that happened.

Too hard? No, she wasn't. She wasn't too hard on him, she'd been too hard on herself for too long. Maybe the video hadn't been the smartest move on her part, but in all honesty it could have been a whole lot worse.

The weird thing was that video didn't bother her anymore. She was more angry that she made the video because some guy told her he wanted someone more exciting— she'd actually tried to change herself for a guy. What the hell was she thinking?

And now... now the guy she loved wanted her to change something she did in her past. She somehow wasn't good enough. Again.

She wasn't changing herself. Not anymore. She was not changing for anyone. Ever.

"Hello? Anybody home?" her father bellowed from the front door.

Definitely not the person she wanted to see today, or any day for that matter. Another man who couldn't accept her for what she was. Another man disappointed in her. She was getting that from all sides these days.

"Karina. I'm looking for Mike. Are you home alone?"

"Yeah. I'm allowed to stay home all by myself now," she said before her filter had a chance to shut them down.

"Yes, I suppose you are old enough." He sat down at the table. Nerves zinged as she watched him play with the Lazy Susan in the center of the table. He hadn't sat down to talk to her for over a year. Since the incident.

She missed him. Missed having her daddy in her life. Missed the conversations. Missed having him to rely on. How many times would she have liked to ask his opinion? She would have loved to get his suggestions on her classes or her career choice. He'd built a successful career and law practice. She would have benefited from his experience. But she couldn't talk to him about any of that. She couldn't talk to him about anything. Not when…

"Can I ask you something, Dad?"

"Of course." He rubbed his palms on his gray golf pants. He must've had another "playdate" with Mike, the child he still loved.

"Do you love me?" Tears pricked her eyes.

"That's a stupid question. Of course I do." He ran his hands through his dark blond hair. The hair that matched hers.

"Then, do you like me?" A tear slipped down her cheek as she looked into the hazel eyes. The eyes that matched hers. She was so afraid of the answer, but she needed to know. She couldn't go on with him like this. She couldn't hurt every time she saw him. She couldn't handle being shunned. Something had to change.

"Karina, what's with these questions? Of course I like you."

"Then why can't you look at me anymore? Why don't you come to visit me? See me when I'm home. Talk to me."

"I just…"

"…can't stand to be around your slutty daughter." It always came back to that.

"No." He jumped up, fire blazing in his eyes. "I will not let you talk like that about yourself."

"Then why?" She seemed to like that question lately. Of course, she should be careful— the last time she asked that, she didn't get the answer she wanted.

"Karina." He sat back in the chair and rested a hand on hers. "You have always been my little girl. And then I saw that video, and—God. You were so grown up. *Are* so grown up. It took every ounce of strength I had not to beat the crap out of that little creep for what he did to you."

He breathed in deep, his eyes haunted. Every word seemed to break him down. "I had so much trouble knowing I failed you. I'm your father.

It's my job to protect you from creeps like Craig, and I didn't. One day your little girl in pigtails turns into an adult, and you find you can't control them and you can't protect them and you wonder how you can possibly go on." He squeezed her hand as a tear glistened in his eye. "You are a beautiful woman and you mean so much to me. It just took me by surprise. One day I'm pushing you on a swing, and the next you're with boys doing God-knows-what."

"Kathy's been dating since she was twelve," Karina argued.

"She was my daughter, but she was a mommy's girl, she was never my little girl. Not like you. You were my little girl, and all I saw was me losing you. I couldn't handle it."

"You didn't lose me, Dad. I'm right here."

"I know and I wasn't there for you. I'm sorry."

"It was just a video…"

"It's not about the video. It was the way you handled yourself. You didn't complain, you didn't blame anyone for your mistakes. You would have taken the punishment they dealt you, and let Craig get off free and clear. You handled a bad situation better than most adults, and then I realized…you didn't need me anymore. So, I fought to make sure Craig would pay for his part. At the very least, you deserved that."

"I loved that you fought for me. I needed that. I needed you. I always have. I always will." Karina felt tears slide down her face.

"I'm so sorry." Her father's eyes sparkled with moisture.

"I'm sorry, too."

"Come here, Kare Bear."

She moved into his arms and hung on. "You haven't called me that in a long time."

"Are you too old to be my Kare Bear? I can stop." He sounded sad as he asked the question.

"Please don't." She sniffled on his shoulder. Hopefully, he didn't need this shirt for anything, because it was going to be covered in tears.

"Thank God." He squeezed. "You will always be my Kare Bear. I love you."

"I love you too, Dad." Karina sat on her dad's lap, listening to his breathing. Her head rested on his chest, rising and falling with each inhale and exhale.

"What's on your mind Kare Bear?"

"I'm not sure you want to hear about it."

"Let me guess. A boy."

"A stupid boy." She nodded her head for emphasis.

"If he doesn't see what an incredible person you are and worship at your feet, he is stupid."

"You have to say that, you're my dad." Karina snuggled closer. He was her dad. She finally had him back. And he could exaggerate about her being an incredible person or the most wonderful person on the planet. It didn't matter if he was biased. It still felt amazing.

"Legally, I'm required to feed and clothe you, but the Department of Children and Family Services doesn't require me to pump up your self-esteem with lies."

"But you are a lawyer. Aren't lies part of the job?" She always could joke about things with her dad. Even his job wasn't off limits

"Speaking of which, I hear from Mike you're going pre-law."

"I am. I watched someone close to me fight for those who couldn't do it on their own and I thought, 'I should do that'."

"I'm so proud of you."

Karina's chest warmed at her dad's words. Her dad. For so long she'd called him Father, like he was Darth Vader— cold and distant, a beacon for the dark side. Now he was her dad again. At least one part of her life was getting back on track.

~»ΨP«~

Chapter Thirty-Four

Ryan

RYAN SAT IN English, staring at his phone. Not the best use of time when he had finals next week. But he couldn't get his mind off of Karina. No incoming texts. No incoming calls. She wasn't taking his calls. He wasn't sure he blamed her, but that didn't mean he was going to stop trying.

He missed her. He still loved her. And the fact that he hurt her was killing him. After she left the party, he followed. He drove to her house and thought about knocking on the door. But that haunted look in her eyes—the pain he caused with one stupid omission— Why the hell hadn't he called her his girlfriend? What was wrong with him?

He hadn't been embarrassed or thought less of her because of that damn video. He just didn't want his mom and dad to look at her differently. No—he didn't care what his dad thought. It was his mom. He wanted his mom to like her as much as he did.

When he eventually settled down, he wanted a woman his mom approved of or at least liked. She was the reason he turned out semi-sane. She was the foundation of normalcy for his life. And she was all he had. His sisters were fine, but they never quite understood him.

Settled down. Crap. He had thought he would settle down with Karina. Some day. It had actually crossed his mind. He had no idea if that would ever happen now.

His teacher finished rambling and mercifully let them leave the class early. He walked next door to Karina's psychology class. He'd driven her there a few times and pretty much had her schedule down. He would talk to her today, even if he had to wait outside every single class or camp out at her dorm.

Stalkerish? Yes. Was he desperate enough to try it? Unfortunately, yes.

Her psych class emptied into the hall, and he watched her walk toward him. Her hair was held back in a ponytail, showing the soft curve of her neck. She was beautiful. And he'd had her. He hoped he hadn't lost her.

She looked up. He could tell when she saw him, because she stopped moving and stared. Her lips turned up into a sad excuse for a smile. "Hi, Ryan."

This was not good. "Hi." He tried not to fidget. "I'm so sorry about Saturday."

"Thanks." She moved her books from one arm to the other. "I'm glad you're here. We should talk."

"Yeah." He followed her outside, dread wreaking havoc on his stomach. The frosty December air nipped at his soul as she walked to a secluded area and sat on a bench. She put down her books and knotted her fingers in her lap.

The cacophony of silence was clawing at his nerves. He needed her to talk. He needed her to forgive him. He needed... Wasn't that what got him into this situation, worrying about what he needed?

What about what she needed? He would give her anything. She just had to ask. She just had to talk to him. He watched her wipe her eyes. Did he somehow make her cry again?

Crap.

He couldn't take the quiet any longer. "I missed you." He reached for her hand. His heart broke as she pulled away.

"I don't think we should see each other anymore." She turned glassy eyes to him.

"I'm sorry, Karina. I was so nervous that you were meeting my family and I was thoughtless..."

"Maybe, but you shouldn't have to work so hard when you love someone."

"I do love you. We can work this out." He was desperate. "Take some time to think about it? We can talk after German tomorrow."

"I don't think we should date or be friends." She picked up her books.

"What about tutoring?"

"I think I can handle it, and if I can't, I'll hire someone."

"But why hire someone when I'm willing to do it? I'll help you. We don't have to date, just don't shut me out." He was begging. He knew it, but he couldn't just say goodbye. It would destroy him. "Please don't do this." His breath lodged in his lungs.

"It's already done."

"I'm sorry."

"I know. Me, too." She gathered her books to her chest and stood up.

"Karina, I love you."

"Good-bye, Ryan." She didn't turn around. She didn't stop. She walked away and she was gone. Gone from his life.

He bent over and grabbed his head. A headache pounded his skull, leaving no room for coherent thought. Maybe if he just kept the headache, he wouldn't have to deal with the disaster he created. The friend he lost.

What the fuck did he do?

Chapter Thirty-Five

Karina

KARINA SAT ON her bed, running her fingers over the pillow in her lap. "I'm sorry I've been so distracted lately. So what exactly happened over Thanksgiving break?"

Savannah picked up a picture from the shelf above her bed. "I saw Leland, and goodness, he looked incredible. I ran into his arms and kissed him."

"Sounds romantic."

"Not really. There was nothing there. No spark. Nothing. I hung out with him for a day or two, we talked and kissed, but all I could think about was Joe. So we broke up. He was upset, but it wasn't fair to pretend we were heading anywhere else but over." She put the frame in her hand back on the shelf, inching it next to another remaining frame. "I'm a horrible person, aren't I?"

"Not at all. You haven't seen him in months, and things weren't that great before you left. It would be cruel to give him hope and keep things going the way they were."

"I guess. I don't want to talk about me anymore. Let's talk about you and Ryan."

"Let's not. I lost a relationship that was few weeks old. You and Leland were together forever." Karina pulled at the blanket on her bed.

"The forever word…not helping." Savannah picked up another family photo and peered at it. "I didn't realize how many of my pictures have Leland in them." She put that frame into the trunk. Her multitude of pictures was becoming a handful. "So, are you completely done with Ryan?"

"Yes. No." Karina had no idea.

"You're still in love with him."

"Who says I was in love with him?"

"Oh honey, you need to learn to lie better. You have been head over heels for that man all semester. I was so glad you two finally got together."

"Yeah, that worked out well."

"You're miserable. You still love him, don't you?" Savannah sat next to her and took her hand.

"Fine. Yeah. But it doesn't matter. He's embarrassed of me. He introduced me to his parents as a friend. A friend."

"I'm sure he just made a mistake. You know, a heat of the moment type thing."

"You're defending him?" Traitor.

"Yes. You two are good together."

"Can we talk about something else?" Karina refused to cry. She'd never get rid of her roommate if she was crying. And she wanted

Savannah to go out and take Gabi with her. They deserved to have a fun night out, and she deserved to have a cleansing wallow in.

"You should come out with us. Last celebration before the hell of finals."

"No, thanks. Not ready to celebrate."

"See, that is why we should be talking about your love life. I'm fine. I think Leland and I were over a long time ago. It was just convenient. Expected."

"How much of it was that it pissed your dad off?" Karina giggled.

Savannah sniffed. "A lot. But that's not a good reason to try to build a life together."

"How's Joe?"

"Adorable. We're going to that nasty frat, and then we're going back to his place."

"Really? Decided to finally give it up to the boy." Karina laughed at the look on Savannah's face.

"What are you talking about?"

Karina shook her head. "Seriously? I know you haven't slept with that poor boy yet. Hell, you haven't slept with anyone."

"How did you know that?"

"Savannah, *honey*, speaking of learning to lie better.? You never changed your sheets after any of those guys left, and there were no condoms in the trash. You're a neat freak, so I could see the no condom if you tossed them elsewhere, but Gabi rests a foot on your bed and the first thing you do is wash your sheets. And you know Gabi. I figured if you slept with some guy, the least you'd do is wash the sheets."

"Why didn't you say anything to me that you knew?" Savannah closed the trunk and pushed it under her desk.

"I figured you'd tell me eventually."

Now that she was done packing Leland away, Savannah got dressed for her date. Karina had trouble lifting her head these days, and Savannah was like a toddler on pure sugar, energized by her new freedom.

Gabi knocked on the door. "Hey, ladies. Ready for a night of drinking and dancing?"

Why aren't you dressed?" Gabi glared at Karina.

"I'm not going. I am in no mood to party." Karina leaned back against her bed. She didn't mean to be the place where fun went to die, she just wanted to sit alone with her depression and nurse it with ice cream and chocolate. And probably another round of tears. She was more like where fun went to curl up and take its last breath.

"Come on," Gabi coaxed. "You can't sit here and pout."

"I can and I will."

"Fine, but I'm not putting up with this much longer." Gabi waved a finger at Karina. "You can't continue to leave me alone with her. After finals? We're going out."

"Hush, Gabi." Savannah grabbed her purse and followed Gabi out the door.

"One last chance," Gabi yelled down the hall.

"Have fun." Karina laughed as she looked around the room. She loved her friends, but could not wait to start her own party. "A pity party."

Ugh. Her jokes were bad when she was battling a broken heart.

She grabbed her shower basket and walked the barren halls of the dorm. How relaxing. It was so nice to be alone. Once the water was running in the shower, she stepped under it, letting the spray beat against her face. She wrapped an arm around her stomach and gasped for air as the tears came fast and furious. What was wrong with her? Why was it that men seemed to run away screaming?

In high school, she'd convinced herself that if she was better, hotter, smarter, Craig would want her. He didn't. Then again, she really couldn't blame herself for Craig's preferences. That was on him, not her. Then Robby happened, just some jerk trying to get with the easy chick.

She thought once she came to Ritter things would be different. College was supposed to be better, but so far...not so much. First Kyle, then Ryan. She replayed all the time she'd spent with Kyle, and then the time she spent with Ryan.

The two of them were night and day. She knew it—now she did, anyway. All Kyle ever wanted was that bump and run. He used those corny quotes and bullshit compliments to get in her pants. Like Robby. But in Robby's defense, he never even tried to slather her in bullshit compliments. Which was why she'd thought Kyle was different. Not so much, it turned out.

But Ryan—Ryan was different. He was real and warm and loving— and gone. She hated to admit it, but she missed him. She missed the way he saw her, the real her, and didn't hide or laugh or cringe. Well, he didn't cringe until that night in front of his parents.

Maybe she'd been wrong about him. The tears streamed down her face again, until her fingers pruned and she had to leave the water or join the California Raisins singing group. When she got back to the room, her eyes were burning, but she didn't want to go to sleep. She wanted to wallow. She pulled on underwear, sweats, and a T-shirt before checking the fridge for cookie dough.

She looked up when someone knocked, and Megan stuck her head in the room. "Hey. Want to go see a movie?"

"I thought you went with Savannah and Gabi."

"Oooh, a night of being the fifth wheel. No thanks." Megan walked in and closed the door.

"I don't think I'm good company tonight."

"That's the beauty of a movie. We don't have to be good company." She sat on Savannah's comforter, not that Karina was going to tell Savannah. "I just need to get out of here."

"What's wrong?"

"I think I like Danny."

"Why?" Maybe that came out a little harsher than she intended. But Danny? Female-mainliner Danny? "How did that happen?"

"Poor judgment. Too much time together." Megan threw her hands up. "He really is a great guy. We talked the other night. I see why the brothers like him."

"Yeah, he's awesome if you have a penis." Oh look, she was channeling Parker. Bad. Megan couldn't choose who she fell for any more than Karina could.

"He's nice to you, and you don't have a penis," Megan said.

"I know. I'm sorry. I just don't want to see you get hurt."

"I know. Me either." Megan took a shaky breath. "So, I need to find something else to do besides think about him."

Karina tried to think of reason not to go. She wasn't done wallowing, darn it. Then again, her eyes were dry. Maybe she was done. Maybe it was time to get out of the room and stare blankly at old movies.

"Okay." Eye drops, socks, and gym shoes, run a hand through her hair—that was as far as she needed to go. "Ready?"

"Yep." Megan jumped to her feet. Karina threw on a jacket and walked out the door. This was just what she needed to move on.

~»ΨΡ«~

Chapter Thirty-Six

Ryan

RYAN STOOD BY the table where Brent had set up beer pong. He watched the ball sail through the air, watched it swoosh into a cup, but he couldn't seem to get excited about his friend's win.

Brent waved him over. "Ry, you're up."

"No thanks." He held up his own beer.

"Fuck, Ry." Brent slapped the ping-pong ball into Ryan's hand. "Go take a Midol and snap out of it." He pulled one of the women standing around the table closer to Ryan. "Brittany, honey, you're on Ryan's team. Can you use some of that super-fine mojo and get him to smile?"

"Sure." She giggled.

Ryan tossed the ball at the rows of beer-filled cups, but the ball bounced off a lip and flew off into the room. Brittany laid a hand on his arm. "Good try. You'll get it in the next throw."

He smiled and drank more of his beer. Like he cared about this stupid game. His eyes kept wandering to the door. Gabi and Savannah were coming tonight; Joe and Brent wouldn't shut up about it. He just hoped Karina came with them.

He still missed her.

An arm wrapped around his waist as he stared at the empty doorframe. He tried to wiggle free. "Brit, let go."

"Do we need to talk about this Brit person?" Parker purred in his ear.

"Nope." He drank from his cup as he watched what seemed like everyone from campus walk in the frat. Except the person he wanted there.

"Something interesting at the door?"

His obsession with the entryway was obviously getting out hand if Parker noticed. "What do you want?"

"You're up." Brittany held out the ping-pong ball.

Ryan pulled away from Parker as he grabbed the thing from Brittany's outstretched hand and tossed it across the table, missing the cups altogether. Shit. He turned to Parker.

For some reason, her usual smirk wasn't there. She looked...he didn't know how she looked. Kind? Concerned? "Why don't you just go talk to her?" she asked, with none of the sarcastic lilt he was used to hearing.

"To who?" He had a feeling he knew where this was going, and he had zero interest in having this conversation with her. He didn't need to hear how Karina was beneath him, or how Parker would be willing to comfort him.

She rolled her eyes. "Seriously? You need to ask who?"

"Fine. She's not talking to me."

"Make her. Don't be such a wimp."

"I thought you were trying to convince me she was trash." It was like spitting out a hot coal.

Parker sighed. "I didn't think you'd fall in love with her. I've never seen you like this."

"Butt out. Haven't you caused enough trouble?" He turned watched another group of coeds walk in. None of them Karina.

"So who told you? Gabi? She's such a bitch." Parker shook her head.

"Told me what?" He drank more of his beer while he waited for an answer. "Parker?"

"Don't be too mad, but...I'm the one who posted the video at homecoming."

"You what?" He nearly spit his mouthful of beer on the floor. She couldn't have just said what he thought she said. She posted the video? Dammit.

"I'm sorry."

"Why are you apologizing to me?" He gaped at her. "Try apologizing to Karina. How could you do that? Do you know how much that hurt her?"

"I know—and I did apologize to her."

"No. She doesn't know it was you." Ryan's chest hurt. "She would have told me."

"She knows." Parker laid a hand on his arm and he pulled away. Dammit. He always knew she had a mean streak, but he never thought she was this much of a fucking bitch.

Parker took a deep breath. "I was so angry at her. But she had every chance to turn you against me and she didn't." She looked away, mouth tight. "I'm sorry. I hope you can forgive me." She kissed his cheek and walked away, toward the front door. If he didn't know better, he'd swear she had tears in her eyes.

How could Karina have kept that from him? Guilt, anger, and frustration had a mini cage match in his head while he stared after Parker. He called a truce when a familiar brunette walked in the door— Gabi, followed by Savannah. No Karina.

He pushed his way through the crowd over to Gabi and Savannah. "Does Karina know who put that video of her into the homecoming slides?"

The two of them looked at each other, and Ryan had the impression they were getting their stories straight.

Gabi raised her eyebrows at him. "Hi, Ryan. It's so nice to see you, too." Sarcasm dripped from each word.

Maybe he could have said hello, but his mind was on Karina and that damn video, not manners. And he sure as shit didn't have time for the attitude. "I'll take that as a yes. Can I assume you both knew as well?" He stared at them. They stared back. Another, yes. Great. "So, was someone going to tell me? Or was this just a way to have fun with dumbass Ryan?"

"No." Savannah gripped his arm. "No. She made us promise not to tell you. She knew how much Parker meant to your mom, your family. She didn't want to take that away."

"That's ridiculous." Then again—

Savannah let go of his arm and heaved an exaggerated sigh. "Honestly, if she told you about the video, would you be able to face Parker at the club, or family functions, or any other goofy thing the two of you were invited to? Could you pretend to be friends for the sake of your mother?"

Ryan hesitated. "I don't know."

"Exactly."

He couldn't believe Karina kept that from him. He understood. He would do anything to protect his mother. But he wanted... Oh, who the hell knew what he wanted at this point? Well, besides her. He still wanted her. And the fact that she wanted to protect his mother made him want her even more. "Is she coming tonight?"

"No. She's miserable," Savannah said, and Gabi nodded.

"You both match. You should call and grovel. A lot," Gabi suggested and walked over to Brent.

Ryan chewed his lip. "She won't take my calls," he told Savannah.

"Why don't you stop by in person?" Savannah asked.

"How do I get her to listen?"

"Despite the stupid move at the country club, I know you're a smart guy. You'll figure it out. Call me if you need my help."

Ryan actual felt a little bit of hope bloom in his gut. "You'd help me?"

"Yeah, deep down I know you're a good guy and she loves you. And you love her, too." Savannah smiled, eyes glowing, and Ryan wondered about that until he saw Joe come into view. "Just do me a favor? When you get her back don't mess it up again." She ran into Joe's awaiting arms.

Ryan stared at his empty beer. Losing himself in liquid amnesia sounded fun, but he needed to come up with a plan. Once and for all, he needed to either get her back or move on.

If he only knew how.

~§~

Ryan sat at a back table in Casciani's staring at his phone. His parents would be here any minute, and he still hadn't heard from Savannah. This was going to blow up in his face. He just knew it.

He tried sending another text to Savannah. Where r u?

Dorm

Will u b here soon?

OMG we'll B there.

When r u leaving?

When some id10t stops texting me so I can get ready.

Ryan smiled despite the static buzzing in his spine and put down his phone. He needed tonight to go perfectly. He really wanted this to work.

It had to work.

He watched his mother walk in the door, a smile lighting her face when she spotted him. Ryan stood and pulled a chair out from the table for her.

"Hi, sweetheart." She kissed his cheek and sat.

"Are you alone?" Ryan heard the disappointment in his own voice. His father had a real gift for disappointing his children.

"I'm sorry. Your father had some work at the office. He couldn't get away." She kept her eyes on the table as she picked up the fabric napkin and smoothed it onto her lap.

"So, he doesn't have time for lunch." Or better yet, he didn't have time for his son.

"Oh, honey, he means well." Her hand flew over and covered his, and her smile faltered.

"Why do you defend him?" he asked before he fully thought it through. The way her eyes darkened told him what a dumbass question that was.

"Honey, I hope you understand. He loves you. You know your grandfather wasn't the easiest man, and your father never learned how to be—comforting or supportive. That doesn't mean he isn't proud and he doesn't love you. He is. He does."

"I'm not so sure. He wasn't too happy that I was taking architecture courses. He said he's not paying for school anymore."

"Well, don't you worry about that." She patted his hand. "I'll make sure your school is covered. He just worries about you and your future. I think he was more concerned with getting you and Parker together than your sudden change of majors."

"Why? She's not that great." He picked up his glass of water to give his hands something to do. His parents had always loved Parker and her family. No matter how dysfunctional they were.

"You're right. She's not."

He could feel his eyebrows lift as he stared at his mother. She'd never spoken that way about Parker before. She hadn't said anything negative about her, ever. She and his father were too busy trying to get the two families married, resulting in some social and financial dynasty.

"If she's not that great, why have you guys been trying to send us down the aisle for the past ten years?"

"That was your father and Parker's parents." She squeezed his hand. "I love Parker, but she's not very nice sometimes. Don't get me wrong, if you came home tomorrow and told me you loved her and I could see it in your eyes, I'd accept her with open arms. But you don't love her... Don't look at me like that. I can tell these things." She took a sip of water. "The same way I can tell you have feelings for that Karina girl."

"I'm in love with her."

"I know, honey." His mother squeezed his hand again.

"She's not talking to me," he said, the buzz of nerves turning to a rush of pure energy. "She wasn't too happy when I introduced her as a friend at the Member party."

"So you're dating her?"

"I was." *Until I screwed it up.*

"And she's the girl from the video."

"Yes. Is that a problem?"

"If it's not a problem for you, it's not a problem for me." His mother's mouth curled up on one side. "Lord knows I can't sit in judgment of anyone. We've all made our share of mistakes."

Ryan's mouth dropped open.

His mother shook her head at him, still with that odd smile. "Don't look so shocked. Everyone makes mistakes. Some are just better at hiding them. Even your father has his share."

"Really? Care to tell me all about them?"

His mother laughed. A hearty, heartfelt laugh that Ryan felt in his bones. It was so good to see her so happy.

"Oh, honey. You won't be getting your father's and my secrets without a few more glasses of wine. But nice try." She laughed again and patted his arm once more before taking her hand away.

A waitress walked up to the table, setting out a basket of warm bread and small plates in the center. "You're waiting for more, correct?"

"Yes."

"More?" his mother asked.

"I invited Karina and her roommate. I want you two to meet— for real."

"I'm sure she'll forgive you, honey."

Almost on cue, Savannah and Karina walked in the door and his throat dried like jerky. He took another drink of water, and it went down like jagged spikes.

"I wish I shared your optimism." He stood up and waved. "But I guess we're about to find out."

~»ΨΡ«~

Chapter Thirty-Seven

Karina

KARINA HAD ASKED Savannah if they could go anywhere but here. Yet here was where she stood, right on the edge of that familiar abyss of sadness. Oh God—and now she was turning into a drama queen. She had spent so many days dragging herself out of that hole. Having to concentrate on finals next week helped, but coming back here...?

She couldn't do this. Karina reached out blindly and caught her roommate's wrist. "Savannah, can we go?"

"Just wait." Savannah towed her toward the back of the restaurant. Karina looked up, and there was Ryan standing next to a table. The same table Savannah was dragging her toward.

Karina dug her heels in and jerked back. "Savannah?"

Savannah took hold of her arm and leaned closer. "Do not be a brat about this," she hissed. "Give him a chance."

"Since when are you his Labrador, jumping when he says jump?" Karina let the flare of betrayal burn away the sadness. How could Savannah do this to her?

"Whatever. You are a whiny mess and you need to get over yourself. He said something stupid. So what? He's a guy. If you're going to get mad every time a man says something stupid, you're going to be mad an awful lot." Savannah gave her arm a squeeze. "Now, follow me to the table and listen to the love of your life try to dig himself out of this hole he's made for himself."

"Fine," Karina said, shaking off Savannah's hand, "but we are not okay. I am not okay with any of this." She forced a smile and walked toward Ryan. She would not let him know how much it hurt to see him. She was strong. She was not heartbroken. She was fine. At least she would be in Ryan's version of the story. He would not see her as a weak, heartsick woman who couldn't live without him.

As they approached the table, she noticed an older woman sitting next to Ryan. His mother. Fear yanked her makeshift smile right off her face. Great. He called his mommy to explain how his precious bloodline couldn't be sullied by a trampy lion-straddler. And how Parker was God's gift to the world. Good times...

"Hi, Karina, Savannah."

"Hi, Ryan." Savannah grabbed the chair across from Ryan, next to his mom. Karina was left with the chair next to him. Savannah was so on the shit list. Traitor didn't even cover it this time.

"Mom, I want you to meet someone. This is my ex-girlfriend Karina and her roommate Savannah."

Ex-girlfriend. The reality of those words cut deep.

"It's nice to meet you both." His mother smiled at them. "Karina, I've heard so much about you. I do hope you can forgive my son for being an idiot. I did raise him better, but apparently he still makes stupid mistakes."

Karina had...nothing. Nothing to say to that. What does one say to that?

"I apologize that my husband couldn't make it today. He had some pressing issues at the office."

Karina nodded. She still had no idea how to respond to any of this.

A waitress came to take drink orders. Despite an overwhelming urge for something laced with vodka, Karina ordered a soda.

"So, what year are you dear?" Mrs. Kent asked her.

"Ummm... freshman." Karina glanced at Ryan. What the fuck?

"Mrs. Kent" Savannah said brightly, "I heard that you know the owner of this restaurant. Would you introduce me?" She stood up.

"Sure, dear." Ryan's mom got up too. "Are you interested in becoming a chef?"

Savannah ushered her away from the table. "No. I'm studying education with a focus on English."

"So, you're a foodie?" His mom must not have been in on the plan. Even Karina could see through her roommate's blatant attempt to give Ryan time alone.

Karina turned to the great schemer. "Why am I here?"

"I wanted to say I'm sorry."

"I think you said that already." Karina lifted her chin. "I really should go."

"Please don't. I was an ass and stupid, as my mother so kindly pointed out. I was asked who you were and I freaked. I was afraid my mom wouldn't like you..."

"So, you have mommy issues. Phew. Dodged that bullet."

"Really?"

Given the health problems his mom had in the past, that might have been a bit harsh. But she was feeling a bit harsh right now. A bit hurt. A bit raw. "Fine, sorry. I don't know what all of this is supposed to be, Ryan.

You came out to your mother. Mom, I'm in love with a girl who took her clothes off in high school. Did your mom give permission to bang the local slut until you get it out of your system? Tell you you'll make a better husband for Parker that way."

"Enough. I hate when you talk that way about yourself. I don't think that way about you. None of us do." He must have read the disbelief on her face because he added, "None of us that matter do. Your friends don't. My mom doesn't. She knows I love you, and she wants us to work it out."

"So what if your mom accepts me. What happens when the country club set questions your relationship? What about your father?"

Ryan leaned forward, and his voice was low and hard. "I don't care about the country club or what my father thinks." His eyes held hers. No evasion.

No. she was not falling for this. "You really believe that, don't you? But you do care about what your father thinks. You're still a business major."

"So, if I switch majors for you, will you believe me?" He actually sounded disappointed.

"No. But you should switch for you. Whatever you choose, you'll be stuck with for the rest of your life. Might as well be something you love."

"So what about us?" His mouth twisted.

"Truth? I'm scared. You were so quick to turn your back on me. My dad did that, Robby, Craig, Kyle—they all walked away without a backwards glance. I honestly thought you were different, and then you proved me wrong. I don't want to be wrong again. How can I ever trust you, when I'm scared to death you'll bail again?"

He slid out of his chair and knelt down in front of her. She thought about pulling away when he gently took her hands in his, but her body wouldn't listen. It was too busy humming with the warmth of his touch. Every little movement sent electric jolts to her tattered heart.

"I lost you once. That was enough. I've been a mess without you. I don't ever want to go through this again. I can't. I won't. You are everything to me. I can live without you, but life's not worth living if you're not with me." He must have sensed her resistance waning, because he reached a hand to her cheek, inches from her lips. Her eyes closed at the intimacy of his touch. "I love you, Karina Wolfe. Please give me the chance to show you how much. Let me prove to you I'm here for good."

"But..."

"No buts. There are no guarantees in life. You can't guarantee that you'll never be sick of me or that you won't find me repulsive once my hair turns gray. But I'm willing to take the risk. You're worth the risk. We're worth the risk."

Karina couldn't speak. Emotions banged and clanged against each other in some crazy version of flying lottery balls. Fear. Anger. Happiness. Love. Each emotion warring in her internal moshpit. She could only nod.

He leaned up and wrapped his arms around her. The unwavering grip of those strong arms held her tight, promising to never let her go. He nestled his face into her neck, placing a soft kiss at the base.

He loved her. She could feel it. And despite the last week, she loved him, too. He never gave up on her. On them. Her heart lightened as the pain of rejection and loss floated away with every feather-light kiss.

He pulled away. Too soon. Always too soon. He ran a whisper-soft finger down the side of her face, his lips edging closer to hers...

"Get a room." Gabi walked up to the table with Megan in tow.

He ignored them and pressed his lips to Karina's, sealing his words in place. With one hot, chaste kiss, he managed to tell everyone, including Karina—I love you, I want you and I won't let you go.

Ryan pulled away, a smile lighting up his face.

"What are you doing here?" Karina looked at her friends, resisting the urge to fan her face like a Southern belle.

"Reinforcements. Savannah told us what was going on, and we're either here to tell you what a great guy Ryan is or help you kick him in the balls. Whichever would be most appropriate." Gabi smiled. "Although, given the way you were sucking face, we'll go with he is a great guy and you should give him another chance."

"Did you want to join us for dinner?" Ryan grinned as Gabi pulled over a chair and sat.

"I thought you'd never ask."

Ryan moved to his chair just as Savannah and his mother returned to the table.

"We have company." Mrs. Kent replaced the napkin on her lap.

"This is our friend Megan," Ryan said, "and you know Gabi."

"Of course, it's nice to see you again, Gabi. Megan.

Ryan wrapped his hand around Karina's and squeezed as laughter and conversation ebbed and flowed around the full table. Savannah inhaled a breadstick, food no longer being wasted, as she shared a story about one of her brothers and their harvesting shenanigans. Ryan's mom laughed as Gabi turned to say something, probably inappropriate, but sipped her water instead.

On her best behavior.

Karina's face nearly hurt from smiling so much as contentment settled in her stomach. She never felt so accepted, so at home. And this was her home. Here with her friends, her Ritter University family. She finally found the place where she belonged.

EXTRAS

Thank you for supporting an independent author. It would be great if you could leave a review or a rating wherever you purchased this book, or on Goodreads.

Would you like to know when my next book is available? You can sign up for my new release email list at http://www.vanessamknight.com or like my Facebook page at http://facebook.com/vanessamknightauthor.

<u>Other Books by Vanessa</u>

Chicago's Finest Series (in order)

Second Time's the Charm

Stark Raving Mad

Ritter University Series (in order)

Major Renovations

What Happens in College...

Christmas Breakdown

Rushing In

Sophomore Slump (Out Summer 2016)

~»ΨP«~

Christmas Breakdown

Chapter One

Nica

NICA BRADLEY GRIPPED the steering wheel as she flew past the sign she knew so well. WELCOME TO SCOTTSDALE. MOST LIVABLE CITY.

Maybe the sign was right. Life had been a heck of a lot better when she lived on this side of it. The familiar sloping chocolate peaks of the McDowell Mountains and the caramel-brown landscape welcomed her back. Cacti and palm trees adorned with plastic holiday lights lined the well-travelled road, bringing color to the neutral monotony. Home.

Frankie Goes to Hollywood belted out their suggestion for Nica to "Relax" from her cellphone. She glanced at the screen. Megan from Ritter University. Shiitake. Like getting a call from Megan was going to make her relax. Not after what Nica did.

The ring tone quieted. She really wasn't ready for that lecture. She thought she had a bit more time before everyone found out. Then again, Nica gave Megan a key to her room last semester, probably why Nica's phone was blowing up with calls—oh, and now texts.

Call me.

Now.

We need to talk.

Nica sighed and reached for the phone. Megan wouldn't give up. She'd call and call until Nica answered the blasted phone. Or threw it.

Whichever came first.

Nica pulled over into a convenient store parking lot along the road and clicked on her contacts. She sifted through the names, but before she could find Megan—

Blasted Frankie was singing again.

"Miss me already?" Nica cooed into the phone after she clicked accept.

"I'm not laughing, Nica. Why is your stuff in boxes?" Megan's voice was high-pitched, angry. Megan never got angry.

"Why are you on campus? Shouldn't you, like, be at home with your family?" Nica should've had more time. She should have had time to come up with some logical reason why she wasn't coming back. The real reason was so, so pathetic.

"Umm...I'm—uh—just running late."

"Really?" Stammer much? "The stutter takes away some of the credibility."

"We're not talking about me. We're talking about your empty closet and the boxes lining your room." Megan must have moved the phone as the earpiece sputtered. "Shhh..."

"Who should shh? Are you with someone?"

"No. Stop trying to change the subject." Megan's voice was laced with guilt. She was with someone all right, but Megan would never talk about that when she was on her soapbox, attempting to clean up Nica's life.

"I'm taking a break." Nica sighed.

"A break? Why did you take all your clothes and box your crap?" Silence thundered across the line. "Nica? Is this because of that stupid class you were having trouble with?"

"No."

"Dammit, so you retake it. It's no big deal."

Yeah, if only things were that easy. Hot tears stung Nica's eyes. She didn't want to talk about this. Not with Megan. Not with anyone. "I have to go. I'm running late."

"Nica, you can't quit school."

But she had to—the class—the GPA. She had no choice, really. Well, she had a choice, and this was hers.

"I'll call you later." She clicked end and leaned her head against the headrest. She didn't want to quit school, but she couldn't go back. What did he say? Oh yeah.

Some people just don't have what it takes to be graphic designers.

She didn't have what it took to do what she loved. She was on the verge of crying when he'd said that. Her whole world crashed around her, so she'd done the most logical thing. She'd headed home.

Nica pulled out of the parking lot and headed back toward her gran's. She'd come home a few times since she left for college, but this time felt different. It was different. This time, she wasn't sure if she'd make the drive back to school in Indiana.

She swerved as a truck cut into her lane. A box of bread crumbs jumped out of the grocery bag in the backseat, landing on the floor. Darn truck. If that box broke, she was not going back to the grocery store. A week before Christmas, and the place was a nightmare of shoppers and long lines. She wasn't living that hell again, not even to make her brother's favorite meatloaf.

She pulled up to her gran's house. Not much had changed. Large flower pots filled with dead flowers lined the crooked porch. The siding along the left side of the house was still sagging, the mailbox was held together with electrical tape. Her grandfather's 1955 Chevy Bel Air still darkened the parking spot in the carport, and her grandmother's car was parked right behind, exposed to the elements. Same as always.

She parked along the street and leaned into the back seat. Dropping the wayward breadcrumb box into the grocery bag, she pulled the paper sack into the front seat and angled out of the car.

A grocery trip was a necessity when Nica came home. She loved her grandmother, but between the search and rescue dogs' training and care, she sometimes forgot the simple things, like cleaning and food shopping. So, whenever Nica came home, she used a portion of the money her grandmother sent her and bought groceries and cleaning supplies. After all, her food and dorm were covered by her Resident Assistant gig. With the exception of the multiple hair dyes she used to change her look, she didn't have many expenses.

It had been five months since she'd been back, so Nica could only imagine how bad the house would be this time. Her brother's clothes everywhere, dog toys covering the floors, dirty dishes lining the countertops. Five months' worth of cleaning would be waiting behind that front door.

She couldn't wait to get started. Most people probably found that weird, but she loved to clean. Cleaning had always been a respite for her, a great way to think about upcoming decisions. One's future—or lack thereof.

Silence met her inside her childhood home as she threw open that door. "Grandma. I'm home."

No dogs, although their familiar smell permeated the air. No horrible polka music. Nothing.

"Ben?" She looked around the living room. Grandpa's faded striped recliner sat against the front window drapes, looking directly at the TV set on the table against the wall. She put the bag in her arms on a side table and lowered herself into the seat. No one was allowed to sit here. Even her gran hadn't sat in Grandpa's chair in years. It was his and his alone. She ran a hand down the arms of the chair and sat back. It still smelled like him. Musk and evergreen cologne mixed with his signature peppermint.

I miss him.

The rough material scraped along the palm of her hand. It had been three years. Three years since they lost him. Three years and her grandma still kept his car in the drive and his chair enshrined in the living room.

She jumped up when a car door opened outside. She pulled back the blinds. Thank goodness. Not her gran. She'd flip if she found Nica in the sacred throne.

Nica grabbed the bag of groceries and slid it onto the kitchen counter. She looked out the sliding glass doors to the back yard. The state-of-the-art dog obstacle course stood empty. Her grandma wasn't training the dogs. Her brother was probably still in school. She had the house to herself.

Perfect. She'd get a chance to clean up before they came home. It would be a double surprise. Not only was she home for the holidays, but they'd celebrate with a clean house.

She pulled away from the doors and headed to the sink. Emptying the dishwasher was first on her agenda. She pulled the door open. Empty. Not one dish.

She closed the door and looked around. The counters empty. All the large utensils were sticking out of a wooden caddy. Things had a place. And everything was in that place. In fact, everything looked clean. Maybe her grandma finally hired a cleaning lady like Nica had suggested.

"Who are you?" a deep male voice demanded from just inside the open sliding doors. When had those doors opened? The owner of that voice ran a hand through his dark hair. His tan skin glistened with sweat. Hot. The man was gorgeous. Deep brown eyes. He moved forward.

Crap. She saw TV. She knew how these things worked. He was probably a serial killer that broke into her grandma's home, and she was drooling. Death by gorgeous psycho. What a way to go.

"How did you get in?" She turned to the knife block... No knife block. That damn wooden caddy full of kitchen gadgets sat in its place. Was a slotted spoon threatening? Not so much. Where did her grandma move the darn knife block? She grabbed a meat tenderizer from the caddy and held it up. She might not have a knife, but she could tenderize the heck outta this guy if she had to.

"The door was open." He rubbed a towel over his forehead.

"So you just walk into someone's house? Who are you?" She twisted the weapon in her hand. He might be hot, but the smokin' Latin-truder was going down.

"Cruz Lazaro. Who are you?"

"I'll ask the questions here, buddy. Why are you in my house?"

"Your house?" A small smile turned up the side of his pink bow lips, and now she noticed the shadow of a beard lining his chiseled chin. "You must be Veronique."

He said her name perfectly. Perfectly. Most people butchered it. She was called varying forms of Veronica or other stumbly forms of Veronique, but it just rolled off his tongue. Her name rhymed with Monique. And when he said the word, it sounded delicious.

Although she didn't go by that name any longer. "Nica. How do you know my name?"

"Lo said you weren't coming home for Christmas this year." He walked to the kitchen table and put down a towel and a bottled water.

"Lo?"

"Your grandma, Lori. She was pretty disappointed, too. I'm glad you changed your mind." He popped the top on the water bottle. Chocolate eyes met hers over the plastic. "Is it safe for me to drink, or are you going to use that thing on me?"

Gosh, she was a sucker for chocolate.

"Uh...sure, go ahead." Nica slid the tenderizer to the counter as Cruz guzzled the water. "My grandma talked to you about me? How do you know her?"

"I live here."

"Here? Since when?" Nica played with the red and green bangle bracelets on her arm. It was just one of her many odes to the holiday.

"About four months."

Four months? He'd lived with her grandma for four months? Right after Nica left for college. How the heck hadn't she known about this? Why hadn't Gran told her?

"Oh my goodness! My goodness, Nica darling. I thought that was your car on the street." Gran walked into house, long gray hair hanging loose down her back. Bruno and Snowball scurried in front of her. Somehow, the three criss-crossed without stepping on each other. "You came home for Christmas. I'm so happy."

Nica ran up to her grandma and leaned down, arms wrapping around her neck.

"I'm so glad you're here. It's not Christmas without you. Your hair's amazing. Is that green?" Gran leaned back and twirled a finger through the green tips of Nica's hair. The tips that took all day to do, between bleaching her dark brown hair and applying dark green glop. But the smile on her gran's face was worth it.

"Totally—and check out my nails." Nica raised her hands, showing off her green and white nails with the red berries painted on each one.

Her gran squealed and ran a hand over them. "Oh, my, they're beautiful. The berries and stems are so lifelike."

"That was my friend Savannah's handiwork. She's, like, a genius."

"Gifted girl." She dropped Nica's hand. "I see you've met Cruz."

"I did." Eyes narrowed, Nica watched the American psychopath—closely.

"He's a godsend. He helps out so much around here."

Yeah, boiling bunnies and eating brains. Nica listened to the Cruz-worship as she leaned down and called to her favorite Akita. "Come here, Bru-baby."

Bruno and Snowball sniffed and nudged Cruz instead. Tails wagging. Tongues hanging. Each dog fighting for his share of attention. The man's long fingers flew from one dog to the next, rubbing the soft fur back and forth. Nica couldn't keep her eyes off the dogs squirming on the floor. Did he have that effect on everything he touched?

She shook him from her mind. Not that it mattered. These were her dogs. Her babies. They had to miss her.

"Bruno. Come here baby." She tapped her thighs and called. The honey colored dog with a white covered stomach ignored her words and drooled over Cruz.

"Go say hi to Nica. She missed you, boy." He ran a hand down the dog's fur.

Pity. She could feel the man's pity as her dog ignored her. She didn't need pity from anyone, especially, the dog-stealing housecleaning jerk-wad.

"Whatever. You don't have to beg him." She stood up and crossed her arms.

"Honey. You've had a long drive." Her grandma rested her arm on Nica's shoulder. "Maybe you should lie down."

Nica felt a yawn build. Today's fourteen-hour drive from Oklahoma was exhausting on top of yesterday's thirteen-hour drive from Indiana to Oklahoma. With only a four hour nap in between, she was dead on her feet.

"You're right." She walked out the door to her car. Fatigue seeped into her bones making her movements slow and choppy. Of course, maybe that was just her mind. Thoughts were getting jumbled. She couldn't wait to sleep in her own bed again.

She grabbed her overflowing suitcase and kicked the car door closed. She walked in the house and passed her grandma and the Latin annoyance in the kitchen. "I'm going to my room."

"Umm, honey?"

Nica stopped and turned to her grandma's guilt-stricken face. "We need to talk about your bedroom. You see, well, Cruz needed a place to stay."

She couldn't have.

She wouldn't have.

"I'm sorry, but you moved out. Cruz is staying in your room. You can stay on the pull-out couch in the living room."

She had.

How could she? Nica's own blood gave away her bedroom, and

expected her granddaughter to sleep in the living room. On the guest couch. While that—that stranger slept in Nica's bed.

Fudge. Fudge. Fudge. She hated swearing. Well, she didn't technically swear, it had been ingrained in her to never use swear words. Her inner monologue was G-rated, yet she still had no bed to sleep in.

"Why don't you lie down on my bed for now?" Gran smiled as she rested a hand on Nica's shoulder. "Things can get a little loud after your brother gets home from school."

"Shouldn't he be home already?"

"He has Spanish Club today. He'll be home in an hour or so."

"Fine," Nica growled and headed to her grandma's room. She knew this visit home would be a hard sell with the whole "moving back" thing. But Cruz and his Goldilocks ways was making things a heck of a lot harder.

A few minutes later, Nica lay down in her grandma's bed. The familiar smell of Jean Naté and peanut butter covered the room. The Jean Naté was her grandma's, but the peanut butter was all Bruno and Snowball.

They loved peanut butter treats. And her Gran loved making them happy. It was a heavenly match. Even if it did make the room smell like a peanut-processing plant.

She stretched and snuggled closer to Gran's pillow, her sheets and her blanket. She missed her gran, too. Five months was too long to be away. She wasn't tired anymore. She should be, but the rollercoaster of her life was spiking her heartrate at every turn. She stared at the dark room as the sun peeked through the blue floral curtains, casting orange light along the door. Almost made it look heavenly. But it wasn't, and despite her inability to sleep, she had no desire to leave the safety of this hideaway.

Her gran gave away her room. That added a whole layer of complicated to the situation. Shiitake.

What was she going to do?

She didn't have what it took to stay at school, but she didn't have a room to stay here. Her family had replaced her. They'd given away her bed. Even the dogs liked him better.

Surrounded by family, she was more alone than she'd ever been before.

About the Author

Vanessa M. Knight has always enjoyed writing, and once she found romance, she was addicted. She props her laptop in the suburbs of Chicago with her husband, son and menagerie of four-pawed claw-babies (AKA cats and dogs.) That laptop has partnered-in-crime to write contemporary romances with a dash of humor and splash of snark.

When she has a few moments to spare, you can find her singing off-key (but she assures everyone it's still considered singing), reading, kickboxing or killing a few brain cells as she stares at the many sitcoms and dramas available through the Internet and TV.

For more information on Vanessa, including her Internet haunts, contest updates, and details on her upcoming novels, please visit her website at www.vanessamknight.com.

www.ingramcontent.com/pod-product-compliance
Lightning Source LLC
Chambersburg PA
CBHW072205130726
47910CB00011B/1916